1

Karma

by Michael Albee

First Edition
Printed in the United States of America

West Coast Publishing
Manhattan, New York
www.westcoastpub.com

For Dad
Rest in Murder

Twine Time

I wasn't always abysmal. I used to be normal; as normal as any of you are, I suppose. I started out as a young boy full of energy. My world was as quiet as the words spoken by my grandparents. My grandmother and grandfather both lost their hearing at different stages of life.

My grandfather was the ripe old age of three when his world fell silent. He was a child of poverty, and, growing up during the 1920s where a small illness could take a man's life, losing your hearing didn't seem all that bad; at least it never did to him. Grandpa always had the biggest smile on his face. He was diagnosed with meningitis and the potentially fatal disease left his life intact, yet very different. He was, like me after the accident, changed forever. He would never hear the chirp of a bird or the wheels of a car as the acceleration goes from forty, to sixty, then to seventy miles per hour, and so on. His life's journey wouldn't allow him to hear the leaves shaking hands during a light wind.

My grandmother was older. Her world was silenced when she turned eighteen. Her cherry-red Mercedes was whistling down 24th Street in Phoenix, Arizona, when a yellow car—I was never told the make and model—heading in the opposite direction started to drift, then drift some more, then drift all the way into the far lane, striking my grandmother's car head on. She remembered waking up in the hospital two days later and reaching for the radio. She turned the dial until she found her destination: station 97.5fm. Her favorite show was *-Twine Time* with James Buckley, and as luck would have it, the rotary clock hanging on the wall pointed to *Twine Time* with its big, black hands.

That was the moment she said she burst into tears. She nearly broke the radio dial trying to spin it all the way to the right at full volume. She told me that for months, the only sound she could hear was the screaming inside her own head. She, like my smiling grandfather, had taken a different path to a somewhat more peaceful world.

Growing up with deaf grandparents bore challenges. My mother was working, and my father was deceased—more on that little tidbit later—meaning I spent most evenings at my grandparents' game nights: rooms full of deaf people playing poker and bridge, smoking cigarettes, and passing around salami, mustard, and American cheese sandwiches on egg bread. If I had the choice of a seven-course meal donned with French truffles, honey-glazed carrots, pureed celery root and a bleeding piece of cow flesh cooked to perfection, or my grandmother making me one last shitty salami sandwich with Plotchman's shitty yellow mustard, I would choose the sandwich every single fucking time.

But I do not miss the smell of those game nights. One sneaky trait of the deaf community is that they will shamelessly fart anywhere and love every second of it. Walking behind my grandmother at the grocery was like waiting behind a semi-truck on the highway whose horn may go off at any moment.

My accident gave me what many people would consider gifts. Those people are idiots. But one "gift" I didn't receive was the ability to bring people back from the dead. If I could bring people back to life, I wouldn't hesitate to bring my grandparents back. I wouldn't be in so much pain if they were still alive. I wouldn't think about taking my own life on what seems like an hourly basis. Now, I have to stay focused. If I help people, the pain goes away—for a few seconds, anyway.

If I can help all the people who provide more breath and light to this world than the trees and the sun combined, the pain will go away—it must.

I'm not as strong as my grandparents were. They made deafness seem like an ill-placed, permanent pimple. After my accident, I can't even go one fucking day without putting something toxic in my body. In order to help the lame, I must succumb to the suffering. There's no other way except to put myself in the middle of the abuser and the abused.

The ironic part is now the only time I ever feel even a small semblance of peace are the seconds of silence after I've mutilated one of my victims and the sheer relief on the face of the aggrieved.

The quiet in the room after everyone has been shown their truth. The truth that people will never understand the pain they cause until the knife they hold slits their own wrist.

Masks

I used to wear so many masks. I never knew when one came off my face and another went on. The masks helped keep the pain away.

I would put on my happy mask. Happy me was full of love and tenderness, available to those who gave me even a sliver of daylight to improve their mood. My angry mask was obvious. I have a strong inclination if I were to see it in the flesh it would be green in color, with my marred, red eyes shining through.

The scariest part of my many masks was not knowing the person underneath them all. I could consciously put on a mask, then forget the person underneath them all. The only—and I mean, only—thing the accident allowed me to do, was shed myself of my masks.

I never knew if I was a nice person wearing angry masks, or if I was always angry, but able to put on my happy mask at the drop of a hat. I never met the real me. I lost touch with the reality of my face as if the masks were each lined with thorns, and each time I pulled off a mask, a piece of flesh tore off my cheek, or nose, or forehead, leaving me scarred and scabbed. An unrecognizable face staring back at me mortified in the mirror.

A small part of me is happy now, knowing that there is no question I have a monster living inside me. The monster is no longer hiding, but it is worn on my one and only face for all to see. I used to be a series of different people confusing themselves as the embodiment of a rational person, but there is no confusing the truth now. The masks I wore molded me into a disfigured monster. Now, instead of running from them, throwing each mask to the ground and stepping in the other direction, I must embrace them.

I must embrace the masks made of gold and titanium. I must embrace the masks made out of recycled tobacco and celery root. The core of my being was once a naked baby—loving, hoping, wishing for beauty to appear in the sky. Now, the core of my being is somewhere, buried beneath the many materials making up my masks. The core of me is my monster.

Shattered Ankles

My father was born on March 10, 1962 and died on March 24, 1984. He was twenty-two. My mother was barely enjoying her first bouts with morning sickness when he was murdered. The idea of aborting the fetus (a.k.a. me) floated among various family members. Honestly, it wouldn't have been the worst idea. At the time, my mother didn't have an education or even a home to live in. My paternal grandparents were the primary proponents of the birth-prevention method where my mother would sit, legs open, while I was sucked out of her vagina until the notion of me becoming a baby was just that—a notion.

The night of my accident I stood at my father's grave at the Paradise Memorial Gardens near the base of Four Peaks mountain in Arizona. It was a tradition to visit the grave every year on my birthday. For me, it was a way to reflect. I could quite literally see where I came from, spend some time in the present moment appreciating life, and envision where my future would take me.

October 30, 2020 was a rainy night. I had plans to meet my girlfriend and some friends for cocktails later, before going to see a live action performance of *The Night at the Roxbury*. I parked my white Toyota truck along the right-hand side of the cemetery, as I always did. I'd been to that cemetery over a hundred times in my relatively brief life.

That night was particularly dark, but my eyes could have been sealed shut with liquid glue and I still would have found my way. My father's grave was exactly six gravestones to the left of the tall oak tree that stood proud in the middle of the open field. The rain poured down hard, and I thought twice about skipping my traditional visit to my father's resting place; however, I'm not the type of person to let a little water scare me away. Witches melt, not me. At least, I didn't think I was capable of melting.

Emerging from my truck, I was immediately struck with huge explosions of water. It wasn't just raining cats and dogs; I'm pretty sure I could see gerbils and hamsters and aardvarks coming down too. I sloppily trekked towards my father's grave, the wet grass ruining my brand-new, black, alligator-leather tassel loafers almost immediately. *Shit.*

You know the slight nervousness that vacillates between your spine, throat and stomach when you land in a faraway country? The nervous anticipation that crawls up your back like a thousand fire ants, vertebrae by vertebrae, as you anxiously await your adventure? Before the accident, I felt that way all the time; always slightly nervous, whether my time was spent with close friends, distant relatives, or complete strangers. The most comfortable I ever felt was in a coffee shop; alone yet surrounded by foreigners, hiding in plain sight feeling fine.

All I ever used to feel was fine. I deeply regret losing my sense of being fine.

Before the accident I saw physical beauty in the world and in humanity: white chocolate-covered Swiss Alps; swimming in the Pacific Ocean with humpback whales so close I could feel the water shooting out of their blowholes; watching a woman, with no motivation other than pure, unadulterated kindness, take time out of her evening to retrieve a blanket for a homeless man. During every experience, no matter how grandiose or tear-jerking, all I ever felt was fine. Now, as my mind crumbles underneath the burden of knowing the monster I am, I would do almost anything to feel fine.

My entire wardrobe was soaked. My new shoes, my crisply ironed checkered shirt, my jet-black pants, and my off-white leather belt were all ruined because I had this insatiable desire to follow through with the stupid fucking tradition of seeing my father's grave on my birthday in a goddamn monsoon. I thought again about turning back, but my outfit was already ruined, and I was steps from the tall oak tree which signaled it was time to go left. One, two, three, four steps, marked by one, two, three, four gravestones. Two more to go, then I could kneel on my father's gravestone, reflect as quickly as possible, and make my way to my birthday shenanigans.

And that's when I fell.

The fifth gravestone was no longer in place. Instead, a giant, six-foot hole was there with me now stuck at the bottom, with what must have been two fractured and shattered ankles. The pain in my ankles felt as if a god had taken a worthy hammer and smashed my fibula into a thousand pieces. I tried to stand but crumbled to the wet soil screaming, as my foot was somehow inches away from my chin. I yelled for help but the howling wind and pouring rain ate the sound before I could even hear myself. I was trapped. I was fucking trapped.

I did everything I could that night to emerge from the hole. I tried jumping on my broken legs. I attempted digging my way up. My phone was drowned. I pressed my thumb so hard into the reset button that my nail split, sending blood shooting into the air. Apparently, electricity, water and blood are a poor combination. I was exhausted and in excruciating pain. I did the only thing I could think of next: I closed my eyes, I tried to meditate; I focused so hard on surviving and waiting out the rain.

I knew if I could wait out the rain, someone would eventually find and help me. Even if I had to wait until morning, I knew I wouldn't die in that hole. Through my eyelids, I could see a bolt of lightning as thunder boomed in the sky. My eyes opened and all I could see was a falling branch from the tall oak tree crashing down on me. The branch was struck by the lightning, cracking me in the head before collapsing onto my chest. It was so heavy, and despite my best efforts I couldn't budge it even an inch. To make matters worse, the grave was starting to fill with water.

I was going to drown in a grave on my birthday.

Hot Chai at the Bar!

Hours of pure contentment are my favorite; moments of pure serenity.

Voices echoing around. "Hot chai at the bar!" Sitting in a coffee shop holding onto every breath of the long day. "*However far away, I will always love you,*" spitting out of the speaker system connected to the DJ's MacBook.

Nights that make me feel like I am free.

I don't seek out happiness. I seek out the ability to be; I find that to be much more of a challenge than happiness.

Being still in the night. Seeing a single leaf fall in the fall. Watching the effortless aircraft career slowly toward the runway in the most usual of ways.

Trying to Find a Cure

I've searched nearly everywhere for a cure. I've tried
gamma radiation, chemotherapy, and shock therapy. I've removed
the toxicity from my body. I've eaten clean, I've eaten like shit, I've
seen psychics, I've tried counseling; and I've seen ten different
therapists and have been diagnosed with ten different disorders.
I've tried killing myself.

And don't fucking judge me. You would have, too.

I've tried methods for coping with addiction. AA was
fun—even more fun after a few beers. I thought maybe, just
maybe, all this shit was mental. Maybe I was similar to a heroin or
cocaine addict and maybe this was all one giant game being played
on me by my cerebral cortex.

During one of my research binges, I read about an ancient
drug brewed by the Incans called ayahuasca. The drug was
supposed to be able to cure people, and not just anyone—but
really fucked up people like me.

I made it to Peru a few weeks later. In Peru, the voices in
my head, while still present, sounded more like whispers than the
usual screams of terror. In Peru, I was present. In Peru, I took
deep breaths of fresh air each day, inhaling my strength and
exhaling my fears. The voices still lurked inside me, but they were
easier to control. I couldn't completely silence them, but I felt
better. I felt more awake, more alive; almost fine. And, if I listened
closely with a stethoscope, I could almost hear my heart beating

again.

My journey for healing started at nine pm on a Thursday night, 40,000 feet in the air. From Phoenix, Arizona, to Los Angeles, California, to Lima, Peru, to Cusco, Peru, I set my course to the small, South American country where I would enjoy lodging at the Etnikas Clinic of Integrative Medicine—the number-one ayahuasca retreat in the world. As each drop of fuel burned on my winged transportation, I was one step closer to the unknown, deeper into uncertainty.

Every cloud and star that passed caused an anxiety that I would never live without the monster inside of me.

On the flight from Los Angeles to Lima, I sat next to a middle-aged Japanese couple. The language barrier between Han and Leia, my super-original nicknames for them, could not be broken despite numerous attempts. However, the thick wall between our audible sounds quickly dissolved with hand gestures, smiles, and a common final destination: Cusco, Peru. I could discern that they were heading to see Machu Picchu. Meanwhile, I shyly informed them that I was going to have my mind bent with the most powerful hallucinogenic on the planet. Other than our different reasons for travel, the cultural differences, different skin colors, and ages, they were very relatable.

Unfortunately, as I sat next to Han and Leia, the voices screamed bloody murder. I wasn't able to control my facial expressions and I casually excused myself to the restroom where I lay crying on the floor in the fetal position for the remainder of the flight, wondering how the trip would be if I wasn't in so much pain. I let my fantasies run wild as I imagined enjoying the trip to Peru with a beautiful wife. I imagined my jokes sticking more than my recent conversation as Han and Leia didn't particularly understand my sarcasm or the word "the," for that matter.

I think I would have been happy if it weren't for the fantastic, fucking five in my head. I think I would have been better

16

than fine.

The final flight to Cusco was on an Airbus 320. The plane was built anywhere from ten to seventy-five years ago. To be honest, I wouldn't be surprised if the original Redenbacher brothers worked on the plane that took me from Lima to Cusco. Wait, was it Orville Wright or Orville Redenbacher who first put mechanical wings into the sky? I've never been much of a science buff, but I do love popcorn.

Surprisingly, making matters more comforting, the Airbus 320 was parked directly next to a prop plane from the 1950s. Somehow, it made me feel safer knowing that at the very least, our plane was better than a plane being held together with duct tape and hope. It reminded me of how women would go out with less attractive women to make themselves look better. At least I wasn't about to ride in the ugly plane.

I was trusted with the emergency-exit row, which ordinarily meant more leg room. However, based on the frailty of the vessel, I put the odds at fifty percent that I would be forced to put my emergency-exit skills into action. When the engine was warming, it sounded like chains were dragging along the ground. In full gear, the engine emulated the buzz of a handheld fan, only if that buzzing sound was being pushed through loud concert speakers. I couldn't decide if that was a good sign or a bad sign.

As the bird finally did take flight, I, along with the rest of Flight 2039, closed our eyes and prayed our way toward Cusco, Peru.

I'm a Goddamn Fucking Monster

The most ironic part of people thanking God for me is knowing that I was raised with the Devil living inside me. Seeing shapes everywhere, no clear lines in sight, my vision is all but a bright light with floating objects in all directions. As I drift, I discern nothing. My eyes grip shut with fluorescent bulbs burning inches away from my eyelashes. It feels like having hot embers stuck inside your pupils.

The hardest part is living with the idea that I will never be enough.

I know I will never be enough.

I'm a monster. I'm a goddamn, fucking monster.

"Join me, ladies and gentlemen, for a rousing rendition of one of my favorite accompaniments. I, Chester C, ChesterMcCuntCunt, bring to you, with the help of my four best friends, 'You're a Goddamned Fucking Monster!'"

Chester coughed loudly as I toyed with the barrel of a Smith and Wesson 500 Magnum in my mouth like an adolescent boy would lust for a fresh nipple. Chester's song had no tune.

"You're the biggest goddamn fucking monster on the planet! We all fucking hate your guts!! You're worthless, you're worthless, did I mention you're fucking worthless? We all fucking hate your guts!"

What have I become?

Spoiler Alert

Spoiler alert: I survived the accident.

I lay there, pinned under the branch. I couldn't move; my physical strength wasn't enough to push the huge branch off me. And, despite being mentally tough, that didn't help much either. Surprisingly, mental toughness doesn't do much to move a 300-pound tree branch, and unfortunately, no experience I've had in the past, and all of my built-up mental toughness, could help me move the giant limb. Mental toughness is bullshit.

I started to cry. The water was filling the grave faster than I could breathe. I was going to die.

I tried to be calm. I tried to think about *savasana* in yoga, otherwise known as "corpse pose." How fucking ironic. I was currently in a pose named after a cadaver as the water started to tickle my ears. I thought about my daughter, and at that point it felt like my tears were filling the grave faster than the torrential downpour of rain. My little girl was going to grow up without me as her father. She was going to have her first period and talk about it with a stranger. She was going to learn how to drive and what college is like from someone other than me; be walked down the aisle by someone other than me. Another man was going to take her to school, prepare her dinners and make her laugh every day.

I cried even harder.

As my tears flowed out, I tried to use my thoughts as

inspiration. I focused all my energy and every ounce of strength I had on moving that goddamn branch.

One, two, three!

Nothing. Not even a small budge to lift my spirits. Not just one sliver of movement to give me hope. I couldn't even move a splinter.

Hope was not springing eternal as the water was now spilling into my mouth. I screamed again, hoping that someone was around. This would be my last opportunity to call for help.

That's when the sky broke open with lightning. Without the customary passage of time, a baritone of thunder crashed down on top of me. All I could see was a violent, bright light filling the sky through the water. Then it hit me: a rush of electricity all over my body. It felt like someone was tattooing my entire body all at once; a mix of the most intense pleasure and pain I've ever felt in my entire life. It felt like taking a handful of MDMA and orgasming after a night of raw, intense love-making while scorpions scrupulously stung at my feet. The sensation lasted for hours, with my body fully engulfed in water. I wasn't alive, but I certainly was not dead. I could feel everything.

Eventually, the rain stopped pouring. The water seeped into the ground and my mouth was now tasting breath for the first time in hours. How in the hell was I still breathing? How the fuck was I still alive?

And then, I heard them all for the first time: Chester, Margaret, Ophelia, Brit, and Tetro said in unison,

"*Hello, sir.*"

The Victim

I tried to give her everything. I tried to show my little girl the world; fill her with inspiration. I did my best, my fucking best. There were times when it felt like I wasn't doing enough, times when I felt like I should be doing more. It's so hard to not feel like a failure in a world that loves the victim.

There Was No Sacrifice

Watching her playing in the water, her smile as wide as the Pacific Ocean, I am trying to wrap my head around that level of happiness. The confusion is overwhelming. For the life of me, I can't understand how a ten-year-old little girl who is maturing, evolving and turning into a woman, can sit in the ocean and just smile. Doesn't she know her period is going to start in a few weeks? Doesn't she know about how hard life can be? The only place I am even remotely close to finding that level of happiness is when I'm watching her smiling and laughing in the blue ocean.

The closest relationship I have had with anyone is with my daughter. I was the first man to love her marveling at her beauty as I bathed her with nervous anticipation. What was life going to look like outside of the hospital walls, knowing that as soon we told our nurses the final goodbyes, it would be her and I alone? The lone wolf now had a cub, even though we were both young enough to resemble Mowgli.

I couldn't fathom the amount of sacrifice this relationship would take, and, in hindsight, each moment I spent caring for her and loving her was like hitting the jackpot on a slot machine. Her laughter mimicked the sound of the coins hitting the bottom of the pan and the lights flashing, "*WINNER!*" In hindsight, there was no sacrifice.

After a few hours, the large waves crashed against her,

causing her to fall face-first into the ocean. Our time was up and she had spent every smile spit out by her cerebellum. She collected herself and walked over to me, grinning with a mouthful of sand.

"Hi, Daddy! Do you want to go for a walk with me?"

I've found parenting works best with simple rules. I have two for these situations: first, if your daughter ever asks you to dance, you unequivocally, without hesitation, turn on her favorite song and put on your dancing shoes. For the record, I don't actually own any dancing shoes.

The second rule I follow closely is that if your daughter ever asks you to take a walk with her, you put on your favorite pair of walking shoes and you go for a walk. For the record, I also don't own any walking shoes.

I put down my book and she grabs my hand and pulls me up from the ground. We walk nearly two miles before either one of us even thinks about turning around. Both of us are barefoot. The warm sand slightly stings with every step.

We talk about everything under the Hawaiian sun. She tells me about her best friendships and the girls who pick on her at school. She talks to me, at length, about the boy she likes. She uses the word "crushin'" seven times when talking about the boy. She questions the world in an organically youthful and curious way, asking me about the purpose of the crab's life that crawls across her foot. I make a joke about how the crab's purpose is to scare little girls who are walking along the beach so that they will listen to their father. She makes a point to tell me the crab did not scare her.

As we walk, she pauses every few minutes to take a breath, look up at me with her green eyes and says, "I love you, Daddy."

My heart is full.

We spend the better part of ten days wandering the little island of Kauai. During the trip, I see every facet of her personality. Her intelligence shines as she grabs a book to read instead of the remote to watch TV. She sits on the balcony reading for an hour, only looking up briefly to lose herself in the soft drops of rain that fall from the sky. Her strength is on full display as we trek through four miles of the Kalalau Trail. Neither her feet nor her mouth stops during the strenuous stretches.

Her spirit captivates me the most; she emanates good. The highest vibrations pour out of her. She doesn't discriminate. She richly values each and every soul and will thoughtfully remind people why they are important. She does so effortlessly. This quality spills out of her soul as she asks me if she can meditate with me.

She wakes each morning, excited to go to this certain spot on the beach—our spot on the beach—where we close our eyes for twenty minutes in gratitude. Afterward, she confidently communicates her feelings of joy.

It's hard to imagine this little girl will end up putting me in jail. It's hard to imagine her view of justice will end up being so fucking skewed. How can she not see the good I've done? How can she not see the veracity through her stubbornness? Stubbornness passed from my DNA to hers.

Space and time separate me from her stunning adolescence. She put me in this electric box, negating any possibility of my escape. However, despite the distance between now and her juvenile laughter, I still love her. I unconditionally love her.

Blue

Veronica stared blankly at the ceiling. She couldn't move her neck as she had tubes sticking out of every crevice in her body. They were shoved down her throat, sticking out of her arms and poked into any other place doctors could stick a tube. Apparently, the doctors were trying out a new treatment. Neither her nor I were extremely optimistic. Her mind appeared to wander in disbelief. Finally, she spoke around the ducts in her esophagus:

"You did what? That's fucking disgusting. She must have been covered in bugs."

However, in the end, Veronica agreed with me that "she" deserved her fate.

Blue—or Bette, according to her driver's license—was seventy-eight years old and she had murdered most of her family forty-three years before I even met her. She committed one of the most heinous crimes imaginable and went grocery shopping for green beans the next day. I met this fucking bitch at Walgreens about eight months prior to telling my cancer-riddled friend about her. Bette was one of the only people I'd befriended since the horrible creeps started whispering in my ear, dictating my every move.

I stood in line next to Blue at the pharmacy. She was purchasing a topical ointment to help her arthritis. I was in line buying two large-sized bottles of Nyquil so I could sleep that night, and reloading my prescriptions of Percocet, Xanax and Viagra. It can be difficult to spark an erection when Margaret is nagging.

"Sir, you really shouldn't put your boogers on the bed. Other people sleep here too. It's very disrespectful."

It should go without saying that Blue spoke to me. I rarely talk to anyone anymore, let alone old women with skinned knees. I can't even remember the last time I talked to my daughter. Candidly, I don't even know if she's still alive.

Blue looked at me with her weathered, ice-cold eyes. I could still see the youthful blue underneath the clouded layer of gray from a lifetime of pain and suffering. She slowly said, "Isn't it a travesty?"

Before I could nod and turn away, Ophelia piped up in my head and I, erratically and nearly yelling, shouted, "Isn't what a travesty, Blue?"

A few hours later, we were enjoying our third cup of coffee at my favorite coffee shop. This was yet another one of my favorite pastimes stolen from me on that rainy night. We sipped Caramel Cappuccinos at a café called Comida. It was completely empty except for a twentysomething barista who should have just tattooed the word *"Hipster"* on his forehead. His efforted outfit consisted of hand-stitched and plaid pants, a checkered vest with nothing underneath but a shocking amount of chest hair, and clear glasses, which may or may not have been prescription. For the record, I did like his glasses.

Blue and I talked for hours about politics, relationships, different cultures—she was fascinated with Mexican history—and anywhere else our caffeinated consciousness would take us. It was lovely. It was the first time in forever that I felt fucking lovely and, by estimation, the first time in over three years—1,206 days, to be exact—since I'd had a real conversation that didn't include me trying to fight or fuck somebody.

We started meeting at Comida once a week, on a Thursday, for as long as the conversation would last. There was nothing taboo or off-limits during our conversations. We talked about sex, violence, past and current drug use, candy corn, *Friends* (not ours, but the television show) and whether or not we believed in aliens. For the record, we both hated candy corn, and both believed in aliens. Unsurprisingly, she had tried fewer drugs than me.

I told Blue everything. The only small, itsy-bitsy-teeny-weeny-yellow-polka-dot-bikini secret I kept from Blue was the fact that I had the ability to transform into any person, object or thing on Earth, and the fact that each night I inflicted my version of justice to people around the world. Blue's only secret would shortly be discovered.

It was Thursday morning. I was at Comida drinking Café Americanos as I waited for Bette to slowly creep through the door. Scott, the simpleton hipster with stupid tattoos, tried talking to me. After two hours had passed, I couldn't keep listening to him describe his new tattoos and meticulously lament the decision of whether to put them on the inside of his biceps or on his calves. Plus, if he said the word "Dude" one more time I literally would have snapped his middle fingers into two halves. Chester was even worse. He was so fired up I may have shoved both of his fingers up his ass afterwards. I was worried and over-caffeinated and needed to find Blue.

Blue's house was only a few minutes from Comida. I used the caffeine surging through my veins and sprinted to her house. I didn't even need to transform into a stronger version of myself. I had been to Blue's quaint blue house a handful of times, bringing her groceries and dropping off medications. She lived in a docile domicile in Mesa, Arizona, that was covered in old-lady knickknacks. Her stove top was an original from 1936; she had a sewing machine that she claimed was salvaged from World War II;

27

and, most prominently, she had vibrant Mexican masks on each wall.

I didn't knock when I arrived. Instead, I jumped over her six-foot wall with the same ease as if I'd turned off gravity for a few seconds and went to her sliding glass door. I peeked in and saw my friend sitting in front of the television watching CNN. When she wasn't running errands, having coffee with me, or striking up conversations at Walgreens, she was watching CNN. She often joked that if she had a younger pussy—her exact words—she'd fuck the jew out of Wolf Blitzer: also her exact words.

I slid the door open and saw an ice-cold Blue. My friend was dead. I touched her withered skin and, based on her temperature and the horrid smell of cat litter which had gone unchanged, it appeared she'd likely been dead for about four days. I covered her with a nearby University of Arizona blanket and started looking around. I'd been in her house, but I'd never fully explored Blue's intimate world. She had pictures of a family on the wall. Curiously, I reminisced about our hours of conversation and in all that time she had never mentioned a family; no husband, no kids. Not even an estranged aunt. Yet, here on the wall with her, stood timeless photographs of what appeared to be her with a husband and, presumably, six of her children.

I moved into the kitchen, aimlessly opening drawers, hoping to find a treasure chest or chocolate bar containing a golden ticket. Disappointingly, all I found was an appointment book with scribbled names and numbers in it. Blue didn't have many friends, but there were two names circled with a dark, felt marker. I took out my phone and dialed the first number. A woman answered lightly saying, "Hello, this is Belinda."

I muttered, "Umm... Hello, Belinda. You don't know me, but do you know a woman named Bette?"

Belinda's voice firmed. "Of course I know that cunt. She's my mother. What is this regarding?!"

I asked Belinda if she lived in Arizona. She said yes and to my surprise she lived 2.7 miles away from Blue. She lived within three goddamn miles of her mother and she had avoided her for over forty years. What the fuck was wrong with Belinda? I asked her if she would meet me and she agreed.

The following Thursday I met Belinda at Comida. Scott kept asking me about Blue and finally I told him that it was none of his goddamn fucking business, and if he didn't shut the fuck up, I would break his precious piano. Other than his tattoos, his prized possession was the broken piano he kept in the shop.

Belinda and I talked until Comida closed. By the end of our conversation, my face was red and I was crying hot tears of rage. This old fucking Blue bitch had lied to me for months. I was her only goddamn friend! Hell, she was my only goddamn friend. The first person I had cared about in years was a monster.

Belinda told me about the truth about Bette, the lying woman hiding behind the broken, blue eyes. Belinda was five years old when the tragedy occurred. It was Thanksgiving Day. Bette, her husband Bruce, and their six children sat down to enjoy stuffing and cranberries and turkey, and everything else people eat on Thanksgiving, each member of the family joyfully boasting about their gratitude while stuffing their face with mashed potatoes, green bean casserole, and lightly salted and buttered asparagus.

Belinda remembered waking up groggy and finding herself strapped to the chair at the kitchen table. Everyone's smiles had been replaced with thick pieces of duct tape. In their holiday cheer, no one had noticed that their sweet mother, Bette, hadn't eaten one bite of food. Nobody noticed as she sat maniacally drinking her red wine, waiting for the arsenic to kick in. Bette had found a recipe deep in the recesses of the internet that used a poison dart frog, and used it to drug her entire family and tie them where they sat.

29

When they all awoke, Bette took the sleek, silver slicing knife used to cut the turkey, and slit Bruce's throat in front of her children. Belinda told me she could still remember her mother cackling with excitement as the red blood sprayed their white tablecloth. She told me about how the sound of her father's skin tearing open resembled the cutting of the turkey and how that was the last Thanksgiving she had ever enjoyed. Bette went on slicing each one of the children's throats, in order, from oldest to youngest, before arriving at Ben, Belinda's eight-year-old brother. The one mistake Bette made that night was forgetting to tie Ben's leg down.

Ben kicked Bette hard and fell to the ground, breaking free from the chair underneath him. He then took the large silver platter holding the prosciutto-wrapped asparagus—for such an atrocity of an evening, knowing Blue, I'm sure the food was impeccable—and hit his mother directly in the face, causing her to fall to the floor. Ben freed Belinda and they ran to their neighbor's house. The next day, the police arrested Bette while she was shopping at the grocery store for green beans.

Bette ended up serving forty-three years in prison. She served her time, but my research showed she was never really serving. She enjoyed prison. The little, blue-haired woman turned into a queen and revelled in the glory her cell bestowed upon her. She became a bit of a kingpin.

She deserved to be punished.

I went to her grave, where she now lay, and unburied her mangled carcass. Bette didn't deserve to rest in peace. She deserved to burn in hell. I took her carcass and dropped it in front of Wolf Blitzer's home with the story. The last memory of her would be one of embarrassment, having her dreamboat tell the story of her life with disgust on his face.

Justifications

My anger is consuming. I've been in therapy for years trying to stifle the small outbursts, my justified reasons for acting like a piece of shit. I've never taken a fist to anyone or pushed anyone to the ground. So, I'm justified, right? I must be some sort of saint, right? Saint Michael, the knight-in-shining-fucking-armor, here to save the day and make you cry rivers for hours. But at least you don't have a black fucking eye!

I've locked my daughter in a closet, but only for a second. I've screamed at the top of my lungs, but she triggered me. I've thrown a full cup of water and ice through a glass door, then, in an act of insanity, I walked barefoot across the shards, cutting my feet in the process, but she yelled first. Each sliver of glass penetrates my feet, but the pain feels like cool refreshing ice and is oddly relieving.

Soon-to-be-Teenage Daughter

My mind drifts to taking my own life; seductively daydreaming about slitting my wrist with a razor blade or ruminating the sweet relief found in asphyxiating myself with coarse rope; intentionally inflicting impairment to my homeostasis by throwing myself off a tall building. And so on.

My choice of building is not overwhelmingly famous: located at One North Central in Downtown Phoenix—my old law school. The rooftop was twenty-two stories high. Through a small staircase only a few of us knew about, you could access the roof and walk right up to the ledge. Despite the ideations, I never did succumb. I could never bring myself to commit *hara-kiri*. Granted, there would have been no ritual.

My life isn't glamorous; my job is difficult. Recently, I wasn't enough. Sometimes I never feel like I'm enough. One of my clients, Thom Jones (hereinafter referred to as "TJ"), called me hysterical. He could barely breathe, and the connection was muffled because of TJ's tears and his short, frantic breathing. The pain in his breaking voice was evident. He told me he was standing on the edge of a cliff in Sedona, Arizona. He told me that he'd run out of options; that the monster within him had grown too large. I asked him what happened.

TJ and his ex-wife were in what some people call a toxic relationship. Toxic relationships are emotionally unhealthy, usually resulting in emotional and physical damage by one or both partners. TJ and his wife were both emotionally and physically abusive to each other. They were addicted to the cortisol releasing during their stress, and the dopamine dumps when they would spend all day making love, fucking and cumming all over each other. They were tangled together like two, arm-wrestling squid squirting ink all over each other.

The night in question was a disaster. TJ told me he had a long day at work. One of his employees "severely fucked up," causing nearly $1,400,000 dollars in damage. TJ ran a construction company with locations in Arizona, California, Nevada, Oregon, and Washington. He was notoriously OCD. Whenever I would say his locations were in California, Washington, Oregon, Nevada, he would correct me because I didn't list the locations in alphabetical order.

He was flying home from his Oregon location and his wife was going to pick him up at the airport. She had good qualities but had no idea how to provide him comfort. When TJ was upset, his wife would try to comfort him for about five minutes, mostly telling him his feelings were dumb, and if his mood didn't change in that limited period of time she'd snap.

This particular night they both snapped. TJ told his wife about his day and she became terribly upset. She walked upstairs and packed her black leather travel bag full of clothes. She came back down, and TJ told me he was sitting on the couch waiting for her so they could talk. She said that she was going to her mother's home in Tucson, Arizona, and would be filing divorce paperwork in the morning. The conversation about divorce produced prompt pandemonium. TJ told me he grabbed her keys and went upstairs to their bedroom. He told her she was too hysterical to drive and begged and pleaded for her to calm down so they could talk. He really loved her and would do anything for their marriage.

The door to the bedroom was locked and TJ's wife kept screaming for him to open it. He kept pleading for her to calm down. She did the opposite and broke down the door, rushing into the closet to start breaking things. She threw his shoes and favorite suits all over the ground. She broke his sunglasses and his iPad. He grabbed her to restrain her, but it wasn't enough. She punched him twice in the face and ran back for her keys. She was determined to leave like a tornado, and he was determined to keep any dignity in tack that he had left.

At the end of the fight, TJ tallied the damage. His wife broke his iPhone, iPad, his talking Alexa, an entire box of expensive cigars, and pieces of art that were hanging on the wall. She also punched him numerous times in the face, kicked him once and told him about how she cheated on him multiple times during their marriage.

TJ told me he wasn't innocent either. He restrained her, but hard, way too hard, likely causing bruising all over her body. He also told me about how he broke her things. He broke her iPhone (after she broke his iPhone), her Bose headphones (after she ripped the art off the walls), and her bag of makeup (after she destroyed the cigars and iPad). As I listened to him, I wondered aloud how he would excuse any of his actions.

Now, TJ stood at the top of Bell Rock sobbing on the phone to me. He told me that it was all his fault. I tried to explain they were both at fault; they were in too deep and they were too tangled with the raw, negative emotion they'd lived in for far too long. He wouldn't listen. He kept screaming, "It's all my fault!" He'd scream the mantra in between telling me about what he should have done differently, how he should have just let her go, how he should have been more patient, how he should have taken antidepressants or mood stabilizers. I told him none of that mattered and then the phone went silent.

Seconds of silence turned into minutes before a loud gunshot broke the lull of explosive emotion, followed by the equally loud thud of his body. My client, a man who slowly became a friend, had committed suicide. He ended part of the toxicity the only way he thought he knew how. Instead of causing his wife to suffer anymore, he took the route he thought was best.

At the funeral, I heard people calling him a coward. They talked about how he took the easy way out. I vehemently disagreed.

There is nothing cowardly about a person taking their own life. There's a point where people can't take the pain anymore. They can't take the screaming inside their own head. They can't handle the angst and the anger that floods their senses and makes it feel like your entire body is covered in hot fire. The overwhelming cascade of emotion leaving a person drowning on the inside and forces them to drown themselves on the outside. A merry go round of misery.

The Voices

The motherfucking, cock-sucking, piece-of-shit voices.

It's a bit hard to explain how I hear them. They all come in at once, talking all the fucking time. I haven't learned how to shut them up. The best I can do is get a few of them to kind of whisper, occasionally. (That's in the absolute best conditions and has only happened a handful of times.)

Once they gave me an entire Sunday afternoon of quiet after I pulled a guy's dick out of a girl's vagina while he was in the middle of raping her. I won't lie, it felt great extending my sharp fingernails, reaching my hand back and slicing off his manhood while it still wriggled inside his victim like a dead chicken with its head cut off. They gave me a whole afternoon after that fucker got what was coming to him.

Chester is the first voice. He's the critical one. He'll say things like, "*What the fuck did you even do? She still got raped. You didn't do shit except get blood on your new jeans. You are a fucking idiot.*"

Chester never stops making me feel worthless and he never hyphenates words. I blame my locked jaw on him as I vacillate between anger and a burning desire to clean up this entire goddamn world and chop off every rapist's dick, in every fucking city, in every fucking country, on every fucking continent, no matter what Chester says.

Fuck!!!

Margaret is a goddamned nag. She'll bite into my ears, asking questions like, "*Wouldn't it have been better to extend your teeth and bite off his cock?*"

Yes, it probably would have, Margaret, but his dick is still in a puddle in the alley, isn't it?!

She also constantly asks me where we are going. It's like having five children in the back of a suburban on the way to Disneyland, if Disneyland were on fire in the middle of a pandemic. Two minutes after I tell her we are heading over to a surgeon's house to scare the shit out of him and puncture his lung, so he stops cheating on his wife, she'll ask me where we are going.

"We're going to the fucking surgeon's house, Margaret!"

Five minutes after I tell her we are heading to a chiropractor's house to break his hands so that he doesn't keep beating his kids, she'll ask me where we are going.

"We're going to the fucking chiropractor's house so that he'll stop giving his son a bloody fucking nose, Margaret!"

The most bearable of the bunch is the overly optimistic Ophelia, or O, as I like to call her. She sees the good in everything. Absolutely everything. I love her in doses, but when my hands are covered in blood and I'm holding a rapist's shriveled dick, it's hard to take her seriously when she says, "*That is the loveliest shade of red!*" with the same tone as when she marvels at a garden of sunflowers. I can't help but feel like the sunflowers drip the same, red-colored blood.

Brit acts like my sidekick and has a bad English accent. He's fucking charming and overly obnoxious. I can never speak for myself because he's always fucking telling me what to say. After I lift a horrified victim off the ground and return her to the safety of her home, Brit will implore me to whisper corny lines like, "*Sleep until you can see the light. You are the light.*" All I want to do is roll my eyes so far into the back of my head until my retinas tear off. He can be helpful, but his true value is when I am trying to get a free coffee at the local coffee shop. It's the only time I appreciate the Shakespearean wordsmith.

The last voice is Tetro. Tetro is a giant, speaking MapQuest of demons and disaster, all the time telling me where to go and what to do. Well, he tells me where he *wants* me to go and what he *wants* me to do. No matter where I am, or what situation I may be in, Tetro will spout, "*Woman being raped in the first alley on the southeast side of Indian School and 44th Street.*"

In the middle of lovemaking, Tetro will speak to me in his dial-up tone, "*Deadbeat dad just gave his three-year-old little girl two black eyes.*"

In the middle of a five-course meal, Tetro will sadistically state, "*Woman drowning five-year-old girl in a pool only four blocks away.*"

Ever since the accident, these are my five worst friends; the only friends I have left and the most detestable five friends a person could ever have. They are always talking, criticizing me, and telling me what to do. They talk over each other; they bicker with each other, and me. They yell at each other. They yell at me. They laugh when I am lying in a ditch with my arm falling off. The tell me I'm being inefficient when I slice a rapist's dick off and tell me I should use my teeth, and of course they're fucking right. Using my nails is cleaner, but there is something priceless about the look in a man's peepers while my eyes rage with fire and blood from his dick-drips down my chin.

The simplest and easiest way to explain the voices is that it is like someone is taking five hundred and fifty-five needles and nailing each one into my ear drum with a hammer at the same time.

I'm so fucking miserable.

Before the Accident

Other than my little girl, I have some healthy relationships. Honestly, I have a few select friends whom I hold very close. They are the types who help you move. They support you in any way they can listening to your good days and bad. I meet my friends at little coffee shops filled with optimism and life—mostly because of the abundance of caffeine—and enjoy three shots of rich espresso sitting next to an everything bagel smothered with low-fat cream cheese.

I have a wonderful family. My daughter is the closest person in my world. Goddamn, she is the sun. Her curly blonde hair and awkward, broken smile. Her teeth go in about fourteen different directions. They are big too. She has really big fucking teeth. She can make a basket (in the basketball hoop) from twelve feet away. She plays Mozart on the piano. She is nine years old. She's funny; not quite in a Mary Tyler Moore or Lucille Ball way, at least not yet.

I have a good career. I'm an attorney. I wake up most days ready to work. Although, I never feel like I work enough. In fact, I'm pretty sure I don't. It's an ebb-and-flow work life. Three weeks in a row will be long, heavy weeks. Two weeks are pretty nice. Most days, I work from 9 am to 5 pm and 5 pm to 9 am. It's your common 9 to 5, 5 to 9.

I don't have a significant other; girlfriend or otherwise. However, it doesn't bother me all that much. The only time it really affects my mood is from 2 pm until about 3:57 pm on

Sundays. Sometimes the bad mood lasts until 5 pm. I love the idea of meeting a woman right where the ocean meets the music; the crashing of the music against the bright sounds of the ocean. I want to meet a woman in that little sliver of silence right before the powerful sounds meet: our love.

But odds are I'll just slide into her DMs or something.

People mean the most to me. Some people want gold and riches. I want more people in my life. I feed off people.

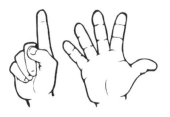

Peruvian Dirt

Ayahuasca is an entheogenic brew made out of the *Banisteriopsis caapi* vine and the *Psychotria viridis* leaf. For the record, I don't know what the fuck any of that means. I do know the active ingredient is dimethyltryptamine, otherwise known as DMT. DMT increases your heart rate, elevates your blood pressure and makes your temperature rise. It also puts you into an altered state of consciousness; a very colorful state of consciousness.

Ayahuasca is known among the Amazonians as "the grandmother", for its ability to gain access to human consciousness and to teach us to do the best we can with the precious gift of our life on this Earth.

In the sixteenth century, Christian missionaries from Spain and Portugal first encountered indigenous South Americans using ayahuasca; they claimed it was the work of the devil. That was right before they sodomized little boys against their will.

The plant itself has been used in the Incan faith as a religious healing tool for what many anthropologists believe to be at least three thousand years. Some anthropologists suggest it's been used for as many as five thousand years.

Ayahuasca is a medicinal plant and is effective in treating patients with PTSD, depression, anxiety and addiction. Facilities in North America are opening. There are clinics in Vancouver,

Seattle, and Salt Lake City, Utah. The word "ayahuasca" means "death's rope." The goal is to not hang oneself, but to use the rope for rebirth. Ayahuasca activates the amygdala, acting as a missile silo for emotional memories. They erupt within the consciousness, causing the person to feel and experience that exact moment in time.

My second ayahuasca ceremony was calm. It took me about fifty-five minutes to finally vomit. If I didn't mention it earlier, along with the all-healing nature and mystical wonder, there's also a ton of vomiting and shitting. They leave that part off of the brochure.

I was amazed at the low volume of Chester, Margaret, O, Brit, and Tetro. They were like low-volume static now. The medicine was working. My mind was being cleansed.

While the normal ration is one dose, on the second night, I, along with one other member of the group, took two doses. The thick liquid sat at the bottom of my stomach. A wave of grace hit me, and I pleaded with the grandmother, asking her to heal me. A thought struck: maybe I don't need healing, maybe I just need control.

The grandmother took me to her factory where it appeared that Willy Wonka was the architect. Laying down on a conveyor belt, I moved through the factory, room by room, with my awareness absorbed by the dancing vines and colorful clouds up above me.

Suddenly, the black tar sitting inside my stomach began to burst out of me: my mouth, my pores, my eyes. Black tears were running down my face. Dazed and a bit confused, I allowed myself to go deeper as the grandmother pulled me through the factory, removing all the black mold inside my body. Immediately, I felt lighter. I could feel the reds and purples and greens and blues inside my soul as they danced in the sky.

The grandmother shepherded me into the next room,

which was touched by Midas; every wall, every inch of space was covered in gold. As I looked around, the walls and ceilings began to bubble like the Grand Prismatic Spring in Yellowstone National Park, and the walls and floor started shooting geysers in every direction. From the ceiling, long, golden tentacles began to spiral down, until they clung to me like leeches, filling me with heaven's meter money, pumping the newly created space with pure magma, pure liquid gold. I could feel the precious metal running through my veins, moving through my fingertips to my feet through my face and to my stomach. The darkness was being filled with gold.

Abruptly, I was outside of the factory, lying in the grass staring at the stars. The grandmother was softly whispering to me. The gold didn't repair me. The gold filled the cracks and made me anew, but she reminded me that you can never fully repair what's already been broken, no matter how pure the reincarnated alloy may feel.

Two days later, I had my third ceremony. My selfish mantra repeated itself until I finally begged aloud, "Show me what I need."

At the end of my third ceremony, I needed help walking up the stairs. I asked John, one of the staff, to help me as I paraded up to my temporary home on the third floor, and asked him to hold my book and candle so I could hold on to the railing. I was still so drugged that my drawstring pants had fallen around my ankles and he made a joke about how I should hold on to them instead of worrying about the railing.

The third ceremony pushed me to the edge, despite only taking a half a cup on this night. I met grandmother ayahuasca almost immediately. She had big, bulbous black eyes and Medusa hair. The snakes and vines from the night before made up her scalp. I was afraid. She led me by the hand into the darkness and obscurity, pushing me to the very edge of the black abyss. We were wandering together silent in a spaceless void, tiptoeing on the rainbow clouds that weren't dancing anymore. They were rigid, like bright floating cubes in space. I started to pulsate, and I could feel my heart pounding inside my chest trying to force its way out, but I had to keep going. I pushed deeper.

I looked into her vacant eyes and begged the grandmother: "Show me what I need. Show me what I need. Please. Show me what I need!"

Energy exploded all around me like a gamma-ray burst. The pressure was crushing and delightful at the same time. It felt like an orgasm. It felt like every orgasm. I shook on the ground in ecstasy until I was covered in sweat. Removing my long-sleeved Henley, my *Captain America* T-shirt which I was wearing underneath, and eventually my drawstring pants, I tried cooling my body. I was so hot and couldn't stop sweating. It felt like I was having a heart attack.

Standing up with the help of the nurse, I made my way outside of the hut to try and cool my body. As soon as my toes touched the cool blades, I fell to the grass, clinging to Gaia, a.k.a. Terra, a.k.a. the Great Mother, a.k.a. Earth Goddess, a.k.a. Ge; a.k.a. the one, the only, Mother Earth. My hands gripped the black Peruvian dirt as if the soil were one-hundred-dollar bills.

John found me on my back doing snow angels and helped me back inside. He quietly tucked me back into my sleeping bag, my cocoon, and I tumbled back into the void, landing on the floating cube. I couldn't contain my fear that I wouldn't be strong enough to keep going further into my journey.

I stood at the edge of the cube watching thousands of movies in the distance: my childhood, me as an adult, my future self and who I could be. I started sweating again. It felt like my sleeping bag was tightening around me as sweat dripped down my nose. I couldn't take it anymore. I felt like dying and must have said something, because at that moment the nurse came over and rubbed cool lavender oil on my skin. It smelled like menthol and I was able to breathe, filling my lungs with what felt like the biggest breath of my entire life and stepped back from the edge of the cube.

Without warning, Maestro Paulo, our shaman for the evening, walked over to me, smoking his tobacco. He put his hand directly on my forehead, chanting. The notes escaped his lips, dancing their way into my ears. Every note that sambaed out from his being was absorbed into mine. Through his broken English, he repeated over and over again, "Wow. Wow. Wow. So much energy."

Then I felt her there with me. I can't remember the last time I could feel her with me, but she was in space with me the entire time. I thought about pouring this new love into her. I thought intently about her future. I saw her blue eyes smiling back at me. I saw her blonde turn to gray. I saw her standing over my coffin crying tears of joy for having a father like me.

Was I foreshadowing or fantasizing about a life I'll never have?

The next day, the group reflected on their individual journeys. Maestro Paulo looked me in the eyes and I told him about the energy I'd felt. I told him about being pushed to my edge.

He said, in perfect English this time, "Your attitude lets you see in the darkness. Not all who wander in the darkness make it out."

He also told me I must use my gifts. He told me to take control.

Happy Hour Menu at Chili's

The voices act like fucking children! Yelling at each other, yelling at me, draining every ounce of energy I have inside of my human form. Some days are so bad. The worst days cause my vision to blur and I fall into a lucid rage, with delusions of a life I once had. My head pounds as hot oil runs through my veins, until I'm burned alive from the inside out. All the while, I'm supposed to be curing the world; pretending that my purpose is anything other than eating, sleeping, fucking and shitting in various orders.

The only thing that gives me an ounce of peace is inflicting justice on some fucked-up soul. My only other option is suffocating my own soul with as many bottles of brown liquor or multi-colored drug as possible. Currently, I am able to consume two liters of vodka while maintaining any form. Sometimes, when I drink too much, the punishment I render, pursuant to certain documents and the Geneva Convention, may be considered cruel and unusual. I say that, pursuant to me, the world can be unusually cruel and someone needs to stand up for justice.

I've never been a fan of cheaters. It's one of the few things in my past life, before the accident, that always made me proud: I never cheated on anybody. In tests, sure, I'm as bad as anyone. One time, I paid a guy who looked like me to take my math test. But in my entire past life, I never once got too drunk and accidentally kissed some girl in a nightclub. I never flirted with my receptionist enough so that my cock ended up in her mouth in the office kitchen. There were no improprieties in my dating life. I have a blanket moral code that cheating causes more suffering than it is worth; not only to the person who is being cheated on, but also the cheatees, the victims of the cheater, and the person who is seduced into believing they matter for a few hours. Everyone is left wondering what the fuck they did wrong to deserve to the pain.

Tetro buzzed: *"Dentist in Anthem sneaking back into the house after spending the night with one of his 'girlfriends.' Kids are asleep. Wife is shopping online..."*

Usually, I ignore these types of alerts. I'd say at least sixty-seven or sixty-eight percent of Tetro's alerts are about someone cheating, or some kid being a kid. Fireworks, hazing, an adolescent trying the first sip of alcohol that will eventually lead to years of self-loathing and hatred, and hundreds of thousands of dollars trying to harden their liver—that sort of thing. You're not going to believe this, but I'm pretty fucking jaded.

However, an old friend had told me about some sick-fuck dentist in Anthem who drugged her and cheated on his wife with her. My interest was piqued and I pressed Tetro for more information.

It took me a while to figure out how to talk to him. Somehow, Tetro is not just plugged into disaster, he's plugged into everybody. He can tell me my target's name, blood type, and even BMI. It's like he lives inside people's minds. He can tell me if my target prefers decaf or regular coffee, their entire ancestry, and whether or not they prefer blondes, brunettes or redheads. If this whole thing weren't so miserable, I'd actually be impressed.

I implored Tetro to give me more information. He told me my victim's name. That's all I needed. It was the same fucking guy. The same guy who disregarded my friend, slipped GHB in her drink, and took advantage of her because of his own goddamn misery. I cracked my knuckles and slowly stood up from my couch. Anthem is about thirty-two miles away from my condo. I thought about driving but decided against a vehicle. I could use the run anyway.

In addition to the heavy drinking, I had been eating more than my weight in burritos during the last few weeks. I don't even binge like normal people anymore. Yesterday, I went to the local casino buffet and ate six plates of food. If that weren't enough to make me feel disgusting, I wandered into the desert and transformed into a brown bear and went hunting. I ate a whole fucking coyote, bones and all.

What the fuck is wrong with me?

I stood outside my condo, knuckles perfectly cracked, and transformed into a 6'5", 209-pound Olympian from Jamaica and started running along the side streets of my city until I reached the Anthem Asshole's (hereinafter referred to as "AA") house. AA didn't live anywhere special; it was a home in a cookie-cutter community with a brand-new Tesla in the driveway.

It was just before 9:17 pm. I looked through the window and saw what looked like his overweight wife and two kids sitting on the couch. They were fixated on some floating box attached to their wall with flashing images that was barely visible. AA wasn't on the scene. I assumed he was upstairs in the shower, washing off the smell of his girlfriend.

The family watched the television for about forty-five minutes until Mom turned off the floating box. She walked upstairs, presumably to tuck the kids into bed, to be alone with their dreams.

Chester repeated himself over and over again as I laid in the grass, the size of a newt: "*Let's go! Let's go! Let's go! Let's go! Leeeeeet's gooooooo!*"

I sighed and into the house we went.

I really didn't have a plan, other than to wait for Brit to suggest what we should do. On cue, he suggested that we wait until morning and follow AA to work, then when he stopped off for gas, or cigarettes, or whatever vice he stopped for in the morning, we could sneak in the car as something small (like a newt), wait for him to start driving again, take over the vehicle and drive him to the desert for some good, old-fashioned cruel and unusual punishment.

Chester inquired whether we would need to wipe the dust off before or after strangling AA, as the plan would take longer than waiting for a Supreme Court ruling. I agreed that Brit's plan was fucking terrible and we snuck into the house at 11:57 pm.

All the lights in the cookie-cutter were dark. Also, for the record, when I say we "snuck" in, I turned my finger into the exact size of their keyhole, opened the door, and I walked in wearing AA's face. The stairs were right in front of the doorway, and I walked up to where I thought the master bedroom would be. It was deathly quiet in the house, but between my anger—which rumbled like an empty stomach in my mind—and the five Super Friends, I felt like I wouldn't have heard if anyone would have spoken to me anyway. Unless someone was screaming into a megaphone inches away from my ear, I was unlikely to lose my focus. Part of me felt dizzy.

Carefully looking into the bedroom, I saw AA and his wife sleeping in the bed. It would've been best to wait until another day, but goddamn, I was starving and needed the pain to subside. I went back into the living room and found a picture of his kids. These two beautiful little monsters who had no idea that their doting dad spends his weekend fucking women who aren't "Mommy."

My figure quickly modified into what appeared to be AA's son, little Timmy, and went back to the bedroom. "Daddy, I had a nightmare!" I yelled from just inside the door. AA's fat wife

49

yelled at me to go back to bed, but I persisted, asking for, "Daaaaaaaddy!"

Eventually, AA followed me downstairs because "I" was having a bad dream. We walked down the stairs and AA sat on the couch wearily questioning me, his son, about the dream.

Brit piped up, *"Sir, I think it may be prudent to run outside. That way you don't make too much noise in the house."*

Brilliant.

Instead of sitting with AA, my adolescent feet made their way towards the door and into the backyard. *Holy fuck!!!* The Anthem Asshole prick had a better car and a better yard than I did. His pool was majestic.

AA followed me, exasperated and without breath. The cunt could barely breathe. As AA chortled in between deep breaths he screamed, "What the hell are you doing, Adam?! It's three o'clock in the goddamn morning!"

Apparently, Little Timmy is actually Little Adam. I wondered quietly if his stupid mongrel sister is named Eve. As I looked at AA, still dressed as Adam, I turned my pupils into a burning fire. AA gasped and fell to the ground, staring to the sky as if God were going to come down and save him. I thought about changing into AA, reflecting his own image so he could see the monster within, but for some reason I took Chester's advice. He was screaming at me to stay in Adam's form because apparently the *"pig-headed, cock-sucking, fire-roasting, chicken-choker"* would be more upset being tortured by his son.

For the record, Chester is usually a bit more original than *"fire-roasting."* After all, we weren't developing the Happy Hour menu at Chili's.

I jumped on top of AA, still dressed as Adam, but because of my small frame he threw me off like a rag doll. Brit told me to make my arms bigger, so I did so while also adding talons —because talons!—and I was able to get back on top of "Dad." I pinned him down, letting one talon slowly sink into his left shoulder blade, tearing his rotator cuff in half. He screamed loudly and I took one muscly arm off him and covered his mouth. As I muffled the sound, I felt a crack in his jaw, and he attempted to scream louder. A light popped on upstairs, and you're not going to believe this, but Margaret mentioned that I'd better mosey on my way before getting caught. And, yes, she fucking used the word "*mosey.*"

I still didn't have a plan but I bent down and whispered in the child's voice, "Where the fuck do you get off ruining people's lives?!" I screamed for a whole minute about the injustice of him cheating on his wife, the pain and questioning he creates in the young women he defiles, and then lastly, I faked a tear as Adam, and told him he was hurting his kids the most. To be honest, I don't give a fuck about AA's kids. I just wanted him to feel shame.

AA promised me that he would never cheat on his wife again, but unfortunately, his promise meant as much to me as his vows meant to him. I took Chester's advice, turning my left hand into a rusty pair of scissors and cut out AA's tongue before transforming my left hand into a pair of nutcrackers and slowly breaking each one of his fingers like pecans.

I looked to my left and saw AA's wife standing in the doorway, mortified. Her jaw was practically in the grass. She heard and witnessed the whole monstrosity. However, she didn't charge me or threaten to call the police. Instead, she looked blank, confused, as if she'd just learned the Earth wasn't flat or as if she'd found out America wasn't the only country on the planet.

Brit blasted my eardrums, making me stand up to leave, and as I did, AA, with blood gushing from his mouth, brokenly said,

"Fuck you, Karma!"

I beat Brit to the punch and looked AA straight in the eye saying, "I'm your Karma, motherfucker."

If I was a woman, I would have fucked me on the spot, right fucking there in the grass. Obviously, we would have needed to move AA's wife's jaw out of the way. And, obviously, I would have had to transform out of Little Adam's body.

I ran out the back gate and down the street, still clothed in Adam's skin. After I made it a few blocks away, I turned into a Harley motorcycle and rode a few miles before turning into a leopard moth and flying away. (For the record, leopard moths are gorgeous creatures, despite the surprising size difference between males and females.)

I made a few loops, just in case someone had figured out how to follow me, before heading to the parking garage at my office. That's because I always come here. I change into a titan beetle, then climb into my office before changing back into myself. Getting caught isn't an option and, despite it taking me longer to get places in insect form, I appreciate the feeling of an otherwise-small world feeling enormous again while I'm embodying a bug.

I sat in my office chair dressed as me, with the oil in my blood still boiling. I needed another target. I needed to do more than just remove someone's tongue and break their hands.

I wasn't doing enough. I could do more. I had to do more.

Standing up and walking toward the door, I knew exactly where I was going.

I asked Tetro to recall an old client of mine. A guy who not only made me look like a cunt in court but also, and more importantly, beat his wife with both fists until both of her eyes were colored black. I was going to kill Abusive James (hereinafter referred to as "AJ").

Four Thousand Two Hundred

I tried to silence the voices. I tried so fucking hard to stop the annoying daily articulations from the asshole assembly in my head. I looked everywhere and scoured the Earth for a cure. I looked in every fucking nook and godforsaken cranny, desperate to stop their constant cynical chatter. I even did something I promised myself as a youth I would never do: I prayed and asked God for help. Hell, I spent over two years donning a symbol of death—a miniaturized torture device shaped like a T—around my neck, to different sermons and lectures around the world. I tried every iteration of pretending to be a God-fearing man: Catholic, Baptist, Methodist, Lutheran, Presbyterian, Protestant, Pentecostal and Mormon. At one point, I even transformed into a priest from Argentina, and sat in conversation for three hours with Pope Francis, discussing religion.

My journey for silence and solitude only worsened. Chester, Tetro, Ophelia, Margaret and Brit were now not only filling each second of each day with their own individual forms of verbal torture, but now they were singing the praises of Jesus. Just last week they were simultaneously debating the date of the *Book of Ruth,* while calling me an asshat for not moving out of the way fast enough while the train was rushing at us. Why did they care anyway? I was the one who nearly died.

Christianity, as a whole, left me with a bitter taste in my

mouth. Parts were good; the people in the faith were good: men, women and children who would actually bleed for Christ as opposed to the men, women and children just reaping the benefits of the sandal being on the other foot. Other parts felt like dirty water turning into cheap wine. So, I moved on.

I tried out Satanism. You're not going to believe this, but the Church of Satan is a weird fucking place. Everyone in the Church wears black and looks like they are ready to crucify or circumcise me at any given time. Surprisingly, they looked strangely at me when I showed up in a bright-orange shirt. Surrounded by all the men, women and children dressed in black, I looked like a pumpkin on Halloween night.

Curiously, Margaret felt at home in the fiery parish. It was the least I'd heard her complain in months. Her silence almost made it worth changing my wardrobe and donning all black. Plus, ironically, Satanists still celebrate Christmas, so it wouldn't be that bad if I decided to give my weary soul to Beelzebub.

For the record, I did not try all four thousand, two hundred religions around the world in my silly search to silence the suffering; I focused mostly on the popular ones. To me, it was like watching a movie. If you give me the choice between a Hollywood blockbuster or a single-shot, first-person movie about the evolution of the sea sponge, I'm going to pick the Hollywood blockbuster every single time. Although Pastafarianism was tempting; there's something surreal and rather quaint about a group of people worshiping a flying spaghetti monster.

Scientology had Chester hooked. He was ready to not talk for an entire year and honestly had me worried every time I went to sleep that he was going to take control of my body and turn us into Tom Cruise so we would be able to board the *Freewinds* Cruise. My favorite part of the experience was visiting the Czech Republic and practicing with the Cosmic People of Light Powers, affectionately known in my mind as CPLP. If you're unfamiliar, the CPLP is a UFO cult which believes that in 1990, aliens communicated with their leader, Ivo A. Benda. The CPLP believe extraterrestrial civilizations operate a fleet of spaceships, led by Ashtar Galactic Command, orbiting the Earth. They keep a close watch and are waiting to transport their followers into another dimension. For the record, they are not half as weird as the Mormons.

Hinduism was the last religion I tried, and it led me to short stints of relief. I was satiated in silence after months of this shit. Brit, Ophelia and I all were hooked on Hinduism. Life was still misery, but the practices broke up the relentless stream of my miserable life ever so briefly.

Before practicing Hinduism, my life with the voices felt like I was trying to survive whitewater rapids each day, with nothing but a shitty apartment pool's sun-bleached flotation device. No breaks, no air, just years of trying to survive, gasping for each and every fucking breath, while Satan poured hot oil down my throat. My mind was defunct and full of debris. I couldn't remember the last time I remembered a yesterday. Hinduism gave me a sweet reprieve for twenty seconds each day. The religion allowed me to remember the life I once had. Nearly three years of searching through religion after fucking religion and all it did was give me twenty fucking seconds a day of peace and quiet.

Brit and Ophelia remind me to be grateful.

Whatever.

I am most closely related to the *Purusartha*. *Purusartha* is the object of human pursuit which refers to the four proper goals of human life. The four are *Dharma* (righteousness, moral values), *Artha* (prosperity, economic values), *Kama* (pleasure, love, psychological values) and *Moksha* (liberation, spiritual values). Most of my focus and intention are set on the *Dharma*. Everything I was fucking doing was to create order. All I ever did was even the playing field, regulating the natural order of this chaotic fucking disaster that is known as the world.

Each morning, my alarm wakes me up at 5:00 am. On a good night, I've received anywhere from one to three hours of sleep. Most nights, my eyes are wide open, waiting for the alarm to ring. Once it does, I sit up straight at the foot of my California king bed and scream, "*Dharma!*" at the top of my lungs for thirty straight minutes.

"*Dharma. Dharma! Dharma!!!!*"

One time, I was so loud my neighbors called the police. At the end of my howling, I'm usually exasperated, exhausted and sweaty, and my throat burns as if I'm playing chubby bunny with hot embers of coal. That moment, right after my thirty minutes of screaming, is when I have my twenty seconds of silence. Begrudgingly, I thank God for that twenty fucking seconds of silence.

Today, I am going to see Veronica. I need to vent.

Hail to the Chief

So, I feel like I should tell you—I've stolen some money along the way.

About two months ago, Tetro alerted me of a brutish man sodomizing young girls. These youngsters were around the age of seventeen, but still, he needed to be stopped. He treated the world like shit. This guy wasn't just rich; he was really rich. He was one of the wealthiest men in the world. He lived in New York City and was worth three and a half billion dollars. The world was nothing to him. He scammed, stole, fucked, touched, grabbed by the pussy, and narcissistically manipulated the common man (or woman) for pleasure.

When Tetro buzzed about him I couldn't wait. I transformed into a Belgian horse and set off east. I rode the Arizona desert relentlessly hard and made it to New York City in four days. Ordinarily, a horse can only ride about ten miles per hour for up to five hours per day. Fortunately, I'm not ordinary. I galloped at roughly eighty miles per hour, only taking breaks to eat and pee and fuck and sleep for short periods of time.

When I reached New York City, I remained in my horse form until I reached Central Park, where I transformed back into me. I needed a shower and to scope out the area before taking action that night. He wasn't only going to promise me he would never fuck an underage girl again, but he was going to be embarrassed. This guy had an ego the size of Donald Trump's head and he needed to be knocked down a few—if not all—pegs.

After my shower, I made my way to his towering building. I looked up at the fifty-eight-story building where he occupied the entire top floor—which would have been impressive on its own, but he also owned floors one through fifty-seven. My eyes turned into binoculars and I could see a small window in the corner next to where a young woman was pressing her hands against a larger window. There was a woman behind her jamming a 14-inch dildo into her twat. Mr. Fantastic was sitting on the couch grinning and snorting Columbian cocaine as he tugged on his small (2.2-inch) penis.

I turned into a Peregrine falcon and flew into the dark night sky. By the time I'd reached about thirty stories, my wings would barely flap. I was exhausted. The wind was strong, and at my size, I didn't have a chance to make it to the top without coughing up a lung. I needed more strength, so I transformed into an albatross: a strong, flying bird. Ironically, the word "albatross" is sometimes used metaphorically to mean a psychological burden that feels like a curse. So, there's that.

As I reached the open window, I turned back into a Peregrine falcon. Between the cocaine and the show, Mr. Fantastic was preoccupied and didn't notice. I flew over to the far side of the room, near the fully stocked bar. The bar had every type of beer and liquor one could imagine; everything from Natural Ice to a bottle of sixty-year-old Macallan.

The entire room was filled with an awful odor, smelling like a mix of fish and old-man semen. Mr. Fantastic had put down a rolled hundred-dollar bill onto the coffee table and had asserted himself on his leather couch fully naked, jacking off with a belt around his neck. His large frame was slouched into the couch. When standing, he stood 6'2" with blonde hair and a smug grin that never came off his face. He looked very presidential.

I thought carefully as I crafted my plan. It was perfect. So fucking perfect. If there was one thing Mr. Fantastic loved more than drugs or pussy, it was money.

I started to transform from a small bird into a giant, million-dollar bill with legs. As he saw me materializing, he was so fucked up on the drugs that he just smiled from ear-to-ear as he continued tugging on his penis that was no bigger than a slice of mandarin orange. He looked at me and, somehow in all seriousness, said, "Look out baby, I'm going to fuck you!"

I quickly decided to change plans as I had not anticipated—although I probably should have—him wanting to make sweet love to me dressed as a million-dollar bill.

New plan: don't get fucked.

He jumped toward me and I stepped to the side, avoiding him with ease. On top of being completely coked out, he was hysterically overweight. His hands were on the ground and his flabby old-man ass was sticking up into the air. I reflected his voice and said, "Come fuck me with the dildo, ladies!" Then I rubberized my entire body, covering his mouth with my hand and held him down with my feet.

The girls blankly obeyed. It was fucking creepy. They didn't question the fact that a rubberized, seven-foot million-dollar bill was holding down their boss. They didn't run for the door, they just walked over, grabbed the giant dildo, skipped the lubrication and shoved it right in his ass. As his eyes bulged out of his head, I let out the smallest laugh as I jumped off the greasy pig.

He yelled, "What the fuck are you doing?!" as he pulled back a fist and punched one of the young Russian girls in the face without her even flinching. Blood started to drip down her nose, but she never broke eye-contact with him. She looked at him as if to say, "*Is that all you've got, you fucking pussy?*"

That's when the games stopped, and I transformed into Mr. Fantastic. The girls' attention waned, and their eyes drew to me. No facial movements, no reaction, just looking.

He knew exactly who I was, and he didn't hate me for what I was about to do. He hated me because I was the only person in America who received more media attention than he did. He smiled and said, "Hey, fucker," in his droopy New York accent. He wasn't scared like most people. He wasn't scared at all.

In fact, he looked like he was going to kill me.

And then, he tried to kill me.

"Percy!!!" he screamed. Within half a second, another man was in the room directly to my right. He was big. Really, really big. He stood about 6'6" with broad shoulders and brown hair down to his waist. More importantly than his size, he was holding a 9mm in his left hand. He smiled at me too.

Brit buzzed, "*What is with all the people here smiling today?*"

He didn't hesitate to lift his left arm and fire. He knew better than to fuck around and threaten me and we forewent the usual placated and veiled intimidations. I knew Mr. Fantastic would have security, but I didn't expect only one man. I turned my right arm into a vibranium shield and blocked the bullets. As the bullets ricocheted into the air, I transformed my left arm into a sharp hook and threw it at Percy's temple. The hook stuck into the top of his head and split him in half. I quickly retracted my arm and smiled back at Mr. Fantastic.

He gently reminded me a few times that I should go fuck myself before attempting to grab the gun that had fallen on the floor. I put the hook directly through the top of his hand. Like the Russians, he didn't scream.

"*What is with the smiling and silence, sir?*" Brit chirped.

I left the hook in Mr. Fantastic's hand and walked toward his desk, opening his computer. I told him that he had to pay for his transgressions; that despite his logic it was detrimental to society as a whole to defraud students (he funded a fake college); to take advantage of women (he had done everything you can imagine); and to go to Uganda to shoot humans as sport (he had, but it wasn't in the news).

He still didn't plead for his life like most people. He did what he did best: he attempted to negotiate. He told me he'd give me a million dollars to leave. I laughed hysterically. I mean, fucking hysterically. My head was cocked back, one hand was on my stomach, and tears of joy were running down my face. This motherfucker offered me one million dollars.

I told him I wanted three billion, four hundred million dollars. He didn't flinch. He expected it and quickly agreed to the price. He knew that as serious as he was, that I was more serious, and that I would scalp his head, cheese-grate his penis, then remove both of his eyes from the sockets while each of the Russian whores face-fucked him with a strap-on dildo.

And so on.

I slid a nearby computer to him and I watched him transfer 3.4 billion dollars to various charities around the world, with most of the money going to help men and women suffering from starvation. Also, I had him transfer a hundred million dollars into a separate account: my offshore bank account. I didn't kill him, but he did pay heavily for his transgressions.

Buttfuck, New Mexico

Part of being an only child is a never-ending, mostly false belief that you are the most important person in the universe; that the Earth doesn't revolve around the sun, but rather the entire cosmos is suspended in motion because of your massive fucking ego. This was especially true for me, the son of a widow, raised by two well-intended, always-spoiling grandparents. I was so full of myself that, if pressed, I would be convinced the term narcissist was concocted after one of my many therapists interviewed me.

This all changed once She was born. The minute She escaped from her mother's womb, I knew that I was as insignificant as a single leaf in a lavish, green jungle.

It was as if God had reached into my chest and recalibrated my heart, reorganizing the ventricles so that instead of blood being pumped, all I could do was emit care and compassion for her, pouring out love, insight, education, and so on.

My singular purpose was to make sure that she was properly appreciated, if only to make sure that she didn't wind up on a stripper pole in some podunk town in Buttfuck, New Mexico.

"Good" and "Bad"

It took me a while to become accustomed to my newfound powers. The newspapers, news stations, Twitter and Reddit users make me into a hero when I do something good or wholesome, like save a cat from a tree, but when I do something bad or gruesome—like hang fourteen fucking female genital mutilators to a tree in Djibouti by their God-forsaken necks because they had an insatiable desire to needlessly stitch their wives' pussies closed—they demonize me.

I hate the media. They try and separate my actions into "good" and "bad" to drive controversy, as if the media are the ones who determine right and wrong; just and unjust.

Fuck them. Fuck them all.

Sometimes, fate isn't enough. Life isn't fair. The fucking universe is not fair.

Sometimes, people need to have their karma given to them before an untimely death in a car accident or a heart attack. Some people need to be shown how awful they've been to society. They need to see the suffering they have caused firsthand. Ever since the accident, that has been my job, and the only thing that brings me any positive feeling.

At this point, you're probably wondering, exactly what does this motherfucker do? Well, I have the ability to transform my physical form into almost anything. I say almost anything because I'm sure there are things I haven't tried yet. I know that I can turn my hands into knives or any piece of cutlery. I know I can turn my feet into propellers to make me faster in water. I once took the form of an airplane to fly to Philadelphia, when Tetro told me about a ghastly asshole who was dressing up on Halloween and molesting children for candy. He'll never touch another child or look at a king-sized tootsie roll in the same way again.

When I am scarring my victims and scaring them straight, or simply ending their lives, I'll do my best to take their form—face, body, mannerisms—before I say my final goodbyes. I do this for two reasons: firstly, I don't want to end up behind bars. Secondly, and more importantly, I want them to see their own worst enemy. I want them to see the face that has caused so much pain to other individuals.

My masks are similar to before the accident, except now I can quite literally take any face I desire. Before, I had to fake it until I made it. Now, I show people that they have been continuously mistaking the self for what is not the self. I show them their truth that they refuse to acknowledge. The darkness that lies within.

Witblits

So, here I sit in first class, not too worried about the $7,943 bill. My headphones are sitting on top of my head and I'm finishing my first bottle of champagne.

The flight attendant is attractive. She has long, curly red hair and clear glasses like mine. She sits right next to me and I make a few jokes. Her infectious laugh fills the cabin like rich oxygen. She sounds a bit like The Joker, but more feminine. I'm not sure if it's the alcohol, her hard nipples showing through her blouse, or the fact that she has laughed hysterically at every single one of my jokes, but I'm really turned on. I'm going to fuck this woman.

Brit always knows what I should say. Obviously, it grows tiresome when I am tediously removing a person's nipples from their chest using only the strength of my fingers and nails, but when women are involved, he can be worth the trouble.

"Your red hair reminds me of a thousand roses falling to the ground, slowly drifting, as if waiting patiently to catch the bright reflection of the burning-hot sun." The words flow out of my mouth as I play with her hair and move my hand closer to the inside of her leg.

Her lips purse as she reaches forward and puts her hand directly on my cock through my jeans. "Is there anything else I can do for you, sir?" she seductively speaks.

With my hand still wrapped in her rose petals, I pull her

close and tell her to grab a blanket. She returns a few minutes later with a blanket and a change of clothes. Before, she was wearing tight blue pants to match her top. Now, she stands in front of me wearing the same blue top with a short blue skirt hovering just above her knees. As she takes the seat next to me, she covers me with the blanket and utters, "Is there anything else I can do for you, sir?"

I whisper Brit's beautiful words in her ear and before I know it, her head is under the blanket with her mouth firmly around my dick. I look to the right and see an older Asian woman looking in my direction. I give her a wink then start extending my cock in the flight attendant's mouth to make her choke. The entire plane can hear her choking on my dick.

As she comes up for air and wipes her mouth off, she says one final time, "Is there anything else I can do for you, sir"?

This time I don't speak. I lift up the arm rest, pull her flower underwear to the side and slide myself into her. She comes quickly, twice.

For the record, I use my powers when I'm with a woman to perfectly fill them up. Then, like one of those cool $180 vibrators at the store, I rotate the head of my cock while I'm inside them. It drives them wild.

After I finish in her throat, she wipes her mouth, jumps up smiling and fixes her skirt. The Asian woman is now smiling brightly. I can faintly hear Chester say, *"See if the chink fancies a go!"* but I shrug it off and inform the slightly overweight, gay flight attendant I want another bottle of champagne. He returns with the bubbly, and right as I am finishing my second bottle, we land.

I am in South Africa, happy and very drunk.

I stumble off the plane with my headphones blaring as my lips move in synchronization to the music for nobody to hear. It is almost time for happy hour but feels anywhere from four-thirty am to the middle of the universe. On the plane, I'd settled on my accommodations and informed a driver to pick me up at six pm sharp. The old me lived one check mark at a time and, as part of my arrangements, I made plans to take a pen to my bucket list and swim with great white sharks the next morning.

I find a local group that take cash. Their boats aren't as up to par as the travel agency's fine fleet, but they work quickly and according to their brochure and, according to the concierge, I can bring local gin onboard. Did somebody say win/win?

My limousine arrives quickly to the hotel where I am greeted by Simon, the concierge. He is a nice fellow, standing roughly 5'9" with a red mop of hair and a doughy, baby face. Simon takes my bag from my right hand and replaces it with a warm, complimentary bottle of my favorite African liquor, Witblits. The following waiter provides a clean, crystal glass with two ice cubes to occupy my left hand. Witblits is African moonshine meaning, "white lightning."

Simon and I speak for roughly forty-five minutes on various topics, including, but not limited to, the current economic situation of Poland, the proper way to pronounce "wholesome," and whether we should open another bottle of Witblits. However, before the party gets out of hand, I bid my farewells and tell Simon I will be back in more than eight hours, but in no less than ten hours.

I make my way on foot to the coastal fishing village of Gansbaai. By the time I reach the broken, wooden dock, the second bottle of Witblits I stole without Simon seeing has gone, and my eyes are transfixed on shark fins piercing the water roughly fifty feet in front of me. They are right there. The distance feels like inches and the chilly cold from the massive beasts penetrates to my soul. I can't wait until tomorrow. My head feels like it is on fire and I need to touch the fishy.

I hear another rumbling as Tetro buzzes, "*Man in Cape*

Town using a pool cue on his son because the boy ate the last loaf of bread. The boy is being forced to put his hands on the table while the father is taking a belt to his back, ass and ankles..."

Ophelia chimes in, "*I can see the sharks swimming underneath the water. They look like pure beauty.*"

What the fuck is going on? They have been quiet since Peru. I thought everything was getting better.

"*Sir, we really should focus on the task at hand. What exactly are we doing here?*" Brit bellows.

I extend the right nail on my index finger and trace my veins along my left arm until it is soaked in blood. I dip my bloody arm into the water, and almost in unison with Chester, say, "Here, fishy, fishy, fishy, fishy." The frantic need to feed is back.

Chester spouts, "*You just had to take advantage of that redhead in the airplane, didn't you? You fucking idiot! You're a fucking idiot!!*"

I stand up too fast and fall into the water. Quickly and drunkenly, I transform my eyes into those of a great white shark. Their eyesight is impeccable.

To my dismay, my eyesight could have been that of a rhinoceros as the blood beasts are only inches from my face. For the record, rhinoceroses, or rhinos as they are often affectionately referred to as, have terrible eyesight. The great sharks are enormous and they are all lusting after me. Ophelia tells me I should be flattered.

There are three sharks surrounding me, smelling my chum-covered left arm. I heal my wounds and stop the blood from pouring, but the damage is done. They move in a flash, coming at me at roughly thirty-five miles per hour before I can even blink. I am too drunk and haven't transformed in a long time. This is a bad idea. I quickly go from the greatest threat to great white sharks to the least. Unfortunately, I am already in human form and they don't see myself, in my current stupor, as much of a threat.

So, I transform. My bones break from my shins to my elbow. My skin turns rubbery, black and white, as large fins rip through what is left of my human skin. Conical and interlocking teeth rip through my gums and I jump into the air with a still-growing, 45-foot body, roughly twice the size of an average killer whale, and swim 40 mph towards my new friends. The black and white tux feels good. I feel powerful. I am ready to take on the blood beasts.

Tetro: "*Your mother will die in ninety seconds. Natural causes. Her blood is thinning causing a…*"

What the fuck? What the fuck? What the fuck? What the fuck? Why would Tetro tell me that?! Why now?!!!

Chester: "*Hahahahahahahahahahaha!*"

Brit: "*I'm sorry, sir.*"

Ophelia: "*Life is just a beautiful dream. We all have the ability to enter the conscious state of sleep choosing to make the most of the colors within.*"

Margaret: "*Watch out for the sharks!*"

Two of the sharks lunge to bite me. I dodge them and swim straight down towards the black of the ocean as they decline to follow me toward the abyss. I crave the darkness, and when I can't feel their vibrations, I look up towards the sky. The three amigos are swimming in a large circle two hundred feet above my head. I swim cautiously toward the moon above. I have my plan, but stupid fucking Brit has to remind me anyway:

"*Sir, if you remember correctly, great whites are known for being quite docile when turned on their backs.*"

He doesn't even know what he is talking about. He always speaks with confidence but half the time he's wrong. Great whites will literally go unconscious if flipped over.

I start swimming to the surface and my speed approaches 35 mph as I crash powerfully into the side of the first great white.

He flips over instantly and the other two break the circle, zeroing in on me.

The bigger female seems farther away than I thought as her teeth sink into my back. The pain is immense as I send a charge of electricity through my body, frying the chunky female instantly.

The last one looks scared, genuinely scared as we lock eyes. He knows he has no chance; his superior counterpart and alpha has just been fried to a crisp. He spins around, swimming as fast as he can away from the dock toward the vast ocean.

I swim toward a nearby beach and transform into a black man with long dreadlocks. The whole ordeal takes about as long as a seven-course meal, and I am starving and filled with testosterone. My blood naturally pumps hard throughout my body. With each pump of my heart, I feel a deep bass beat in my chest as Chester, Ophelia, Margaret, Brit and Tetro get progressively louder.

I need a drink.

I stumble into the first very fancy hotel lounge I can find on Longmarket Street, named Tjing Tjing. When I walk in, the patrons take a collective gasp. That's when I realize I am still black. My long dreads cover my nipples and the only clothing on my body resembles a Tarzan cloth covering my loins. I lumber to the bathroom and transform, becoming Japanese. My suit is perfectly pressed, my hair combed well. My demeanor screams, "Hand me a martini. Now."

I walk back into the lounge without the same gawking and awkward reception, but still filled with rage. I can't stop shaking. It takes all of my strength to stop my body from shaking. I need to calm the fuck down!

I press my right hand hard into my right knee and stop my jittering from shaking the restaurant next door. To my left, sitting at the bar, are two high-class women desperate for a refill. I swallow hard and motion them over to me with my left hand. They smile coyly and move next to me as I introduce myself as Yakunan, which is actually a woman's name meaning "misfortune." They don't notice anything but my perfect smile, and luckily for me, they can't see the burning in my eyes.

They are businesswomen from Vancouver, Canada, in Cape Town buying gold. They'd traveled around the world together and are good friends. Maria is short, very short. She is Mexican and fiery. She has long black hair and brown eyes. She sounds like a smoker even though she's never touched a cigarette in her life. Her body is curvy, and her red lips are intoxicating. She plays with Molly's hair as she sips her Bombay Sapphire and tonic. Molly is tall and blonde, American-made. Her tits could be one of the seven natural wonders of the world. To be fair, I'm not sure if they are natural.

Molly moved to Vancouver when she was twenty-five to pursue a career at First Quantum Minerals. She is now thirty-two, filled with experience—and probably with silicone—and looking gorgeous. In seven years, she has gone from an assistant to the CFO of a 1.7-billion-dollar company. She also, cutely, takes very small sips of her martini. They are the smallest sips I've ever seen.

I tell them about my history. Well, the history Brit created. I fought in the Japanese Army until I was twenty-two years old. At that point, my father had died leaving me one hundred million Japanese Yen—about a million dollars. I tell the women I've figured out a way to make electric coffee. The liquid causes a jolt sensation upon contact with a person's mouth, creating arousal in their cerebral cortex, allowing them to absorb more of the caffeine into their bloodstream.

They look into my brown eyes as the waters rage beneath them. I have switched to whisky and my Old Fashioned glass is empty while my blood still pumps hot. The women finish their drinks and I excuse myself to reserve a penthouse at the hotel. On my way, Tetro buzzes,

"*Woman had too many drinks and is unwillingly giving a hand job to a man in that bathroom...*"

On my way back to the bar, I pop into the men's room, grab the old man and break his spirit and his tailbone.

Returning to the women, I gather their hands in mine and escort them to the 42nd floor. The room is gorgeous. The ceilings are twenty-feet high, there are giant chandeliers, and—my favorite—there is an ebony Steinway winking at me from the corner of the room. I pour three fingers worth of whisky and take my seat at the piano.

"*Fly me to the moon and let me play among the stars, let me see what spring is like on Jupiter and Mars. In other words, please be true. In other words, I love you...*" croaks out of my hollow throat.

Maria and Molly are kissing on the couch. I sip my whisky, turn a football match on the TV and sit back, admiring the show before me. Maria is on top of Molly while Molly's hand runs up Maria's tight black dress. I walk over and play with Molly's Grand Canyons, set down my whisky, and take off her white gown in an instant.

The three of us pour champagne on each other and make love throughout the night, before falling asleep on the bed made for a king. I wake up at four am, before the women, and step into the bar in the bedroom. I pour three more fingers of bourbon and watch them sleep. My head is a fog.

All at once I crash to my knees. They are screaming again.

Chester: "*NICE FUCK, YOU WANKER!*"

Ophelia: "*THAT WAS A MAGICAL EXPERIENCE. I'VE NEVER SEEN SUCH EROTIC, ORGASMIC BEHAVIOR.*"

Margaret: "*YOU'RE DRINKING TOO MUCH ALCOHOL. YOU'RE RUINING THE AYAHUASCA.*"

Brit: "*SIR, WHY IN THE WORLD WOULD YOU BE*

SO SELFISH? YOU COULD HAVE BEEN HAPPY."

Tetro: "*German man wearing a brown suit in the lounge at Tjing Tjing. He is about to leave the lounge and assault a homeless woman on the corner. He will beat her, as he has beaten homeless men and women in the past, just up to the point where she will die. Then, he will force-fuck her face.*"

I transform immediately and unconsciously. I am standing at the bar pouring another drink, looking at the two women. I am a German man now. I run to the balcony and jump off, plummeting forty-two stories to the earth. I've only done this once before, but who fucking cares?

Who the fuck cares? Who the fuck cares? Who the fuck cares? Who the fuck cares? Who the fuck cares?

This has to stop. I am sure that it has been too long since I've done any good. That's why they are back. That's why they are screaming again. I am sure of it.

I land hard on the ground and while it hurts like hell, the booze soaks up the pain. I pop up as the German. He is on the corner, seeing how far he can fit his fist down the homeless woman's mouth before replacing his knuckles with his dick.

I walk over to him casually and tap him on the shoulder. He spins around and our eyes meet.

"Hallo, motherfucker."

I kick him in the balls, smash in every single tooth in his mouth, and punch him in the face until all that is staring back at me is thick, red blood. I can't tell if there is more blood on my fist or on his face.

I start to open my mouth when Tetro buzzes me again. He is loud again. I can hear all of them, loudly, again. They are even louder now than when I left for Peru.

I thought I had them under control.

Tetro buzzes, "*Man taking advantage of two drunk women in a penthouse.*"

73

My eyes rage. I need to turn it off. I need to flip the switch.
The pain. The rage. The anger.
I'm never going to be okay.

Darkness and Nightfall

I was still pinned under the branch and these new voices wouldn't stop talking. Goddamn, they were fucking annoying, but I was so happy to be alive I didn't really care. I figured they were a result of concussion and they would be gone soon enough.

The light from dawn began to say hello from over the rim of the grave. I tried yelling but my voice was gone from screaming so much the night before. It felt like I had a rotten grapefruit stinging my throat. I was so thrilled to be alive. My body was depleted of energy and emotion, but I knew eventually, someone would find me. The worst was over, or so I thought, and I could wait for someone to walk past the open grave, gasp in horror at the bloody sight of me, then, presumably, help me out.

My mind wandered back to my daughter. I was so overcome with gratitude I started to cry again. How in the fuck was I alive? I still laid in corpse pose, exhausted with the branch still on top of me. These strange voices kept talking clumsily over one another. I tried to put my mind elsewhere.

I've always been a huge comic book fan and my mind drifted to how one of my favorite heroes would remedy the situation. His slight stature would morph into a giant, green freak. A hulking figure. That's when it happened for the first time: my body began to change. My muscles bulged and broke through the skin of my shirt. My bones cracked as they increased in size, sounding like a crackle in a campfire. The pain burned and I screamed in agony, my throat stinging with acidity as I cried.

What the fuck was happening?

I closed my eyes and told myself I was hallucinating. As I peeled them open, I could see the street clearly. My body ached, and I was now standing tall in the grave instead of lying flat. My shoulders were sticking eighteen inches out of the grave; I was roughly eight feet tall. I looked down. I was naked and my entire body was green. I had muscles popping out everywhere. My muscles had muscles. I had transformed into a Hulk. What the fuck had happened to me?

I stepped out of the grave, firmly in the grass, and kept looking at my giant, green hands, audibly saying some variation of, "What the fuck is happening to me?"

No longer did I think I was suffering from concussion. I thought I was dead. I pinched myself. I couldn't feel anything. So, I uprooted a tall oak tree and dropped it on my foot. I barely felt it, but I did feel it.

Could I really be alive?

I started running in a gray haze toward home when I reached Shea Road, a mere couple of hundred feet from the grave, I heard the car tires screech and loud bangs as cars crashed into each other. Seat-belted drivers and passengers alike gawked and stared in awe. I ran in the opposite direction until I reached the overwhelmingly large Arizona desert. Apparently, it's not every day people see a giant, green monster.

I waited in the desert until the light was covered by darkness and nightfall had fallen upon my first-born city. I walked, instead of ran, toward my condo so I could stay out of sight. The last thing I needed was to cause pain and suffering, or for people to be harmed because of this freak instance. I didn't make it far until I saw other human beings. I say "other" because I still assumed I was human. There were people drinking coffee at a Starbucks on Mayo Boulevard, just west of Scottsdale Road. It was a family: a husband, a wife, a son and a daughter.

I thought of my little girl. I wondered if I'd ever see her again.

Everything was a cloud of gloom.

I thought about the last time I saw her when I felt the burst of the campfire again. My bones cracked as they began to shrink, and I covered my mouth to keep people from hearing me yell in pain while looking down at my hands. They weren't green anymore. They were not enormously huge anymore. They looked like my hands.

Then, for the first time since they said hello, I was conscious of the voices.

The fucking voices.

Brit bellowed, *"Happy to be back in your normal figure, sir?"*

Margaret moaned, *"All your credit cards are ruined because of the rain. I'm not sure how you plan on getting home. You're also naked and I can see your shriveled little dick."*

Chester critiqued, *"The green looked much better on you. Plus, you didn't have your gut."*

Ophelia opined, *"You're so fortunate to be alive, sir."*

Tetro buzzed, *"We have five minutes to intercept. Black man being targeted by two white males in Tuscaloosa, Alabama... Men are currently arguing inside the bowling alley and, 'taking it outside...' All three men are outside, both white men are armed with 9mm handguns. Black male armed with Swiss Army knife... Taller, white male, aged thirty-eight, strikes black male, aged twenty-four, in the face... White male number two, aged forty-two, is now grabbing the younger male by the throat and choking him... White male number one steps back, draws his weapon and shoots twenty-four-year-old male in the head twice and once in the stomach. There is no time left to intercept. Time has expired."*

Chester laughed thunderously. *"That kid died because of*

you, you fucking idiot!"

My body was stiff. I felt dead. My legs shook as I nervously walked toward Starbucks. Cars on the street continued to their destination. Surprisingly, onlookers and patrons didn't gawk as I walked by them. I walked into Starbucks and went straight for the restroom. I hadn't peed in hours and, slightly more importantly, I lusted for a mirror. I had to see the eyes that would be staring back at me. I looked in the mirror and saw green. Fortunately, it was the green of my eyes and not my skin.

I was back. I was me. I was standing nearly naked in a Starbucks bathroom, but I was me. I must be hallucinating.

Tetro buzzed again, *"We have fourteen minutes to intercept. Woman on 68th Street and Indian School is holding a gun against her seven-year-old son's temple. Woman is screaming about how life isn't worth it..."*

He informed me fourteen minutes later that she pulled the trigger and the boy was in a critical condition. Broken, mangled and feeling destitute, I made the short, nearly naked walk back to my condo—seventeen miles—and opened the door.

I was home. I was finally fucking home after the worst night of my life and it was time to figure out what the hell had happened.

Madam V

It was one week after I'd fallen into the grave.
Unfortunately, along with having the five friends fumbling
around my conscience, I also had the famous *Mouse Rat* song
reverberating around my recluse reasoning organ. In a way, with
my new abilities, it was like the whole world fell into the pit with
me. Everyone had changed. Every unjust bastard would now
know what it felt like to have their bodies dripping with acid. The
worst part was when the hot liquid crept into the corners of their
mouths, sending hot embers rolling down their esophagus,
burning them from the inside.

The worst part was that I couldn't talk to anyone about
my situation. No level of friendship or relationship would be able
to stand the heart-to-heart that I required to feel heard.

They talked all the time. All the fucking time. It was like
being stuck in a room with your five worst enemies. And no, I'm
not talking about being stuck inside of a mushroom trip; quite
the contrary. It was like being stuck in a morbid mushroom trip
and never escaping. My whole world had transformed from
borderline peace to disharmony and distress at every corner.

Tetro wouldn't stop buzzing and reminding me of life's
inescapable horrors; line after line of lucid language. How I
lamented my existence! After hours of weeping on the couch,
Tetro finally said something that caught my attention:

"Woman draining the blood of three little girls on

Camelback Mountain. All three girls are hanging by their feet. Stomachs have been slashed open and blood is running down their entire body..."

I stopped crying instantly and stood up. If I was going to be stuck in perpetual misery, I could at least do something about it. Maybe that would shut these goddamn pieces of shit up. Maybe if I alleviated suffering, my suffering would be alleviated.

Over the previous week I had done nothing but cry on my couch, and drink bottles of Nyquil to sleep. Every time I awoke, the voices were in mid-conversation, mid-argument and midway through telling me about the horrors occurring down the road. Part of me didn't believe that I transformed into a giant, green freak roughly a week ago. Part of me thought I would wake up from this morbid mushroom trip eventually; I'd awake from a coma or realize I was not in the good place. Unfortunately, part of me was so very wrong.

Tetro kept chugging along like Thomas the Train as I stood helpless in my living room: *"All three girls are eleven years old. They have roughly forty-five minutes left to live before they will suffer too much blood loss."*

I thought about my predicament. If I really did have powers, I would have to use them eventually, right? After all, the stores would run out of Nyquil eventually, right? Plus, what if it made the voices stop?

"We're not going to stop no matter what!" Chester howled.

Brit quickly interrupted: *"I like the idea, sir. Let's go play hero."*

Standing naked (you really think I'd go on a NyQuil bender with pants on?), I thought about how my last transformation happened instantaneously. I didn't know if I could consciously control the body modification process.

"Sir," Brit quipped, *"I've seen enough movies to know mastering our skills could take months, even years. For fuck's sake,*

80

Batman trained for twelve years with the League of Shadows before he even had pubes."

When the fuck did Brit ever see a movie?

Chester chimed in, "*You've been training for years and you're not even a man yet. You fucking pussy!*" Then he laughed his maddening laugh. He sounds like Bobcat Goldthwait listening to a Richard Pryor record from the inside of a wood-chipper.

"*You're never going to make it on time,*" Margaret mused. "*You may as well grab the large Santoku knife on the counter and shove it into your esophagus.*"

Margaret's words of wisdom will never make their way to an inspirational meme.

I set my timer, giving me thirty fucking minutes to learn how to transform on command. If I couldn't figure it out by then, I was going back to Walgreens for my over-the-counter, sleepy-time tea.

But the first time it happened, I wasn't even thinking. I had let go of any expectations and preconceived notions; I was simply ready to die. I focused all of my energy and thoughts on nothing, which proved to be impossible as Tetro went in-depth about how the littlest girl, Alice, just had her large intestine punctured with a large sewing needle.

"*Roughly six of the eight inches of the needle has punctured through...*"

Letting go was too hard and would take too much time.

"*Be patient, sir,*" Brit opined.

I didn't have fucking time to be patient. I had twenty-seven minutes and counting. I needed to take control of the process. I needed to fully engage in terror if I was planning on terrifying the woman torturing the three little girls.

I saw her a few weeks ago on the news. Most channels called her "Madam V of the Bloodhouse." She had killed thirty-nine little girls, all the same way: in a bathroom, hanging from their feet, with cuts and incisions all over their body. All the girls died from blood-loss; however, when police investigated each scene, they determined that half of the blood was missing. The theory was that Madam V was drinking the girl's vital fluids as it dripped off their adolescent bodies.

My mind was racing and my heart started beating out of my chest. My ex-girlfriend used to take Xanax on a regular basis (talk about a red flag) and had left a few pills in my medicine cabinet. I ran to the cabinet, took two pills and laid flat on the bed. I could feel every sensation of the 10 mgs of benzodiazepine shooting through my central nervous system, inhibiting my brain until I was numb from the extreme emotion. My heart was still beating faster than an Etruscan shrew, but I could at least see my thoughts amidst the worry for the girls and the screaming from Brit, Chester, Ophelia and Margaret and Tetro's metallic, robotic buzzing.

I closed my eyes and tried to focus. I needed a plan of attack. Was I going to kill Madam V? There was no way. I'm not a killer. I'm not an anything. I'm just a normal fucking dude with five imaginaries and luminaries running back and forth in my head with the ability to physically mutate into anything, from a blackbird floating in the dead of night to a fucking K2 Black Panther tank.

I thought about it some more—could I actually reconstruct my matter and turn into a battle tank? Who knew?

Margaret reminded me of the Santoku knife on the counter and that I only had twenty minutes to make it to the Bloodhouse. I fucking hate Margaret.

The Xanax wore off faster than a blink of an eye and my heart was still palpitating out of my chest. My mind felt like I was floating in the ocean with drops of acid falling from the sky. I remembered the Grey Goose vodka I kept in the freezer and wearily stood up from the bed, walking towards the kitchen. The bottle was three sips away from being half full. I popped off the cap and started chugging, finishing the bottle faster than it took for the Xanax to wear off and stumbled back, falling down. My hand accidentally grabbed the aforementioned knife and I squeezed hard thinking it was the side of the countertop.

I laid on the ground like a lone wolf, with no one to hear my howls; not a soul who would help bandage my pierced, bleeding hand or hear my cries. The only person ready and willing to save me would be God herself, but, as tends to be the case, whenever she lends her lovely hand, the obsessively compulsive Devil rears her ugly horns.

What had I become? What could I become? What if one of those little girls, trapped and bleeding, was my daughter?

"If it was your daughter, I'd properly remove my jimmy and give her a righteous go," Chester chimed disgustingly, *"because you know I wear a jimmy everywhere, just in case."* He bellowed laughter.

I screamed at the top of my lungs, clenched my blood-soaked hand and stood up, facing the moon shining through my large, corner window.

Margaret was right. They were all right. The voices were too much.

I was going to kill myself.

I had a running start and jumped through the large, corner window, hurtling towards the ground from my eighteenth-story condominium. As I fell, three crimson-soaked girls flashed into my head, hanging by their ankles with blood running down their face, coagulating with their tears. Images of my daughter rushed into my brain, then Madam Blood sadistically laughing.

For the first time, I saw her clearly. I saw her surprisingly sweet disposition; her pink cheeks coupled with her skinny, wry smile. When she smiled, she pursed her lips and they resembled a soft, tiny, red kite. Beneath her pursed, red lips were four veneer vampire teeth where her canines would ordinarily be. This bitch was trying to be a vampire.

As is usual with long falls, my mind drifted even further into the abyss with the pavement a mere seconds away from my face, and I thought about the Maori warriors—another section of society known for being brutally aggressive and eating humans for mana. However, these warriors, while sadistic, would never drain the blood from an innocent child. The Maori would only eat their battle opponent. They had a code of ethics; a morality that set them apart from some crazy bitch who thought she was an evolved version of a bat.

Maori warriors were covered in tattoos, known as mokos. Spiral shapes covered their arms, legs and faces. But their skin was not punctured with hypodermic needles; rather, the warriors were tattooed using a mallet and chisel, with their skin being imprinted like a Beatles record. The men used mallets in battle and, more specifically, they used mere clubs to crack the skulls of their victims.

After the skull was cracked like an egg, the warrior would drain the blood and eat the brain. It is said that no matter where the Maori warrior struck using the jade cracking tool, their victim's head would crack open like a ripe cantaloupe. The Maori kept the heads of their victims and placed them on walls like black, brown or grizzly bears trophies hanging in the cabin of a proud Montana hunter. The Maori were deranged, diligent butchers, ingesting every part of their victim. Sometimes they would even eat parts of their opponents while they laid on the ground, alive, screaming in agony.

I crashed into the pavement and felt the most excruciating physical pain I've ever felt in my life. Every bone in my body was crushed into dust. My simple regret was that knowing the present pain meant that death had escaped me.

Brit bellowed, "*It's time to move!*"

I rematerialized to my feet without hesitation.

What the actual fuck was going on?

I could still feel the excruciating physical pain, but I was fully functional.

I looked in the window of a building and couldn't believe my face; my moko-covered face, my long black hair. My arms were as big as tree trunks and my hand was slightly green and shaped like a mere club. I had transformed into a Maori warrior.

Margaret whined, "*You're going to fail anyway. There are only ten minutes left before those girls are dead.*"

I fucking hate Margaret the most.

Tetro buzzed, "*Victims have eight minutes of life left. Madam Blood is on the fourth floor of the Optima, located at 24th Street and Camelback, in condo number 425.*"

I couldn't believe it. The bitch lived in my building.

Killing Madam V

Some idiot cop fucking beat me to it.

I was five minutes late. Five fucking minutes!

Allegedly, according to Fox News, CNN, *The Huffington Post*, *The Wallstreet Journal*, *The Houston Chronicle* and the *Gibraltar Times*, Madam V was arrested by some dumb new cop who was delivering Uber Eats on his day off. Apparently, even psychopath vampire wannabees need to eat and the perfect side dish to a liter of blood and an engorged kidney are delivered nachos from the local cantina.

All the media praised him. Thank God he found and arrested Madam V. What a fucking saint. Hallelujah! Now the cunt was going to rot in a cell eating moldy bread for the rest of her life where she'd be surrounded by women to mutilate, convince to take their own lives and fuck.

"How the hell is that justice?" Chester moaned.

She was charged with twenty-four counts of first-degree murder without a bond being issued and transferred to Central California Women's Facility, a neighbor and close friend to San Quinten Prison, the most dangerous prison in America. Half the population of the prestigious penitentiary was sentenced to death row, prior to California deciding death was inhumane. Madam V, or Karen Bukowski, as her Indiana birth certificate read, was sentenced to make the Central California Women's Facility home for the rest of her miserable fucking life.

Tetro buzzed, "*Guard in Central California Women's Facility raping...*"

I raged.

Moments later, I was headed west to Chowchilla, California, dressed as a Tesla. I needed some time to digest the moment.

The prison itself was a joke. I wouldn't have any trouble finding my way in. For such a band of thieves, CCWF had minimum security. In the entire thirty-two-house campus there were only three guards for over two hundred and fifty of America's most dangerous women.

Brit and I talked for a bit while Margaret bitched about why we couldn't just fly like an eagle.

"*Shut the fuck up, Margaret! The men are trying to think!*" Chester yelled in an abusive tone.

I stopped about ten miles away from the prison. Brit came up with a brilliant plan which would most certainly go to shit within about five minutes of execution. He wanted to bribe the guard with cookies from a local bakery and then turn our fingertips into telsons, grabbing the guard's neck and injecting him or her with a non-lethal, yet powerful dose of rohypnol. Then, we would enter, find Madam Karen's cell and shoot her in the head, before turning into a hudsoni, the world's fastest insect, and scurrying out of the prison unseen, like a bunch of hooligans. For the record, he did use the word, "*scurrying,*" but did not use the word, "*hooligans.*"

"*What a lame idea,*" Margaret stung. She wasn't wrong. It was hot and we needed to move.

By my estimation, I could break my way inside, kill Madam Karen and have seven minutes before law enforcement arrived. I started to transform in the desert, my internal organs shifting organs into gears, creating metallic fibers where tendons

87

should support the elbow; my eyes melted down and reorganized into a marble visor giving me perfect sight. I still resembled a human, but my size had increased by nine inches and roughly 260 pounds of contorted chromium alloy. My hands were blocky and my fingers hard to move, but with an accurate one-two punch, I could easily punch through any of the stronghold's walls. The rest of my body and frame was large and ready to deform if needed.

Tetro buzzed me in with the information that Madam V was knitting in her cell, located on the south side of the prison, roughly six miles away. Brit wanted us to crawl, and while I am never a fan of taking our time, we did walk through the hot summer heat in order to cause as little chaos as possible. My body was mostly robotic so instead of worrying about sweat clogging my gears I was mindful of the strong winds and sand, and transformed my hips into small fans, dispelling the dust before it could land.

We reached the fence and I stuck two fingers inside the holes, uprooting the aluminum from the ground and throwing it behind us. The alarm sounded and the prison wall stood two large strides in front of us. With two strides my nose was against the stucco and I reached back with my right arm. The wall crumbled like a Honey Maid Cinnamon Graham Cracker, and there was Madam V smiling and knitting away.

To my surprise, despite the loud alarm ringing—for most it must have been horrific, but for me it was but a hum—there wasn't much commotion. According to Tetro, the guards were still in their original location and we had four minutes before we needed to leave.

"Do you know why I am here?" I bellowed, as if through a megaphone. She laughed and kept knitting. "Why are you laughing?!" My words flung out of me like a dirty exhaust out of a glasspack muffler.

Chester roared, "*Don't let that cunt laugh at you! That dirty fucking rotten...*"

I extended my left arm, grabbing her ankles and easily lifted her upside down. She kept laughing while the alarm rang loudly. I turned my right arm into the Elvenking's Sword of Thranduil and sliced her open at the belly, far enough for her stomach to start pouring out and into her mouth. As pieces of her lower intestine filled her nostrils, she continued her delirious guffaw to the point where it started to drown out the prison's alarm.

"*You have ninety seconds before reinforcements arrive, sir,*" Brit chimed in annoyingly.

"Don't you care?! Don't you see the pain you caused?!" I wailed loudly, as if I was trying to be heard during a hurricane.

Her focus never came, and I turned both of my arms into chainsaws, cutting her in half at the throat.

"*I really do not see a need to raise your voice like that. You're such a fucking asshole. Who cares if she's dead? Do you want a medal? You don't even deserve a participation trophy. You are a fucking maggot...*" Margaret nagged as I transformed my lower half into a motorcycle.

Leaving the exact way we came in, we made it to our rock in the desert and I painfully transformed my body into a tank beetle flying four highways away until transforming into a Tesla.

Madam V was dead, and it was time to go home.

Chicken Parmesan

My stomach turns when people associate something with being the best. People comment about the best Chicken Parmesan to ever touch their lips, then upon further probing about the source of the delightful protein, you find they were dining at their neighborhood "Slop and Glop" Italian restaurant where the sauce is poured out of a half-full jar from a shelf covered in dust.

Sorry—but not sorry—you're fucking wrong and that is in no way the best Chicken Parmesan in the world.

In other instances, people associate the term "best" with other less-than-great experiences. Best isn't relative. Best is indicative of a lack of vocabulary, usually being used by people who either have limited experience or knowledge. Potentially—*po-fucking-tentially*—the Slop and Glop Chicken Parmesan is the best meal *that* person has ever experienced, but their own limited experience shouldn't skew others' view, if they have a wider knowledge of what is or is not good, and have never experienced that particular Chicken Parmesan.

There is only one instance where I find the term "best" to be appropriate in my life: my best day ever. In that moment, I was every emotion I've ever experienced. I had no idea that day would turn out to be in fact the best. I was younger than the usual person experiencing that day, and despite my obvious acknowledgment of the day's importance, I could have never been prepared for what came next. I've heard stories of butterflies emerging from a cocoon but never in my wildest dreams could I have ever imagined a Blue Morpho or Ulysses unleashing her wings upon my life.

I remember the day like it was yesterday, despite my memory inhibiting my ability to know what I had for dinner last night (although I think it was Chicken Parmesan.)

I was watching a basketball game with some friends. I don't remember any of the game, but I remember the phone call I received around half-time, beckoning me to the hospital. Faster than it takes a four-armed man to tie two shoes, I was heading to the hospital as my baby girl was on her way. Gallons of sweat poured out of every pore on my body. I was excited and also scared, nervous, joyous, jubilant, worried; and unequivocally and undeniably freaked the fuck out.

I arrived to see my daughter's mother lying in the hospital bed full of drugs. She could barely keep the smile off her face. She looked like a young child wandering through an American Disneyland with a large cotton candy in one hand and an even larger soft drink in the other. The doctor informed me we had a few hours before my baby girl would experience her first breath.

So, I did what any nervous father does: I paced like a motherfucker. I paced back and forth and forth and back until I was asked to leave the hospital room for a bit. Apparently, I was making everyone, "nervous."

I found solitude in my mother and a few friends who came to the hospital. The last few moments of my life spent without the title, "Dad," were spent in laughter with my close friends and my dear family. I was happy, but those moments weren't what made the date my best day ever.

I made my way back to the hospital room to hear the doctor say, "We're going to start the delivery." She emerged quickly thereafter, covered in liquid, not making a sound, and instantly had me wrapped around her little finger.

I did what I do best and made things awkward shortly

91

thereafter, obsessing over the veiny placenta; playing with it, taking pictures with it, joking about eating it. Then, the nurse told me everyone was mortified and took my hand, asking me if I wanted to give my daughter a bath. We went into the next room with a small tub and I fell in love.

It was at that moment that I understood love for the first time. She was the most beautiful thing I had ever seen, and it was, by far, the best day of my life.

The Most Heartless, Soulless, Worthless Human on the Planet

There were about eighty of us standing around the old man. I'd just finished grocery shopping for my little girl and was driving home. Fortunately, children her age are easy to grocery-shop for and the car was packed with chicken fingers, macaroni and cheese and frozen French fries. She says my macaroni and cheese is, "The best!"

Patiently waiting to make my left turn, my eyes noticed an old man with a bright-orange shirt and duct-taped black sandals crossing the street. He looked like a sweet old guy with an age that would set him somewhere in between his eighth or ninth decade on Earth. Sauntering across the crosswalk, smiling at the sun, a sixty-something-year-old white woman struck him with the front of her cerulean-colored Saturn.

I watched the entire atrocity unfold and rushed out of my car, forgetting to turn off the engine or my left-turn signal. By the time I'd made it through the crowd all I could hear was shouting from the Saturn's owner:

"He just jumped out in front of me! Can you believe it?!"

I couldn't believe it. Mostly because I was sitting in my car, looking directly at the man while the woman plowed into him with her decrepit, oddly colored automobile.

"Ma'am," I spoke up as the cluster of people was nearly at fifty, "I saw you turn directly into the man and hit him with your car. You are clearly at fault."

"He dove right in front of me! He practically wanted to get hit! I bet he's faking it for the insurance money anyway."

She raged in my face for an additional five minutes. She was so angry, I'm not sure if during her filibuster she even took a breath.

I didn't say another word as I avoided the argument and switched my attention to the anguished senior citizen. To my shock, despite the mob of people surrounding him, not one person had provided him aid. He was lying in the crosswalk, face down.

I could hear ambulance sirens in the distance and a voice in my head urged me to go help him. At the very least, I could flip him on his back so he could breathe. From a distance, I saw his lungs functioning, but just barely. He desperately needed help. Anything. Even if it was just someone holding his hand while he died. But we all stood there. frozen and heartless like we were men and women made out of tin.

When the ambulance arrived, their first action was confirming the police were on their way as there was no point in resuscitating a dead body. I tried to retreat back to my car, but my feet were stuck as if both of my shoes were made of cement. I couldn't even feel my heart beating.

How did I just stand there and allow that woman to berate me? Why didn't I, or anyone for that matter, lend our fellow man a hand, or at least provide some comfort during his last gasps of air? We all just stood there. Some people even started recording the morbid scene with their phones.

"Did anyone see anything, or could anyone tell me what happened?" Officer Johnson yelled to the few of us who were still left. I didn't even try speaking. I just shook my head "no" and walked back to my car.

I'm not sure why I didn't do anything. I had three

opportunities to do good and did nothing but stand there like a chump with my hands stuck in my pockets. I feel like I was the one who was pressing on the gas pedal that killed him. I feel like the blood that seeped from his head was reaching out to me for help.

I'm the most heartless, soulless, worthless human on the planet.

Veronica

I visit the cancer center at the hospital once a week. The cold, linoleum floor, the dark hallways. The overwhelming sensation of sadness. Each one of these kids have it worse than I do. Each fucking one of them. They were born with a death sentence: six, seven, eight, nine-year-olds, just waiting to die of leukemia. Their disease is nothing like mine.

Somehow, being here feels good. It's the only thing more relieving than instilling justice. But I can't be here more than once a week, or I will literally slit my wrists with a fucking scalpel. I'm not sure how the parents of these kids survive, to be honest. I don't know how you can read a book, or watch a movie, or have a conversation about the ball game, knowing your little Timmy resembles something from *The Matrix*. Tubes upon tubes pour out of little Timmy's body as the family watches the clock, simply waiting for his time of death to be announced.

It's hard to describe what happens when I'm not instilling justice. If I had to guess, I'd say it's probably like chemotherapy: a small pinch of a needle into a vein, a burning sensation all over the body. It's so fucking hot. It feels like Dante's *Inferno* inside my body.

The voices wake up the disease inside me, the disease that needs to be cured; a hard shot of heroin directly into my jugular with nothing but justice curing the anxieties and complexities. When the disease hits, I have to stop the voices and the pain. The feeling of being hooked and drawn to a bottle or a needle, knowing that the only thing which will truly provide relief is a sweet sip of the brown liquor.

This is my disease.

The only cure, the drug for my cancer, is to do good. I karmically ensure that Joe Fuckhead isn't going to rape another woman. I also come here, to the Phoenix Children's Hospital. I go from little Timmy's room to little Johnny's and I stop by little Mandy's room before I go struggle through another day.

They always anticipate me—the ones who don't die, anyway. They all die eventually. But they have a sort of sixth sense about my presence. I can hear them giggling with excitement in the next room before I've even made my appearance. Most of the children enjoy it when I transform into a dinosaur or robot. One little boy, Jonathan, always begs me to transform into SpongeBob SquarePants. Jonathan has six tumors in his spine, one large mass in his brain, and his lungs function at only forty-percent capacity. The least I can fucking do is turn into SpongeBob Goddamn SquarePants.

One night I was prancing around the hospital. Literally. It was Christmas time and I transformed into Rudolph the Red-Nosed Reindeer. I'd hop around in the rooms for a minute, turn my nose red as a candy cane, then transform into Santa. I told the children that instead of presents, I would grant them each one magical wish. Nearly every kid asked me for some variation of a toy which I would transform into before jumping around the room. However, one little girl did not ask me for a toy.

I galloped into Veronica's room, full steam ahead. She didn't move, lying motionless with a thick tube sticking out of her throat. Her eyes were wide awake, staring at the ceiling. For some reason, even though I see these fucking kids come and go each week, I was overcome with emotion.

She looked just like my little girl: blonde hair, blue eyes, and, despite the fact that her mouth was agape, I could tell she had little dimples on her cheeks. I turned into me and walked closer to her bed.

"*You should wake her up, sir!*" Chester bellowed. "*Fucking idiot.*"

I channeled Ophelia and spoke to the little girl: "The world is not a fair fight. Underdogs are often seen as demi-gods with true power waiting to unfold, rising to every challenge. The world doesn't have time for underdogs. The world doesn't make an exception for the person who doesn't make time for themselves. You cannot hear me, but you have one wish waiting for you whenever you awake; a Christmas miracle for only you to make. It can fit in your palm or sing like a mockingbird. It can shine like a diamond or be a hush of quiet in the storm. Whenever you awake, call on me. I'll be here. Merry Christmas."

I stood up to walk away and as I did, the little girl choked words out through the tube in her throat: "What the fuck was that pansy-ass shit? I want my fucking wish like everyone else. Also, are you that guy from the television? You have to be him, right?"

Brit: "*Oh my god.*"

Margaret: "*Dammit. Now somebody knows about us.*"

Ophelia: "*Remarkable how our words brought her back to life.*"

Chester: "*She was already awake, you fucking idiot!*"

Tetro: "*Timmy next door is going into cardiac arrest from all of the drugs. He will lose his life in three minutes...*"

I looked at her curiously as the thick tube still stuck straight out of her esophagus. "What is your wish, young lady?"

She spit back, "My name isn't 'young lady.' My name is Veronica. I have a simple wish. I wish for you to return each week and tell me about what you've done. I know who you are and I love what you do. Watching the news and hearing about all the people you help is the only thing that makes the chemotherapy burn just a little less."

Fuck.

Inspired Lips

Work was going relatively well—as well as it can for an exhausted attorney who battles severe depression and has five voices talking non-stop in his ear. I'd just returned from my paradisiacal trip to Peru. The fivesome was still talking all the time, but at least they were whispering now. At times, it almost sounded like they were mumbling.

I had a semblance of life. I didn't have to keep cutting off dicks and making people promise to me that they would stop beating their family. I was using my new powers for the most important person in the universe— me— and with the Fab Five silenced, I was going to use my powers for good and, also, whatever the fuck I wanted.

My options were limitless as I fantasized about the opportunities. Even just sitting down on my patio in peace felt amazing. I looked at the sky and heard only a light buzzing in my head; to my shock, I could hear the birds' chirping. It was the first time in years it had been quiet enough in my head for me to hear a fucking bird chirp. The small tweets filling the universe felt audible only to me.

I opened up an online dating account and scheduled a date for Monday, Tuesday, Thursday, Friday and Sunday-morning brunch. For the record, I opened up four online-dating accounts with different faces and bodies. One was even me posing as a tall, slender, black woman seeking a lesbian relationship, which led to Friday's date.

Surprisingly, the real me received the most online attention. My reasoning led me to believe the version of me with fiery red hair and an eight-pack, or the one where I am driving a Tesla wearing a HAUTLENCE HL07 watch on my left wrist, would have garnered the most consideration.

I went out with every single woman on my list that week and had sex forty-two times in seven days with eleven different women. None of them left me particularly satisfied. They all had their own story to tell which fell off their inspired lips, but none made me feel anything other than empty inside as I emptied my balls inside of them.

It was fine though. I was finally feeling fine again. I even caught myself laughing this week at the idea of changing form on the date. For the record, I've watched thirteen people die since the last time I laughed. Now, I was laughing and my mind was wandering as I enjoyed the chirping of the birds; wondering at the idea of fun and jubilation as I lay on the ground of my patio, continuing to stare at the sky from my balcony. Each cloud was magnificent.

Over the previous few months, I had been a frequent flyer, going from Singapore to Pilsen to Scranton to Chicago all in the name of good; punishing people for their crimes against humanity, all in an ongoing effort to get rid of the voices. Nobody knew who I was, and I'll never receive praise, but sitting there, in the silence, watching the white clouds break like ocean waves; that was my victory lap.

I thought about where my peace would take me as orangutans, unicorns and unpeeled bananas floated by overhead. I drifted into a meditative state. I could transform into anything. I could do anything I wanted now that I was free from the constant deafening cries of my five worst friends. In the past, I'd been animals, women, children, insects, cars, and heavy artillery, among other things. They were all fun, but nothing really jumped out at me as the next thing I wanted to do.

What would I do with my new freedom? What would I do with the gift of silence? Online dating was fun, but eventually women just turned into a distraction, taking away from my true fun. I could fuck and cum even with Chester in my ear. Now, I had the ability to be where I wanted to be: alone.

So, I did what any young, dumb, full-of-cum man would do: I bought a first-class ticket to Cape Town, South Africa, departing in less than eight hours.

New York City Subway

Love is a peculiar beast. If I could cure my wretched mind, I'd turn it to love and never look back. I'd take that moment—that kiss, that laugh, that curl of pubic hair that avoided the wax—every fucking moment of love. I'll never feel love again.

This constant sawing into my skull. There's no room for love. There's no version of life where I can't see beyond the fog, the rage, the hate.

It's an endless pit deep within me. I no longer have control of how far I'll fall in the crevasse. I could fall two feet, two hundred feet or two thousand feet, all while staring into a black abyss. I'm not sure how I haven't crumbled yet with the weight of the mountains upon my shoulders. Feeling the weight of every pebble, every rock, every tall pine tree burdening me.

How am I still alive?

Hope.

There are two constants where you can push a person's moral compass: through hope and through fear. It's as if I am walking through a New York City subway, everyone poking me as they walk by, everyone screaming at the top of their lungs.

Somehow hope lies within the tunnel: that one gentle voice. I can barely hear her amongst all the screaming. She begs me to keep hope. She tells me everything is okay.

Your Almond Eyes

We melt into bed, staring at the ceiling after having laid tile all day. I've never been married but I'd put a ring on your finger tomorrow if you asked. The blank, white ceiling filled with stars through our stories, talking about what it means for the heart to expand when it receives love. Therefore, the heart may give even more. We talk about atoms and toasters and things I don't really understand, but I love hearing you talk about the cosmos. Every time I lose myself in the symphony of your words, I gaze to my left to make sure you're real. Your almond eyes always require my full attention. Our hands grip so tightly, veins pop out in every direction. My train of thought is standing on the ceiling as my soul binds with yours in our deep stare.

I'll always be a sucker for your almond eyes.

I talk to you about the ghost: my past that stays haunting; the white glimmer chasing me throughout the day, reminding me that I cannot be what I seek to be; the voice telling me I'm not good enough. His deep, raspy tone shakes me to my core. I'm left wanting. You hear about old Casper whispering to me; how he makes my skin crawl with fear. You remind me he's just my ghost, my past. You remind me that I've learned from those mistakes and that it's time to make some new ones.

I talk to you about the time traveler: the little minion who grabs me by the watch and yanks me into the future. He talks until we reach our destination. He's always reminding me along the way that there are bills to pay and mouths to feed while admonishing me with phrases like, "*You haven't met your goals and never will.*"

You, goddamn beautiful you, direct my attention to a reality, our reality. You remind me of my purpose and bring me back to the present. You move closer and lay your heart on my chest. Somehow, as if fate is playing a harp, our hearts beat at the same speed in unison. I wonder if our thoughts are also on the same wavelength.

You tell me you're worried about work. You tell me about the stress you feel, working in a field full of men. You tell me about your million-dollar presentation next week that you are giving in front of thirty-eight, fifty-year-old bigoted men; including, but not limited to, your boss, who once grabbed your thigh during a meeting. You tell me you've been having diarrhea. You tell me you've been having really bad cramps and spotting.

Eventually, you've talked the worry out and I remind you how much I love you. I lightly rub your back and massage the cramping area for what I know will only be temporary relief. Then we hold each other tightly; the type of tight when you're holding someone as if it will be the last time. I never question whether we could be more comfortable. We lay there, blissful, enjoying the beating of our hearts.

Really Low

One day my heart will stop beating. Daily suicidal ideations and heavy contemplation with the overwhelming burden of having to please people, coupled with the voices taking over my mind, I succumb to the idea of not being good enough. Other people's stress seeps from their pores directly into my soul with every client complaint and question, along with the terror that flees the eyes of my victims as I spoon-feed them justice, one torturous stab into their hearts at a time.

Even my own daughter causes me to have heart palpitations. I'm not sure what's more difficult: being the mediator in an argument between Ophelia and Margaret or trying to raise a curly blonde-haired, crisp blue-eyed little girl on my own. I deserve a fucking medal.

She's the only reason I've never offed myself. No, not Ophelia or Margaret, my daughter. If it wasn't for her, I would've taken a more drastic measure to discover what the ambiguous afterlife really does have to offer. My daughter forces me to be creative in my attempts, mostly because they must look like ambiguous accidents.

I'm sure she's already fucked-up enough. I can't even remember the last time I saw her. I think I see her in my dreams, but I'm not really sure what's reality and what's not anymore. Either way, the last thing I need on my conscience is that beautiful little girl's life being ruined because her daddy stuck a .38 in his mouth and confidently, positively, pulled the trigger.

To be honest, I've only tried once. I was low. Really low.

It was early on in my disfigurement. I was trying to understand how I'd gone from an ordinary alpha to an altered anomaly in the short span of a super storm. Work was miserable. I'd tried three cases in one week and lost every one including, but not limited to, when I represented one of my best friends. I always had a rule to never represent a friend, but he was desperate, had little to no money for an attorney, and my heart bled for him.

The fight was an effort for him to keep his curly, blonde-haired, crisp green-eyed little girl: his daughter. She was lovely and pure; only nine months old with an ear-to-ear smile in every picture available. I assume there were times when she would cry, shit, scream and sleep, but none of those pictures were, thankfully, readily available. His situation was exactly like mine: his baby was born out of wedlock too.

Cue the overcharged empathy and inability to decline representation.

However, unlike my relationship, which was rather brief, they were each other's lifeline for a booty call. Eight years of pure, unadulterated fucking and he never even took her on a date. He told me once that the closest they ever were to actually going on a date was when she ran into him at an Outback Steakhouse while he was on a Tinder date with another woman.

We were sitting in court after countless fruitless attempts at settlement. His ex-fuck buddy was the definition of unreasonable. If you don't believe me, she was upset, and argued in court, that he should lose his parenting time for allowing their toddler to watch *Toy Story 2*. Fortunately, despite her attempts, as luck and skill would have it, we were winning every step of the way. My cross examination of Mom was strong and showed clear alienation of my best friend.

She was left speechless and sobbing as I took her down a

windy road leading to her admitting a history of depression and anger towards Dad because he never put a diamond ring on her left finger. We didn't get as far as determining if she preferred an emerald-cut diamond or if she was pining for a traditional round rock.

After questioning her, I was elated. My friend was going to be able to see his daughter. Then, the opposing attorney stood up and called my friend to the witness stand.

He was questioning my friend about diet and potential neglect to the point where my friend's face turned to a red hue and his grandpa yelled from the back,

"This is bullshit!"

Both grandson and grandpa were so upset, they were more red than Chile de Arbol.

At that moment, the opposing attorney asked the poignant question: "When was the last time you smoked marijuana?"

Marijuana. Mari-fucking-juana.

My friend is an amazing human being and I knew he'd be a great father. He loved spending time with his daughter and fought like hell in court, just like I did, for a few hours a week with her.

He works hard at his job as an airline pilot. He is respected in the community. And guess what? He smokes fucking Mary Jane on his days off.

He froze and sat silent for a number of seconds, which felt like hours. Too long. The opposing counsel ripped in again:

"Sir, why are you hesitating?! When was the last time you smoked marijuana?"

My guy responded, "Ten years ago," despite having a possession charge from eight years prior. We were toast.

By the end of the questioning, my friend was crying so hard the judge called a recess. I tried to console him outside to no avail. His family questioned my legal acumen, wondering aloud why I didn't do this or that. To be frank, I felt I had done plenty of this and more than enough of that, but in the end we lost, and none of the reasons for why seemed very relevant.

I'd let my client, my best friend and a person who put all of their trust in me, down. It would be years before he could see his daughter.

However, this was not the reason why I attempted to take my own life. In hindsight, that was the best day of my week.

The next day I moved slowly around the wreckage of my ego. How in the world could I let my best friend down?

I couldn't stop focusing, fixating; obsessing over my friend's short but excruciating pause when I received the phone call: it was my daughter's former principal. She only called when she wanted sex. Even though sex was the last thing on my mind, I was obliged to answer, as the last time I saw her she picked me up naked outside a movie theater, where I was escaping one of the worst first dates I've ever had.

Her daughter had taken some medicine and was unconscious. I rushed over to her condo where paramedics were surrounding the principal's young girl. I yelled. Everyone was screaming.

It was the first and only time I've ever heard Tetro lose his place while reading his disaster-movie script. Tetro, Brit, Ophelia, Margaret, and even Chester, were all screaming,

"Is she okay?! What's wrong?!! What the fuck is wrong with her?!"

While my relationship with the principal mostly consisted of casual anal sex, I did develop quite a relationship with her daughter. She reminded me of K. I rushed to the little girl's side and out of the corner of my eye, I saw the defibrillator. My heart stopped, and I dropped to my knees gripping her little hands so hard I thought they might break.

This charming, soulful little girl was now a lifeless body, clinging to her very last breath. There was no doubt in my mind that she was about to die. I didn't even think to use any of my powers, but I have no idea how I would have even saved her. The emotions were too overwhelming for any sort of practical thinking. I cried and prayed to God and the Devil, finally screaming with my powerful voice, "Please God, save this little girl!"

At that moment, she burst to life and coughed a deep cough. Her pupils were white as snow, but she was breathing and conscious. Thank God I don't pray often. I felt like I'd saved up my one wish for this very moment. Unless this was the Devil's doing.

I followed the ambulance to the hospital, and when I walked into the principal's daughter's room the little fledgling looked like she was in an aquarium, with tubes deep inside her lungs helping her survive. She was still unconscious, but she had life, and the prognosis appeared okay. I sat there with her mom as the doctor walked in and told us her diagnosis: she had overdosed.

Apparently, she suffered from serious headaches, so much so that she took daily doses of Tramadol to ease her pain and suffering. The doctor informed us that the pharmacist had made a mistake and she had ingested ten times the dosage amount of Tramadol and that the overdose caused her to have an epileptic seizure.

A little girl nearly fucking died because a Walgreen's pharmacist couldn't count. A small child's life nearly taken and laid out unconscious because some asshole couldn't count to fucking one.

He's the only person I've ever harmed without Tetro's advice. I checked to make sure he didn't have a family before I ripped off both of his middle fingers and carefully stitched a calculator to his palm. He did have a girlfriend, but she would be fine.

A helpless child almost died.

That was the worst day of my week.

Karen Hernandez was the end of my week. She stumbled into my office with fresh track marks covering her arms like pins in a map; each small dot a reminder of the otherworldly adventure she took after pushing a needle's contents deep into a withered and tired vein. The thick gauge ripped apart her flesh and mind as the heroin took control over her emotions. On top of her obvious issues with drugs, she also had a welted black eye and her top central and lateral incisors were missing. Surprisingly, the files she brought with her were well-kept, albeit falling out of a large black binder that looked like it was stolen off the set of a Coen brothers' film.

She told me about the nightly beatings by her husband. She told me about how one night, they both drank until each word they slurred rhymed with "fuck." About how he grabbed her by her chunky, matted hair and broke her nose on the bathroom counter. She told me about how the blood was a maroonish color and smelled like burnt sausage.

She told me about how he apologized the next day; how he told her for the hundredth time that it would, "never happen again."

For the record, she had only been what most people would consider horribly beaten eleven times. A shaking shell of a human being, standing 5'8" tall, and so skinny that if my assistant walked in, she could have easily been confused for a hat rack; even if she were standing in my office next to a hat rack. For the record, I don't have a hat rack in my office which, hopefully, would have alleviated any possible confusion.

She told me about her last straw. The remote wasn't working correctly and the Seattle Seahawks were playing the Arizona Cardinals. He was enraged that he couldn't switch back and forth between the football game and the World Series of Poker, which was being simultaneously aired on a separate channel. She told me about the first glass of Jameson Whiskey he drank that day. Then she told me about the second glass, the third glass, and eventually the sixth full glass of Jameson Whiskey he drank.

Eventually, she told me about how their thirteen-year-old daughter walked into the room with her ears pierced. She told me about how he slurred his screams. She told me about jumping back, startled, and grabbing an antique armoire that rested in the corner of their barren living room. A large, worn black couch, a 32-inch Sony television and the antique armoire were all that occupied the tiny room. They used the armoire to store their ever-changing pantry of illicit drugs.

Finally, she told me about how he took his Dorset double Old Fashioned glass from Williams Sonoma, a gift from a previous life, into his right hand and threw it at their thirteen-year-old daughter's face. It shattered, splitting her bottom lip and lodging a hard piece of glass into her right eye.

She told me about how her daughter laid on the ground wailing, and her husband stood over the top of her slurring sorry. As he clumsily apologized, the mother reached into the antique armoire, filled one of the dirty needles with enough heroin to kill a grizzly bear, and walked over to her husband, stabbing him in the neck and injecting him with the brown poison.

Her story took about ninety minutes to tell. She informed me that she'd left with her daughter to stay in a hotel and that her husband was still lying in the living room, dead. I calmly told her that I was not a criminal-law attorney and that I would be unable to help her. She screamed at me, called me a piece of shit and lamented me for wasting her, and I quote, "fucking time."

That was the end of my week.

Moo for a Little Fun

She's the only person in my life who never judges me. It's my favorite thing about Veronica. She actively listens to my frustrations as I gripe and complain about stopping another fucking asshole from touching little girl's assholes, or blocking some squawking bitch from burning children in her basement.

She thinks more of me than I think of myself. She doesn't think I'm a monster or a raving rage-filled beast, she sees the world exactly as I do. Last week, she cackled as I regaled her with a story of my trifecta evening.

Tetro was buzzing all fucking day about a nursing home. One of the male nurses, a nasty nurse (hereinafter referred to as "NN") there was taking advantage of old women. NN would give them their nightly cocktail of Centrum Silver, Marzipan and Ambien, then lube up his hands and slide up their moo moo for a little fun.

That wasn't even the worst part. NN would often remove octogenarians' dentures and put his penis into their unwilling mouths while they were unconscious. Once, he even targeted and requested the shift of one of the oldest women in the retirement house who had extremely bad carpal tunnel syndrome. She was one of his few willing participants and he would occasionally grease both of her hands for a quick hand job in between patients. The patients, for the most part, were oblivious and appreciated that he was attentive, if not overwhelmingly odd, and that he could always find a vein on the first poke when drawing blood.

Honestly, I wouldn't have cared much, but Tetro would not shut the fuck up about this guy. He'd been talking about NN for weeks so I made my way toward the nursing home, transforming into a passenger van. Upon arrival, I found an alley and transformed into a sixty-nine-year-old woman. I knew he'd love me because of my age and because of my new tits. I made my breasts silicone and only fifteen years old.

I screamed, "Cash!" as I walked in and expeditiously admitted myself to the Friendly Pines Retirement Home. Within about thirty minutes I was knitting in my penthouse near the west lawn. The nursing home had two lawns. One was for the people suffering from Alzheimer's disease and one was for people without Alzheimer's disease.

Apparently, they used to allow everyone to enjoy the same lawn, until one of the residents started playing tricks on the patients with dementia. Every day he would ask them for the "twenty dollars" they'd borrowed from him last week. He saved five thousand and forty dollars before finally being caught. At that point, the staff decided on separating the residents to their respective lawns.

My penthouse was adequately equipped with a 70-inch, stainless-steel, freestanding bathtub. I called down to the concierge and requested a sponge bath from NN. He arrived, grinning, in about twenty minutes, then helped undress and bathe me.

If I'm being honest, it was probably the best bath of my life. For such a weird, nasty fuck, his hands were as soft as soapstone. As he rubbed my sagging body, I could see the giant bulge in his pants when he stood up from bathing me.

Chester was even grossed out for the first time. He kept saying with disgust, *"Can we please just get this fucking over with?"*

Ophelia was also on the edge. She was the closest she's ever been to saying something negative. She went into a long

114

lecture about the beauty contained within the elderly but paused every now and then. I could tell she was thinking about the nasty-as-fuck nurse.

As NN poorly concealed his surprisingly large penis, he made a comment about needing to grab some lotion and my medicine, which was grossly accompanied by a maniacal giggle. He left the room and I sat on the bed with my bathrobe on.

When he returned only a few minutes later, he had a handful of pills and a giant tub of Boy Butter. He didn't even care enough to hide the fact that he was getting off on his patients. He strutted in like a doctor about to perform life-saving surgery. When he walked in he smiled, noticing that I'd frozen my hand into the shape of an "O." He was grinning.

"Why do they always have that stupid grin on their face?" Brit opined. *"Every pedophile or assaulter has the same smirky grin."*

In NN's voice, I said audibly, "I don't know why they always have that stupid grin on their face."

NN froze. He looked confused and moved forward slowly. I stood up, still fully nude and walked toward the door. I extended my right arm to lock it. NN jumped toward the door and, in a flash, I pinned him against the wall with my free left hand. He tried to wriggle out of my grip but couldn't budge. If I'd held him any tighter against the wall, I would have snapped at least three of his ribs.

Chester made a suggestion and just for fun, I held him tighter against the wall. To my astonishment, I snapped four of his ribs. Usually, I calculate correctly.

"I don't see the point in any of this," Margaret nagged. *"He's not going to stop with the old ladies."*

"Shut the fuck up, Margaret!" Chester and I barked in unison.

If anyone despised Margaret more than me, it was

115

Chester. She was always a few steps behind and wasn't close to smart enough to see where my plans were heading. I nearly always have a plan.

I transformed into NN and he was staring himself in the face.

"What?" he sputtered nervously. "What are you going to do to me?"

I took my right arm off the door lock and extended it towards the shower, turning the water up to the highest heat possible. Then, I told him that if he made one noise, I would kill him without hesitation. He knew that was the only warning he would receive, yet, like the ignorant fuck he was, he screamed like a little bitch.

My hand moved quickly from the shower to his mouth. I made my hand the texture and color of bubblegum and kept both of his lips tightly closed. Each scream caused an odd pink bubble to appear. As the water continued to become hotter and hotter, I reached for a first-aid kit with a third arm I had grown out of my stomach. I opened the kit and found my prize, grew a fourth arm out of my stomach, and carefully threaded the stitching through the needle. He screamed at the top of his lungs. There was no sound, but the bubble was quite large.

I took the bubble gum off his face and started to stitch his lips together. For a novice with jittery hands, I was proud of my efforts. There was excessive blood flow coming from his face, but what did I care? He wasn't going to die and even if he did, I'd watched people die who had done far less than sodomize elderly women.

I stayed close to the edge of his lips to make sure the thread wouldn't hemorrhage and tear. When finished, I stood back with only my left hand still pinning him down as I marveled at my work. He looked like one of the refugees stranded at the Greece-Macedonia border who sewed their lips together to protest against the restrictions placed on their movement to leave the Balkan countries in 2015. I swear it was the spitting image and if you don't believe me, then look it up.

Steam was filling the room as the shower water was finally scolding hot. Taking my left hand off of NN, he fell to the ground. I told him to stand up and go to the shower so that he could burn off the sins of his past. He didn't move and laid on the ground crying.

Brit said, and I echoed out loud, "*Today is your reckoning. Today you will feel the pain you've caused. The women you have violated have lived a combined two thousand, five hundred and sixty-two years on this planet. Today, you will feel every single ounce of pain they have endured during those years.*"

He was reluctant to move from the fetal position, so I calmly forced him into the shower. He screamed and sizzled for over ten minutes while the boiling water incinerated his skin. He was in so much pain he even broke a few of the stitches trying to scream.

I turned off the water and asked him if he wanted to put lotion on his body. He furiously nodded his head up and down before I channeled Chester and yelled, "Too fucking bad!"

I told him I knew what he had been doing to the old women at the nursing home. I told him that if he ever even thought about defiling one of the women again, I'd be back, but this time he'd be dead. Then, I broke his cock in half and bent his hands backwards until they snapped at his wrists.

Veronica squirmed a bit when told her about breaking his wrists, and while she didn't judge me, I could tell she was displeased. I explained to her that these people needed to learn their lesson and that if I didn't leave them in pain, they would just do it again and again and again and again. She understood.

Margaret implored me to stop sharing my stories with Veronica. "*She's just a little girl,*" she would bitch. "*She doesn't*

117

need to know about the cruelty of this world. She doesn't need to hear about how you stitch up people's lips and break their hands."

Out of character, Chester came to my defense calling Margaret, among other things, a *"crackhead slut who wouldn't even know how to jack off a cow if it came with instructions."*

For the record, I'm not sure I would have used the same vocabulary to voice my displeasure of Margaret's opinion.

Veronica continued to chastise me for breaking his wrists. She even quoted Gandhi: *"An eye for an eye makes the whole world blind."*

I told her to mind her fucking place and reminded her that she was a little kid. Also, what the fuck did Gandhi know? When his wife contracted pneumonia, he forbade her from using penicillin, even though doctors were adamant the drug would heal her. She ended up dying as a result of not taking the alien drug. Yet, when that skinny motherfucker contracted malaria, he allowed the doctors to save his life using a western medicine called quinine.

"I don't want to be like fucking Gandhi. He's a goddamn hypocrite," I retorted.

Veronica kept babbling, telling me I could use other means to teach people lessons. She thinks she's so smart, but what fuck does she know? She's lying in a hospital bed covered in tumors. She doesn't know how fucked-up this world can be. She's never had to look a rapist in the eye before. She's never had to stare a woman in the face who had no remorse for killing twenty babies.

I threatened that if she didn't shut the fuck up, I would stop telling her stories and I would stop visiting her. Unfortunately, she smartly called my bluff and continued to opine about my methods of serving justice. Fortunately for her, I had a soft spot in my broken heart and continued to visit her each week, despite her making me feel ashamed for my actions.

What the fuck did I have to feel guilty about? I was doing so much good for this world. I had taken rapists and drug dealers off the street. I was the one who stopped a terrorist from sniping his way through the freeways of Arizona.

It was me. It was all fucking me. I was Karma and there wasn't one goddamn thing she could say to make me change my mind.

Tetro buzzed, "*Arsonist about to burn down a commercial building with four employees still in the office...*"

It was time to go.

Wretched Voice

I transformed back into a titan beetle and set forth on my quest to find AJ. I'd spent four months defending him, fighting every night for him to see his daughter, only to find out he was lying to me the entire time and abusing women in all the wrong places.

Tetro relayed his exact location and before I knew it, I was masked as a Tesla, quietly making my way toward the other side of town. I often choose the Tesla. Other means of transportation are faster, but they also draw more attention. I transformed into a launch vehicle once and it was all over the fucking news. Plus, my daughter used to love riding in a Tesla.

It didn't take me long before I was sitting outside AJ's apartment complex near the pool, dressed as a twentysomething woman with blue eyes and curly blonde hair. It was a regular complex in Tempe right next to Arizona State University's sprawling campus. If I were to walk about a mile north, I would be standing in front of my old law school; the rooms where I spent hours suffering through Water Law, Employment Law, Family Law and so on. I was a good student with a few very close friends—some of the best friends I've ever had—and a thousand different acquaintances. I've always defined the level of a friendship based on one characteristic: would that person help you move homes? If the answer is yes, then they are a friend for life. If the answer is no, they aren't precluded from being an amigo, but they at least should know better than to invite me to a dinner party or a social event where I'll be left standing in the corner feeling awkward.

I followed Tetro's directions to the south side of the complex and until I stared directly at AJ's unit. My nose was inches away from the number forty-two hanging on his front door. Chester reminded me that reminiscing about law school and better days was a waste of fucking time, and that if I wanted to be a pussy, I could head to a coffee shop and write poetry and journal about all my friends in law school. He kindly told me that I really wasn't that popular and that just because everyone knew me, it didn't mean they liked me. Then he proceeded to name every one of my blackheads.

I snapped at Chester, telling him after I've taken care of AJ, I was going to turn my right arm into a shotgun and put a bullet in my fucking head to finally shut him the fuck up, once and for all. He reminded me, while laughing, that the last time I tried to use a shotgun I missed.

I transformed myself into a cop in full police uniform, hat and all. I grew to 6'6" and roughly 280 pounds of muscle as my right hand went toward the doorknob. The knob was hot from the Arizona summer and I slowly twisted it to open the door, which thankfully was unlocked. I saw AJ first, sitting on the couch watching television. He screamed,

"What the fuck is going on?!"

I looked at him calmly and informed him there had been a call about a disturbance. His wife was sitting next to him. They were eating a bowl of popcorn, watching *Westworld* on the TV. The fact that he was watching *Westworld* was almost enough to redeem him. Not.

As I took a step inside the door, AJ and his wife both stopped eating popcorn, and I told him to stand up. AJ's time had come. He was going to pay for abusing her. He knew who I was and he sat silent.

"I've played as you, ya know?" he muttered, as tears started to fill his eyes. "In the video games, I play as you."

I changed into him while he spoke and by the end of his sentence, he was staring himself in the face directly; into the eyes of the monster he was within.

AJ and his wife were silently crying to themselves when she broke through the absence of sound. "Please don't kill him," she whimpered, and I felt knocked back with a sense of disbelief.

I couldn't believe she would have one single fucking qualm if this wife-beating piece of shit wasn't breathing anymore. Hell, if I were her, I'd be asking for a gun and frantically searching for the trigger.

AJ was shaking violently due to fear, but still not making a sound. He was holding back screams as his tears and piss were now forming a puddle on the floor.

How the fuck could she let him beat her? How the fuck did she run back over and over again only to find solace in his fist? Face-first into a wall of sorrow. He was such a fucking pile of shit. Was she clinging to the memory of the time they had two bottles of cheap red wine, watched most of *Gladiator* and made passionate love, while simultaneously forgetting the time they were watching *Good Will Hunting* and she accidentally spoiled the ending, so he broke a bottle of similarly cheap white wine against her countenance; the same night she cried herself to sleep, bleeding and lying naked on the floor?

Her entire world was a walking illusion, not knowing if a word, a look, or even a memory would set him off; a ticking timebomb where she could only carefully walk on every eggshell, praying to God not to upset the beast. Well, beast, here's the big, bad fucking wolf.

I eloquently broke the silence. "You're a fucking cunt."

Chester roared and applauded me for using his favorite word.

On cue, AJ shouted, "Please don't hurt me! I didn't do anything to you!"

I fumed, "You didn't have to do anything to me! You did it to her!" Even from six feet away, the spit from my scolding was strong enough to stretch to his cunty countenance.

Tetro hummed along: "*Young girl being sodomized against her will at 32nd Street and Olive...*"

Ophelia compassionately cried, "*He's a person too, who struggles with his own demons, sir.*"

Margaret boastfully bothered, "*Perhaps you shouldn't do this. You'll regret doing this.*"

Meanwhile, surprisingly, Chester offered the best advice of the evening: "*Kill the motherfucker!!!*"

If I could, I'd rather have locked him up, snapping my fingers, transporting him into a wooden cage and lighting a match to the roof; his world bursting in flames, living in hell. My eyes were burning red. I bellowed as twisted horns slowly ripped through the scalp at the top of my skull.

Brit fucking loves it when I do the horn thing. "*It always adds to the effect when you make the horns come out slowly, sir. Nice work.*"

"Do you know why I am here?!" I yelled as the smell of the room started to shift; with the only explanation being that AJ had shit his pants. He fumbled his words before I interrupted him with Chester's laughing; laughing uncontrollably as his wife started to yell something about calling the police.

I sent bugs crawling underneath my skin, and his wife shrieked again as it appeared that a thousand burrowing beetles had found their way into my body and were trying to dig their way out from under my skin. Her wretched voice pierced my ear. I couldn't control myself. Like a dog hearing a whistle, her shriek set something off inside me. She pulled my trigger.

Margaret yelled, "*Oh my God, my ears are burning!*"

Chester wailed, "*Kill the motherfucker!*"

My hand immediately turned into a Sig Sauer P226X5 and I pointed the gun and pulled the trigger at her face.

Brit: "*Oh my God.*"

Ophelia: "*Oh my God.*"

Tetro: "*Shooting at Phoenix Children's Hospital on 12th Street and Indian School. Three already dead.*"

Chester: "*What the fuck did you do?*"

AJ fell to the ground, vomiting. Without thinking, I transformed into my own form. He looked up, wiping the vomit from his chin and saw my face, recognizing me instantly. He grabbed for my feet and pulled hard, causing me to hit the ground like a sack of potatoes. I was dazed and he was off, running toward the bedroom, confused.

He came back firing a gun. By reflex, my right arm transformed into a shield, and I stopped his six shots. Standing, meeting him eye to eye, my right arm turned into a Claymore sword and I slit his throat. His decapitated head fell back, and behind him I saw his little boy, who was staring directly into my eyes...my eyes. AJ's son was looking at my real face.

Ophelia: "*Don't do it.*"

Brit: "*Sir, you cannot do that!!*"

Margaret: "*You're such a piece of shit.*"

Chester: "*Don't.*"

Tetro: "*Man kicking his golden retriever in the stomach on 75th Street and Shea...*"

And so on.

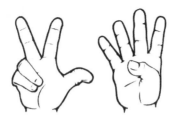

Homeless Man

I walked out, leaving three dead bodies in the apartment. I don't know what happened. If I could take it all back I would, but it was so fast. I just snapped. Shame and guilt washed over me like a hot bath of acid. All I want to do is peel off every inch of my being and start over. This can't be the meaning of life. My purpose must be more than fighting the monsters on the outside and within.

I've been up for nearly thirty hours since leaving AJ's apartment, with my head spinning like plates at the circus, each step causing an involuntary twitch in my mind and body. I am walking, as me, covered in blood and tears; some theirs, some my own. Trying to transform, I can't; I don't have the strength. I walk, looking like I'm homeless to the only place I know will bring me distraction and help me avoid my pain, but first I stop by a liquor store and steal a cheap bottle of whiskey. I finish the handle in roughly two minutes. With each sip, tears fire across my cheeks, faster and faster. By the time the bottle has gone, I have cried so many tears I could fill it once more.

My walk takes me fourteen miles from AJ's apartment in Tempe. By the time I make it to my destination, it is midday; however, I couldn't tell you which day, and would be hard pressed to even identify the month. My surroundings are vastly different than the college campus town of Tempe. I was now looking like a homeless man in one of the nicest neighborhoods in Scottsdale, Arizona. My whole world is a hazy and horrible nightmare, but I've made it to my oasis: Almond Eyes' house.

I am exhausted as I collapse onto her front lawn, barely seeing through the fog filling my mind. I shouldn't be here, especially in the middle of the day, but I need it. I fucking need to feel something other than disgust with myself, or else I'll finally fucking take an axe to my worthless fucking skull.

She has long forgotten about me and to be honest with you, I don't blame her. Nothing about me has ever been easy and my transition made things impossible. The last time I saw her it was in passing. She was with her father, who never liked me anyway, avoiding eye contact while I was desperately hoping I'd simply be able to send her a wave. It was pathetic. She is a yoga instructor and auctioneer, and her husband is a dancer. They own a little home in Arcadia. It's not little, but because of the surrounding mansions, it seems small in comparison. In anyone's reality, the home was perfectly quaint.

They have a modest kitchen with a retractable island that she built. It literally floats. I'm not sure how she did it. Along with being able to glide through the air like a snowflake in the breeze, her mind sees objects and the world with a surreal eye. She could design a building, prepare a perfect Cherries Jubilee for a dinner party of twelve and, frankly the best thing about her, is that she leaves smiles, happiness and abundance wherever she goes.

I think maybe she used magnets or something for the island. The open space of her kitchen is a perfect square with cutting boards falling from the sky on demand and spices sprawled on the wall like tools in a garage. It was a magnificent design, facing the tip of Camelback Mountain, the beautiful apex of the desert. The window over the sink is perfectly positioned to face the mountain. She even took into consideration the sunset and designed the room to maximize the orange light cascading into the space.

The built-in AI sits in the shape of a circle. Aurrie sits on the wall on the far west side of the kitchen facing the entrance of the room. It's positioned so that every morning Almond Eyes greets Aurrie, lightly singing, "Mirror, mirror on the wall, you're in fact, no mirror at all. I made you and you help me. You make me feel like a queen, Aurrie." Then, inauspiciously, Aurrie laughs the same laugh each morning with her maker.

Aurrie is connected to all the machines in the kitchen and prepares a fresh cup of coffee each morning for her maker. After laughing at the quaint song, Aurrie reads an inspirational quote, her maker's daily tasks, and asks her maker what she would like to make for dinner that evening. Aurrie has built-in functionality where she orders ingredients from anywhere in the world and has them shipped to the house. On this day, the little kitchen smells of green chili and cheddar cheese. They are celebrating a birthday party.

The rest of their house dances with music. There are guitars everywhere, hanging on the walls, and racks on the floor. There are bookshelves, so many fucking bookshelves, filled with sheet music from every country. Her favorite song is *Parlez-Moi D'Amour* by Lucienne Boyer.

The entire abode is light and airy, covered in sunshine because of the floor-to-ceiling windows. Almond Eyes even developed the technique of using sunglass technology, where the lens changes shade with the sun, and made it larger in scale. Her windows automatically transition with the sun.

My favorite room, other than the kitchen, is her piano room. It's painted with white walls and emanates grace. The minimized room contains only white paint, a black grand piano in the middle, and one quote on the wall painted in purple. For all of her worldly travels and ideas, her quote of choice is, *"Live, Laugh, Love."*

I've never gone into the bedroom. I'm sure it's immaculate, but it's too intimate.

Her husband seems like a good man, and I'm sure he treats her well. He owns a pharmaceutical company. He cuts fresh flowers from his garden each day for her, and leaves them on the doorstep each morning at 5:30 am. She leaves at 6:00 am. to swim with the kids.

They have kids. Of course, they have kids. They have twins: one girl and one boy. The girl's name is Aurora and the boy's name is Fred. Almond Eyes and I always said that if we ever had children, we'd name them Aurora and Fred.

Sitting outside her little abode is one of the only things that allows me to hang on. I'm so in love with her life and her happiness; it reminds me of what could have been, fantasizing about a life with her instead of lying in the grass covered in blood and tears. I just murdered three people who will never make the news and she is celebrating Aurora and Fred's third birthday party with green chili queso and guests. I can faintly hear, "*Happy birthday!*" in the background.

"*Sir,*" Brit reminds me, "*you really should change or leave before someone sees you. My vote is that we leave.*"

I try to stand and immediately crash back into the earth. My energy is breathtakingly defeated, but I manage to transform, plunging deeper and deeper into the soil nestled into the surprisingly comfortable dirt. I risk easy death in such a weak form, but my mind and my body are paralyzed.

I can still vaguely remember the man I used to be, before I was riddled with the daily shame and guilt stemming from my burden. I remember how that was, the man who would never end a fucking sentence with a goddamned preposition. She brings me hope. I remember the man I used to be through her: a happy man.

I hear kids singing. I hear her playing piano. For a year, she would play our song at the very end of each one of her sets. I hope you'll understand that I'd like to keep that private. I will tell you the song was rudimentary and well below her talent level. She could play Mozart and Bach without effort and move her fingertips as lightly across the keys as she did against a mill. The fantasy was endless. I could have dreamed a thousand scenarios where we ended up happy and together with me staring into her almond eyes for an eternity; her painting on a balcony smiling back at me while I write poetry in bed. Days with her spent in the forest; the garden, the backyard and recitals, each day filled with smiles and happiness. Unfortunately, fantasies don't come true and her flower would never have grown with me watering it. She is a red rose, and I was her thorn.

A small piece of me hopes and believes she knows I'm Karma; that through my abilities, people are better each day. Suffering goes down, despite rare casualties and the occasional murder of three people. I think she'd be proud of me. The world is a better place because I'm in it. I don't save lives, but I enrich them. I make people see their real-life maker. I reluctantly and begrudgingly have to live with, and accept the power of God, when all that I ever wanted was to be normal.

Fuck AA, fuck AJ, fuck his stupid wife and his stupid fucking son. I do a damn good job and sometimes it is a rotating disaster. Ambulances speeding down the highway to save an old man of a heart attack, spin out and kill people.

Just two nights ago, a woman was on her knees in tears thanking me because I broke both of her husband's legs. He was a fucking meth head who would cook then kick. He had a weird thing about kicking a soccer ball at his wife's face until her face was covered in blood. He would yell, "GOAL!" every time the ball struck the poor woman's nose. I broke in, broke his testicles with my right foot then snapped both of his kneecaps backwards.

Just five nights ago, I spent the night at a young boy's house. His name was Stan. He was fifteen years old. He'd been smoking heroin for about three years and was off his fucking rocker. But he was a good kid with a kind soul. He just dealt with demons—demons that sometimes take the form of abuse towards his family. He'd scream and shout and let it all out. He punched walls, he ripped apart bathrooms, he told his beautiful parents that they were worse than a prostitute's popped herpe, and he told them he was going to commit suicide every single night.

Tetro told me about the boy and his family. The boy was throwing couches and his baby sister was screaming in the bedroom. Mom was on the floor and crying with her face in her hands. Dad was yelling, then crying, then yelling some more.

The boy screamed, "Fuck, shit, cunt, damn, pussy, ass, cunt!" And so on.

I walked into the house dressed as an old friend of the boy. His father was holding him down as he was thrashing violently, trying to stand up. He didn't need therapy, he needed a goddamned exorcism.

The father saw me and let go in surprise and the kid didn't miss his moment. He ran towards me and attacked; full speed, right fist, right in the gut. Thanks, kid. I looked into his eyes and couldn't see anyone looking back. He was gone. In his world, ghosts were attacking his soul and the house was melting on top of him. This kid wasn't just fucked-up on heroin, he had taken a handful of mushrooms, smoked piles of pot, and, from the smell of it, had snorted a nostril full of ecstasy.

I did the only thing I knew that would calm him down, and candidly, it was kind of fun. I turned into a snake and made him chase me. I transformed into Morpheus from *The Matrix* and convinced him that he was Neo and, "The One." At one point, I laid him on his back and sang him songs of the Icarus. He cried a lot as the drugs started to wear off about six hours later.

Groggy, his dad brought him a cup of coffee and his mom followed up with 10mg of Adderall. As the drugs wore off, he opened up. He told me about being adopted and remembering at a very young age sleeping in a crib that was barely two feet by two feet. He told me he remembered being "squished." We talked about his drug problems and suicidal ideations. Part of his reasoning for wanting to kill himself was because of the pain he caused his family. He hated himself for hurting them. During his rare instances of sobriety, he would see the cracked windows and the broken doors and hear the echoes of his yelling. He told me about how they made him more ashamed and how they only made him want to get higher.

For the record, the family was fucking weirded out. They knew me as Karma, but it didn't make it any less awkward. It also didn't help that I transformed into Oprah Winfrey for most of the impromptu intervention. His parents and brothers and sister who lived at the house talked about the boy they once knew, the man that may be lost and each one of them had a sweet story about the formerly kind boy. By the end of the night, the boy and his father weren't necessarily patching the holes in the walls together, but I was optimistic I'd taken another junkie off the streets.

Hours have passed and without thinking, I transform into my body. My body; my face, my hands, my feet. I transform into me. It's so hot outside. Staring at me through the dusk, Almond Eyes sits on the edge of the doorstep drinking a glass of Prisoner red wine. Her soft almond eyes catch my beaten red ones. I look down at the dirt realizing she has just seen me appear out of thin air. The night is dark now— it could been her imagination, but she knows it isn't.

She doesn't make a noise, not one fucking noise. She just smiles a wry smile and looks up at the stars. Goddamn, I love her. She winks then says, "You look tired. Go rest."

I try to smile, although I'm sure it looks more like a shrug, before transforming into a Tesla and zipping away.

131

I receive brief glimpses of hope every few months since the accident. Every once in a blue moon, I hear a light voice. I don't think she's programmed into my DNA like the other five. She tells me everything is okay.

I close my eyes and warm light sho-wers me. I feel the hope. I feel the gold shooting through my veins. I feel strong. She whispers, *"Everything is okay."*

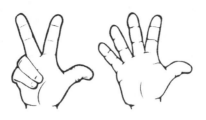

Ship Happens

I was going at about 180 mph on the US-1 as Sabrina fucked me, riding me on top. She clutched me hard, coming all over me as my gaze sailed past her, weaving in and out of traffic.

I didn't come all the way to Miami just to fuck some bitch, do cocaine and smoke a great cigar. I came here to quiet the fuckers and without doing something to keep the order, I knew they would keep fucking screaming about differences and their personal preferences of fat and non-fat ice cream.

In a snap, Tetro reminded me of the other cargo ship. A hundred and eight Taiwanese girls, none over the age of eighteen, on their way to America to live the American dream of giving handjobs and blowjobs to the next middle-aged married man who'd snuck away from his wife and kids on a Wednesday night because he said he was going to play poker with his friends.

Welcome to fucking America, Shūhuì.

I took a hard right up the ramp, speeding towards the Pelican Harbor Marina. By now, my speed was well over 245 mph and Sabrina was screaming at me to slow down, with my dick still lodged inside her pussy. I sped faster and faster and faster towards Shūhuì's vessel, and as we approached the dock, I unclipped my seatbelt and jumped out of the car, holding Sabrina tightly while the car crashed into a parked yacht ironically named, *Ship Happens*. We flew out of the top of the convertible, 1200 feet into the air. I whisper, not quite as confidently as her whisper: "I'm going to set you down now."

I popped a parachute out of my back, and we floated towards the Earth landing on the top of a building four blocks away from the cargo ship. We said our goodbyes, which consisted of her yelling at me and me trying to interject so that she would give me one more blowjob. It was a rough area of town, but to be fair, I've left women in worse places.

I had Tetro give me the details about the boat. There were forty-three armed smugglers on board and a security system designed by the United States government. I couldn't fathom how they obtained the technology. Adrenaline was bursting through my veins as I sprinted towards the ship.

Brit shrieked, "*Slow down, sir!!*"

I didn't slow down. I transformed my body into pure diamond and ripped through the side of the cargo ship with my right shoulder. Bullets started bouncing off me almost immediately. Using my strength, I ripped a railing from the wall, tore it in half, and threw it at two guards' skulls, hoping to split them in two. One piece of railing bluntly hit a guard's head, killing him immediately. In an unfortunate act, the other piece of railing ripped off with a sharp edge and the throw left a 3x3-inch hole where the guard's left eye would have been. He survived and was screaming bloody murder. As my mother used to say, "*Shit happens.*"

I made my way to the top of the cargo ship, quickly realizing there was no way to free all the Shūhuìs unless I killed all the guards on the boat. I disrobed from the diamond and shifted into the body of the one-eyed guard. Picking up his gun, I made my way through the long corridors of the large barge, deck after deck, leaving behind disaster. By the time I made it to the shipping containers, I was covered in Taiwanese guards' blood. In less than forty-four minutes, I'd killed all forty-three human-traffickers on board.

I rounded the corner to the shipping containers and broke

the locks on all fourteen containers. In minutes, there were a hundred and eight Taiwanese women yelling at me in Mandarin Chinese. Fortunately, Mandarin is one of my stronger languages so I could, unfortunately, decipher that most of them were yelling some variation of, "What now?!"

Apparently, unbeknownst to me, most of them had volunteered to be sex slaves. They were planning on sending money back to their families in Taiwan. I wiped the egg off my face as Chester laughed hysterically at my predicament. What the fuck had I done? I thought every action I'd made to date was justified, but how the fuck could I justify killing forty-three men to save the lives of a hundred and eight women, who didn't even want to be saved?

The five synchronously complained as I forcefully held back my tears. The only other thing I'd done in Florida was make a deal with the Devil and spared his drug shipment. I jumped into the Atlantic Ocean and swam the coast until I washed up, exhausted, on the shores of North Carolina.

I needed to find a way out of the misery. I had to figure out a way to stop the pain.

The Aristocrats

My sweet little girl asked me about pain and love one day. She was so tender, unassuming, caring, kind; a heart full of love and curiosity. We took her training wheels off her bike that day. The perfect age. Just intuitive enough to press on if an answer didn't sit quite right, yet she wouldn't settle if seven times seven didn't equal forty-nine. She was smart as a whip. I could bullshit her about the world and people, and why oat milk was the most excellent form of milk for hours, but I had to be honest with her when it came to love.

She still asked me to sing her to sleep. I knew that wouldn't last much longer.

"*Hush little baby, don't say a word, Daddy's gonna buy you a mockingbird, and if that mockingbird don't sing, Daddy's gonna buy you a diamond ring, and if that diamond ring don't shine, Daddy's gonna clean it with turpentine. And if that turpentine won't work...* then I'll have to take it back to the store, which is always a pain because I always lose the receipt and they fucking argue with me because I don't have a receipt so eventually, I end up just buying more turpentine and now I have two full bottles of turpentine, and who the hell needs two full bottles of turpentine?"

Then, after whatever iteration of *The Aristocrats* in combination with *Hush Little Baby* I'd used that night, I'd take a slow breath as she waited patiently with bated anticipation for the final lines: "And, if that turpentine don't work, that's okay we'll make it work. There's one thing I know that's true, you love me, and I love you."

"Daddy," she said one day, through her picket-fence smile, "You never told me about love the other day. What's love?"

I had no choice but to be honest.

"First, my love, as you well know, any advice from me comes with the pretense that I have no idea what I'm talking about and the words coming out of my mouth have only walked as far as my two feet have taken me. Second, I will never be able to fully explain love. Love is not science, nor an equation fitting in a corrugated cardboard box. It's something that can only be felt and attempted to be explained.

"Third, and finally, love is not parallel, love is not blind. Love is fully aware of the light, not just on the surface, but that beams from within. It is the burning of the soul of existence; the acknowledgment that you, floating on this little planet, lying in your little bed are exactly where you're meant to be. Love is found everywhere: in the cracks, in the homeless drifting through Central Park and in the balcony section of Ford's Theater. Love is found in your animals, your friends, your family. It doesn't mean that every burning soul, every gift of life from a begotten star or foreign god is love, but if you look for it, you'll find this fun little planet is teeming with flames waiting to be fanned.

"Love is also aware of the darkness; the inescapable yet beautiful black surrounding the constellations and shooting stars and Uranus, allowing them all to shine."

She giggled and reminded me that Uranus is a planet, not a star.

"Be aware of the flames of people, places and things who have consciously or subconsciously decided to dance with the flame burning within you. The flames, this love, magnifies when

137

combined with similar heat, igniting passion, laughter, and hearty and wide smiles. But the best part, the fucking best part..."

"Daddy, don't swear."

With a wry grin, I looked her in the eyes and said, "The best part is the peace and calm as the flames masquerade with joy across the burning embers."

"Daddy, what happens if the fire goes out?"

"Then it goes out. But, you're still a flame."

Inspiration

Can death be inspiring? The precursor of tears and sadness. Is it possible our fragile mortality, and the proof of how precious each breath is, can be illuminated with the passing of a loved one or friend? Why do we not revel in the time spent rather than lament what was never going to be?

I lost a friend; a great friend. As time evolved, I saw him two or three times a year for coffee or breakfast. We would talk about our lives, our successes and failures, spirituality, and our children, and despite not having an everyday type of friendship, we always had a strong kinship. We had similar childhoods, going to the same schools and living only a few blocks apart. We both had big dreams and goals.

We both had children at a very young age, out of wedlock, and we did what he loved to say was, "*the right thing to do.*" We both owned our responsibility, not only being strong examples for our kids, but doing everything in our power to give them the best possible lives they could live. My heart goes out to his son.

While I loved his music, especially his later, grungier stuff, I don't believe that Norman Greenbaum was correct. I don't believe that when people are laid to rest, they go up to the spirit in the sky. I believe that when people are laid to rest, their spirit lives in all of us. We, the surviving, are given another choice in this sometimes all-too short and chaotic life. We have the ability to live in their spirit and continue to be inspired by a person that was so damn inspiring. I cannot believe that our spirits lose function simply because our heavy meat suit has expired.

Through tears we must see through to inspiration; inspiration from those who walked before and inspiration to those who shall come after, unselfishly running toward compassion for our closest ancestors. We must have a zealous disregard for a normal life, smiling at every opportunity, displaying love, kindness and enthusiasm; remembering to push limits in the kindest way possible and always making sure other people feel comfortable.

This world we live in requires equanimity, compassion and bona-fide conviction, knowing those before us have walked barren deserts, thirsting for water, yet smiling and singing songs with raspy voices. Knowing that the minute source, a natural spring, is within sight, the first sound—after the splitting of chapped lips—is a clear query directed to our neighbor: "Would you rather wait here while I retrieve you some water?"

Good can, and must, emerge from death. For too long people have bastardized death, but what if there are other consequences we aren't considering? What if death doesn't always have to lead to sadness and darkness and destruction? What if there is purpose in death?

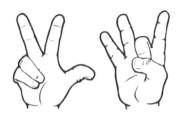

Rats Eating the Cheese Wheel

I'm a born-and-bred American monster. There are three things that matter to me in this world. The first is my estranged daughter, for reasons that should be obvious. The second is my country. So many Americans take freedom for granted. They bitch about lines that are too long and prices that are too high. They bitch about personal liberties and the government infringing on their rights. Needless to say, they are mostly the people who have never stepped foot outside of their county, let alone the country. They moan about how there is nothing to watch on television or how everyone is so negative, without taking two fucking seconds to realize they are part of the problem. They are part of the rats eating the cheese wheel clogging America's arteries. Most of the issues are related to the fact that these negative Neanderthals have never traveled. They've never been to a country where eight people live in a 10x10-square-foot house. They've never suffered while wondering whether their next meal would be a full scoop of rice, a half scoop of rice, or no rice at all.

They are so goddamn selfish, and they have no fucking clue that most of the world would love, and I mean fucking love, a glass of clean water. Entire lives are spent eating Cheetos by the barrel and wondering why they are considered obese according to their doctor. They stuff their faces with reality television, ignoring the very real lives they pretend to lead.

I'm not like them. I love my country.

141

The third thing I care about is my friend.

"What did you do this time?" Veronica squealed as I sat next to her bed. She was in good spirits that day. Such good spirits that a part of me considered undoing her morphine drip and shoving the needle into my own arm.

"Today was a good day, V."

The television in the background erupted: "*This just in!*"

Sean Hannity screamed from the black box hanging in the corner of the room. For such a thoughtful and sweet little girl, I could never figure out why she loved Fox News so much. It was by far the worst thing about Veronica.

Sean Hannity continued, "*The war against ISIS is over. Officials at the White House were shocked to find one hundred and eighteen dead bodies draped across the South Lawn today. The lawn looked like a war zone. ISIS blood covered President Andrew Jackson's Southern Magnolias, Abraham Lincoln's Honey Locusts, and George Washington's Tulip Poplars. No one knows who is to thank for ending the war against ISIS, but sources tell me that we have Karma to thank for ending this worthless war on terrorism.*"

Veronica looked at me in amazement. "What in the world did you do?!" she shrieked.

I looked at her with a wry grin and selected my words carefully. "I ended the fucking war on terrorism."

It started a few weeks ago. I'd gone mad. The quintet nearly caused me to take my own life, and I had locked myself in my condo with four Stella Artois kegs, sixteen handles of Jack Daniels Whiskey—Grandpa would have been proud—and one ounce of the purest heroin in the world. I traveled all the way to Afghanistan to purchase the gooey delicacy.

I didn't intend on taking my own life, but I didn't intend on *not* taking my own life either. All I knew was that I couldn't take the pain anymore. My brain felt like grated Swiss cheese and I was tired of being tormented by Tetro and the troops.

I turned on the television and started drinking and filling needles as fast as I could. I tried smoking the opiate first, but, as anyone who has tasted the Big H will attest, you can only smoke it for so long before you need the rush sooner rather than later. Before long, I was feeding the brown sugar into my veins and chasing it with glasses of my bathtub gin. I'm not really sure why I had the beer. I couldn't drink it fast enough to have an effect and anyone who claims they enjoy the taste of a beer is a dirty goddamn liar.

About four or five days into my binge I was catatonic, lying on the floor with drool coming out of my mouth and my underwear caked in semen. My eyes were wide while Tetro buzzed about rape and murder, and adult males beating off to child pornography. I will never understand why he feels the need to tell me about how they cum. Whether someone wants to put a leather belt around their neck or not when they orgasm is none of my goddamn business.

As if slipping its way through the cracks, I heard the television for the first time in days.
Anderson Cooper was doing an expose on ISIS and terrorism around the world. He identified a new report naming the hundred and eighteen members of the terrorist organization. He didn't divulge his sources, but the way he said the word, "eighteen," made me believe that he was telling the truth. Either that, or the most recent dose of Mexican Mud I'd injected was just starting to slither into my cerebellum. In any event, I'd found a new purpose. I'd found something that would finally stop the voices. If I could end terrorism, they would certainly leave me alone. Right?

I quickly stood up and fell down just as fast. Apparently, when you've been lying in one position for five straight days filling your hemoglobin aqueducts with the White Lady, your legs don't work very well. I transformed into a snake—it seemed fitting—and slithered out of my condo to the street. I knew where I was going, but I wasn't sure how I was going to get there. So, I just kept slithering for hundreds of miles until I reached Oklahoma. By then, the junk had worn off and I was ready to fly.

I transformed into a bald eagle—it seemed fitting—and flew to the Pentagon. I needed information. The building takes special care to guard against chemical, radiological and nuclear attacks. Fortunately, I had no intention of destroying or harming the five-sided edifice and only needed to enter the Information Room (no small task). From my previous endeavors, I knew the Information Room was only accessible by three people, of which I was none. I debated transforming into the President or the Secretary of Defense, or one of the others with security clearance, but decided on a simpler approach and transformed into a cockroach and crawled under the five-foot-thick steel door. For being such a secure facility, they didn't have much in the way of stopping a foreign nation from launching a full-fledged cockroach attack.

Fortunately, the room was empty and I transformed back into one version of myself and started typing away at what looked like a very important computer. Before long, I had penetrated the mainframe and was looking at the faces of the hundred and eighteen terrorists Anderson Cooper had referenced earlier in the day.

Obviously, Chester made note of the fact that I said "penetrated" and discussed my mother in more than one vile position.

I had the faces and I had the names. Now, I needed to figure out how to kill all of them in the most efficient way possible. It would take me years to kill each one where they stood, and by then the number would have grown exponentially.

Brit chimed in, *"Sir, not that I condone or approve of your rampant drug use, but where did you purchase the heroin again?"*

144

He didn't have to say another word. My dealer in Afghanistan was perfect, and I knew just how to draw the entire Muslim Brotherhood to one location.

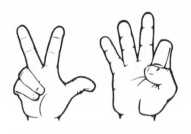

مائة

My drug dealer's name was Mohammad Jaffar Aladdin Mufasa (hereinafter referred to as "MJ"—at least that's how I referred to him). He lived in an Afghan palace about thirty miles outside of Kabul. He knew me as Jaheed, a Palestinian prince with a fierce, fiery and ferocious obsession with anything intoxicating. Heroin was my drug of choice, but he knew me to dabble with speedballs, woolies, flamethrowers (not the weapon), street juice, Charlie Brown's snow toot, Georgia Home Boy, snappers, poppers, whippets and ketamine. Holy fuck, do I love ketamine. The only thing I wouldn't touch is methamphetamine.

MJ was a small man. He stood roughly 5'8" and, from what some of his whores told me, allegedly had only three inches-worth of penis. However, despite his stature and his unfortunate member size, he carried a big stick in the desert. He was known in the region, and in the world, as the foremost authority on illegal drugs. He knew every bad apple and terrorist on the globe, and, most importantly, he knew how to contact every single one of them.

I made my way to his palace and walked right up to the gate. However, I wasn't wearing my usual face. Guards immediately stopped me and upon seeing my face, they bowed—one of the fuckers even started to cry. I had transformed into the only man I knew who could get all one hundred and eighteen terrorists around the globe to congregate: Osama Bin

Laden.

The guards gestured towards a camera and within seconds, the great gold gates opened wide. MJ stood on the other side with an AK-47 pointed directly at my forehead.

"Who the fuck are you?" he screamed in Arabic.

I chortled and walked directly towards the barrel of the gun, grabbing it with my right hand and pushing it down towards the ground. "You ignorant fool! You really think they could kill me?" I added emphasis on "me" to show my power.

"It...it can't be you," MJ said, now shaking.

I assured him it was and relayed information to him I'd pulled from the Pentagon's database.

Yes, to answer your next question, MJ was one of the terrorists; and yes, I was associated and bought many drugs from him, knowing that he was one of the most vile and vicious people on the planet. You can judge me, but if you knew how good his drugs were, you wouldn't question anything. Honestly, part of me loathed the fact that he would have to die too, because I'd have to find a new dealer.

The information I pulled from the database was about MJ's secret vault, located in the basement of the palace. It was where he held his art collection, his rare artifacts; including—but not limited to—the last two white rhinoceroses on the planet; and his crown jewel: a chemical-processing facility and enough plutonium to produce a nuclear warhead. The United States had been tracking his progress for months, but they were unaware how close he was to stabilizing the bomb.

Along with drugs, endangered species and art, he dabbled in arms dealing, but before you judge him, I'd remind you that any financial planner would suggest a diverse portfolio. Also, and I'm not sure I mentioned this, his drugs are out of this fucking world. When I uttered the words chemical-processing facility it was like I had him at "hello." He exploded into tears and hugged me as if he was standing in front of Jesus Christ himself. And, to be fair, I was wearing Jesus sandals.

MJ welcomed me into his palace, offering me an assortment of food, drink, drug and pussy. Chester shouted at me that I should at least be cordial and do a few lines before moving forward with my plan, but I had a mission—and the last time I did coke with a drug lord it ended up ending poorly. For the record, my mission is to shut Chester the fuck up!!!

I told MJ that he needed to call everyone and that we needed a plane big enough to transport everyone to another facility. To my surprise, he didn't question my motives or ask any questions. He pulled out a rotary phone and started dialing numbers, and before I could count to مائة every major ISIS terrorist was on his or her way to the palace, conveniently located thirty miles outside Kabul. As members of the sadistic glee club were scattered across the globe, it was estimated that they would all arrive in roughly forty hours. So, we did what terrorists do best while waiting: we ate, we drank, we fucked, and we drugged ourselves for forty straight hours.

I awoke to one of MJ's minions telling me the good news: the plane was ready, and more importantly, all of our guests had arrived. They were in the great hall, a wondrous room the size of a football field. The hall had thirty-foot ceilings and enough jewelry embedded in the walls to make the Rosenberg Castle look like a Claire's at an outlet mall. Ophelia marveled at the room and gasped so loudly I thought for a split-second other people may have heard her.

My entrance garnered a raucous applause. Some of the men were clearly in disbelief and questioned if I was really Osama Bin Laden in the flesh. For the record, I was not. I raised both arms in the air and the roar of the crowd became even louder; thunderous betas worshiping their alpha. Even the men who didn't believe were excited at the idea that their savior stood before them.

I yelled deafeningly in Arabic, the echo piercing every ear drum in the hall. "My people! Like the great prophet idolized by the Westerners, I have risen from the dead and stand before you with a plan to eradicate all of humankind. I know some of you are wondering how I am alive. I tell you now, that matters not. What matters is that you understand that the air we breathe will soon not be our air, but my air. For, all of you motherfuckers are about to burn in hell!"

Every weapon was drawn and pointed directly at me.

MJ shouted, "What is this, our king? What kind of games do you play?"

I simply smiled and transformed myself into the magnetar, otherwise known as the magnetic neutron star, otherwise known as the Soft Gamma Repeater 1806-20, otherwise, and probably more importantly, known as is most powerful motherfucking magnetic object in the universe.

Every piece of artillery sprung from the hand of its possessor toward me, and I quickly transformed into former U.S. president George W. Bush, it seemed fitting, as the weapons fell at my feet.

From the back of the room, MJ yelled, "RUN! It's Karma!"

They were too slow. I transformed both of my arms into flamethrowers and torched the closest terrorists. The scent of their burning skin made me gag, but I pressed forward. I slit throats, I strangled, I shot bullets out of my eyes. I turned my left fist into a giant hammer and crushed one filthy fuck's skull. I transformed into a twenty-foot rage monster and ripped men into two pieces, and I cut men's hearts out after turning my fingers into jack knives. After the carnage, there was only one man left, my buddy and drug dealer.

He stood in the back of the room, pants full of shit and

piss, begging me to let him live. He told me that he would give me anything I wanted, anything in his possession. I asked him if he could make the voices in my head stop. He told me no. I told him I was sorry and thanked him for the good times before grabbing a 9mm off the floor and putting a bullet right between his eyes.

"So, how the hell did you manage to transport all the bodies from Afghanistan to the White House?" Veronica quipped.

"Easy," I told her. "Remember the plane I made him order? Before I released all of MJ's whores, I made them load the plane with the dead. Then, we flew to North America and threw the bodies out of the plane."

She smiled then asked me my least-favorite question, "Did the voices go away?"

Right as she asked, Tetro buzzed, "*Man on 67*th *Place and Lafayette using a belt on his eight-year-old son because the son spilled a glass of milk. Father is walking into the bedroom to grab his gun. He will use it on the boy first then put it into his own mouth and...*"

I looked at Veronica as a tear dropped down my face. "No, sweetheart. They didn't go away. And I need to go."

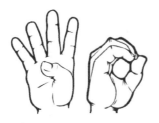

Karma

My powers revealed the burden of obligation and expectation. Before, I could easily move through the world without needing to stay overwhelmingly accountable. I could drift, control small-scale issues, and before any event became too hot to handle, I could move on or through my tiresome, and occasionally mundane, life. There was no boulder of burden on my shoulders to carry everywhere. There weren't five voices making me hate myself more and more, minute by minute, and day by day.

    The hardest part is being viewed as a god. People praise me as Karma. An otherwise humble existence has transformed because of their attention inflating my ego to the point of narcissism. I'm on every network. Half the world adores me, and the other half sits and waits for me to show up on their doorstep one night. Every week, people debate my methods and my value. Each rape I stop, each time I break a dead-beat dad's ankles, the weeks I spend freedom fighting in Colombia. My every step is on international fucking news.

    The tabloids run entire segments trying to figure out who I am. If I wasn't such a nobody, they may have eventually figured it out. My favorite guess was from a scientist who had a theory that I was simply a figment of everyone's collective imagination, which God had embedded through breakfast foods and coffee.

Currently, I am the answer to sixteen questions in various game shows running on major broadcasting channels. My favorite question and answer is, "*What masked vigilante is best known for ripping the dicks off evildoers before turning them into custody? Ding!* 'Karma!'

My least favorite question is, "*Name five of the women who Karma has been with over the last year.*" My sex life is nobody's goddamn business. Honestly, I don't know why any of it fucking matters, but it does. The whole idea of celebrity is comical. Doesn't everyone realize we're just little fucking inconsequential specks floating on a giant rock in the middle of nowhere?

I'd be lying if I told you it wasn't motivating. I jump higher, I fight harder and I try and come up with more creative ways of instilling justice and my own justification of the same. There are times when I will stand in front of my television with my surround-sound system at full blast while every news syndicate exalts me. The fact that no one except for a little, dying girl knows who I am makes it that much better. I'm like Banksy on steroids.

"*Where would we be without Karma?*"

"*Karma cleans up the streets of Minneapolis.*"

"*Ten ways I learned how to orgasm because of sex with Karma.*"

I'd soak it all in. All the fucking words. But, despite all of the praise; despite every person either literally or figuratively getting on their knees and sucking my dick, I can still hear them.

"*You're not good enough,*" Margaret says flatly and repeatedly.

"*You're such a fucking cunt. You narcissistic piece of shit. You have no friends; you have no real relationships. The only person who fucking loves you is the worthless, piece of shit bloke who stares at you in the mirror,*" Chester crows.

For the record, I don't love myself.

Even Brit questions my motives above the chatter,

examining our tactics, preaching about how we could be better and how we didn't need to take people's lives. Ophelia babbles about being present and mindful in the face of blah blah blah blah. How the fuck can anyone focus on the present or being mindful when they can't fucking hear themselves think? When they are constantly listening to five demons banging drums at different tempos in their head?

Everyone else in my position worries about responsibilities. With great power and all that shit. I don't give a fuck about my responsibility to this world. I do what I do for me and to enact some sort of due process to the fuckers who can't keep their dick in their pants or their hands off their wives; and I act to keep the noise down, to keep the thoughts from drowning me in an ocean of despair.

It's confusing chaos. The part that drives me wild, really fucking bonkers, is that my actions don't act as a spark of change. People are filled with wonder and joy and hope when they see that I've stopped a cruise ship from sinking, or freed caged animals in the South Pacific, but nobody else is driven to act. They just debate what I'm doing and grow in their complacency and laziness, polarizing each other. They all just hate each other more. It makes me feel like I'm doing nothing to help anything or anyone. It makes me feel like every time I see a shaking wife's fear leave her eyes, or pull a drowning baby from the lake, it's for nothing.

Like, what's the fucking point to all this? It makes me feel like I just want to grab a gun and...

Women

Fuck, I've used a lot of women.

It's not that I want to use women. It's the complete opposite. I just want to feel anything other than pain.

I long for the days when I held her in my arms, gazing into her almond eyes, by my side. She was the perfect woman. Her feminine drove my masculine wild, and vice versa. Back then, even without powers, I would transform into a rock, withstanding each emotional outburst from my warrior queen. Now, I mostly just fuck to keep the voices down. They don't completely shut up, but they do quiet when I'm balls-deep in some random blonde or blue-haired beauty. I don't discriminate. I've fucked women from nearly every country in the world and made each one roll their eyes in ecstasy. At least, that's what I tell myself. I once joked with Blue—for the record, I never fucked her—that if I could put the heads of my women on the wall, I would have a collection making the tapestries filling the Louvre seem plain. She laughed hard at that joke. At the time, I was unaware she'd slaughtered her family.

My alluring collection would be more famous than a museum housing the Dresden Green diamond, the Graff Pink diamond, the Hope diamond, the Koh-I-Noor diamond, the Star of India sapphire and the Tiffany diamond. I've fucked models, singers, celebrities, princesses and small-town country folk from New Hampshire. I've had my dick sucked by seventy-four yoga instructors, my favorite standing 5'6" with a perfect stomach. She had a tight little four-pack that seemed to become stronger as she rode me faster. She would do the cutest little thing when she orgasmed: she would start singing. She was one of the few women whom I made love to more than once. Although, it's been seven hundred and twenty-four days since the last time I saw her. During that orgasm, she serenaded me to Sisqo's *Thong Song*.

I've had threesomes in forty-five countries around the world. In Belgium, with Dutch twins, fucking twins, I was up for three straight days. We fucked, humped, banged, bonked, copulated, fornicated, masturbated and got it the fuck on, snorting cocaine the entire time and doing a very little bit of heroin. I couldn't help myself. When I met them on the street, they were both freezing because of the weather, yet despite the weather, they both had on the most scandalous, matching black dresses. I may have walked past them, but their four matching hard nipples were too good to be true.

I have used every excuse under the sun not to see someone again. I've said, "It's not you, it's me," in a hundred and fourteen different languages. I've told women I'm gay. I've told older women that I desperately want to have more children. The hardest Chester laughs is when I use that line. I've told women that I'm emotionally unavailable. And I've ghosted women. Ghosting tends to be much easier when I'm not in my own form.

That's another thing – I've fucked a lot of different women in a lot of different forms. I've been black men, Chinese men, Japanese men, Russian men, Latino men. And so on. The weirdest thing I've ever done—and I swear to God I only did this one time—is halfway through sex with an Indian woman, I changed forms into a horse. I know what you're thinking, but I couldn't help it. It was so goddamn funny. Well, it was funny enough to make Brit laugh.

Tetro buzzed, "*Man pretending to be a horse against a woman's consent in the W Hotel in Spain.*" Ironically, it was the same hotel where I was staying.

Fifty-cent-piece-sized Heel

"*Everyone in the room is dead,*" Brit says to me, as I leaf through a hallway bookshelf.

A family of eight violently torn apart, the papered walls painted with blood. Every other step of my foot elicits a loud squish as the orange carpet is transformed into a clotted swamp of cruor. The police won't know about the bloodshed in this rural home for four days. In four days, the neighbor will come over, inquisitive why the youngest child, Wyatt, aged six, hasn't been in school with her son, James, aged six. After finding eight coagulated bodies, she'll turn to hard drugs to cope, and she and her husband will divorce.

"*Do you think it was a murder and/or suicide?*" Ophelia opines. About an hour earlier Tetro buzzed about the murder occurring in East Mesa.

"*This was simply a murder, O,*" Brit articulates further. "The furniture is thrown about as if King Kong was a dinner guest and the only dietary options were vegan. There are body parts torn apart in every room. Furthermore, the father's face looks like he went through ten rounds with Mike Tyson."

Chester cackles with laughter. "*Who the hell references Mike Tyson?! You also missed the most obvious clue, Sherlock! Every person was shot in the back with a 12-gauge shotgun! Even the most flexible son of a bitch couldn't reach a heater around his back and off himself like that! Fucking idiots!!!*"

"He's not wrong, Brit." I chime in. This clearly is not a

murder/suicide. The killer walked out proudly, holding his shotgun over his shoulder. I look around for clues as to who murdered the family of eight. All the bodies are collected in the large living room toward the front of the street. The killer propped them up on the twelve-foot leather couch in what appears to be descending order, from oldest to youngest. Most of their eyes have been gouged out; however, it is impossible to tell if they were gouged during the altercation or after they were modeled on the couch.

Other than the father, the bodies themselves have no discernable evidence hinting at our slaughterer. Some of the children's limbs were cut off in the bedrooms and appear to have been chopped off with a machete. The bones are cracked, and the skin looks like cut, pulled pork.

"*Someone's bitterness and mania has manifested into this family being violently and viciously attacked and brutally murdered,*" Brit observes.

"*No shit, you fucking cunt!*" Chester comments.

"*Great observation, Brit,*" Ophelia notes. "*Who do you think would have committed these murders?*"

"Someone with a limp," I stammer.

The four horsemen inquire in their own annoying ways as Tetro presses on with his monologue of suffering.

"Look right here," I say, extending my finger towards a half-dollar-sized impression. "This impression is throughout the entire house. Our killer used a walking stick."

We go to the front door and I turn my body into an ultraviolet light.

"*Holy fucking shit! The blind, no-nut squirrel found his acorns,*" Chester compliments.

As we Pacman our way through the house, the light shows a series of dots that connect each room and end up in the living room.

158

"*This person must have wonderful eye-gouging skills. Each brain is barely hemorrhaged, and the eyes are removed perfectly from the skull.*" Ophelia sounds as though she is singing a heavenly song.

Right as I am about to chastise Ophelia, Brit yelps, "*Look, sir! Look at the family photo on top of the fireplace!*"

The picture is clear as day; a living version of the family of eight featuring scattered grandparents with gray hair and yellow smiles, and one crossed-eyed, mid-forties-looking man with a Fritz-handle wood cane.

We find the father's cellphone and, after putting his face back together enough for facial recognition to work, begin our search in his contacts and social-media accounts, carefully crossing every other member of the family off our potential-murderer list.

Our primary suspect is forty-two-year-old Jamie Frost, the younger brother of the family's father. Jamie looked like the kind of person whose breath always smells like onions and from the look of Jamie's social-media accounts, and in the words of Chester, he is a "*total loser!*" who lives alone in an apartment in Tempe, Arizona working as a pharmacist. He has two cats and an Instagram account for each cat. He also has an Instagram account for both cats impotently named, "*My Two Cats on Instagram.*"

The father's text messages with Jamie were brief and full of bitterness. Jamie's messages were often ignored by his father and the last message from Jamie said, "*You're going to get what's coming to you someday! You never cared about me or anyone! You selfish piece of shit.*"

Brit giggles hysterically at his own joke, "*Jeeze, tell us how you really feel, Jamie.*" Neither Chester, O, Tetro or I laugh.

I change the password on the father's phone, slip it in my pocket and we head out the door towards Jamie's apartment in Tempe, Arizona. When we arrive, no one is home. We call his work and find that Jamie will be working for another three hours. I transform into the father and we wait on the steps for his pharmacist brother to return.

It is the first time I've sat down in hours and I haven't slept in days. I think about meditating like I used to before the accident; closing my eyes and trying to silence the assemblage of assholes reminding me every second of the day how much I hate my life.

Observing my surroundings, I do my best to find my breath. I feel sleepy and yawn. Within a minute, and for the first time in a long time, I fall asleep without a pint of liquor in my belly.

"Brother. Brother!" I hear, as the long end of a stick pokes into my stomach. "Brother, wake up!" I shoot up groggily, rubbing my eyes.

"Hey...brother," I stammer. "What's going on?"

"What's going on?!" he shot back. "You're sleeping on my steps. How about you tell me what the hell is going on? Are you okay? Where is Becky? Where are the kids?"

"Why is he asking about how we are doing? Didn't he kill us?" Brit whispers.

I can't speak as my eyes are still peeling apart, and a few seconds later, Jamie sits clumsily on the steps, putting his arm around me. "Brother, you're scaring me. Why are you crying? What's going on?"

For the record, I haven't realized I am crying. "I'm okay, Jamie, I'm doing fine. I feel bad that we haven't connected in a long time. I miss you, Jamie."

Jamie starts crying too, "I miss you too, brother. Why don't you come in and we can have some tea?"

Margaret burps acrimoniously. *"He better not only have black tea. Black tea tastes so gross. Also, where's his other walker? The killer used two walkers."*

160

I spew back at Margaret: "*What the fuck do you mean, 'two walkers?'*"

Margaret's tone is dripping with animosity. "*If you men would ever stop fiddling with your dicks for two seconds you would've heard me back at the house. There were two fifty-cent-sized imprints throughout the house, not one. One was always six inches to the left and about a foot and a half in front of the one we traced.*"

I scream audibly and Jamie cocked his head at me. "Why the fuck didn't you tell me about the second set of prints?!!!!"

Jamie and I walk inside and as I sit on the couch, taking out his brother's cellphone, he walks into the kitchen.

"I only have black tea," Jamie yells from the next room.

"*Of course he only has black tea,*" Margaret says, annoyed, as she clamors on negatively commenting on the surprisingly complete collection of antique *Happy Days* figurines sprawled throughout the apartment.

"Sure! Black tea is fine!" I yell from the living room as I rifle through the cellphone. What did we miss? *Who* did we miss? I had checked every text message, Instagram DM and Facebook message that I could access, searching for clues. Now, we're supposed to be looking for a man with two canes!

"*What if it's not a man at all?*" Ophelia opines. "*What if it's a woman?*" As she finishes her query, Jamie walks into the room with two full glasses of iced, black tea.

"Hey Jamie," I inquire, "can you think of any women who would've been upset with me?"

Jamie looks thoroughly puzzled. "Women who don't like you? Brother, you run a lobby attempting to defund Planned Parenthood. I can think of a zillion women who would want to see your head on a platter!"

As he completes his statement, he throws his head back in laughter. I move through my lie carefully. "Well, obviously them, but anyone personal that you could think of? Any old flames?"

Jamie slams his iced, black tea on the table and stands up. "I'm not sure why you're here or if you think this is funny, but it's time to leave, brother!"

I shoot back: "No, no, no. What did I say? Please, Jamie. Help me!"

"Firstly," Jamie roars, "nobody has called me Jamie since I was five years old. Secondly, I haven't seen you in six months and then I find you sleeping on my steps. Thirdly and lastly, you know better than to bring up Dolores! Now get the fuck out of my house!"

I finish my delicious iced black tea, to Margaret's dismay, and walk out of Jamie's apartment. Dolores? Who the fuck is Dolores? I rifle through the cellphone again. Not one contact even remotely close to Dolores.

"*You scroll too fast!*" Margaret chastised. "*Slow down so we can read it too!*"

Rolling my eyes so that she can feel it, I go back to the top of the list at Margaret's demand, and scroll through the names at a considerably slower pace. We make it through the Ds and I slam the phone into my pocket out of frustration.

"*You can't even make it through to the end of the list. What's wrong with you today? Show some patience.*" Margaret will not leave the list alone.

I pull the phone back out of my pocket and scroll through the contact list again slowly. Nothing, nothing, nothing and then, as if appearing for the first time, I see the contact: "*Rhymes with.*" I click with my heavy thumb and see a phone number and an address. Peculiarly, at the bottom of the name, I find that "*Rhymes with*" has been blocked from making any incoming calls or text messages.

"*We must go to the address,*" Brit bellows.

Tetro buzzed, "*Four girls being raped in Florence, Italy...*"

My head is pounding. These motherfuckers never stop

and even with a little sleep I feel myself slowly slipping, succumbing to a world where the voices don't go away and I am stuck between a rock and a hard decision to end my own suffering.

Pressing forward, we head to Rhymes With's address until I reached downtown Phoenix. I check the address and head into a tall building towards the fourteenth floor. As the elevator doors open, a receptionist greets me warmly:

"Welcome to Amaze Co. How may I help you?"

I forgot I am still dressed as the brother, but there is no turning back now.

"I'm here to see Dolores," I convey calmly

The receptionist strikes a few buttons and the speakerphone comes to life.

"Hello," a female voice says.

"Good afternoon, Ms. D," the bubbly receptionist recites. "Jamie's brother is here to see you."

The other line is deathly silent until Dolores breaks the tension. "Pick up the phone now!"

I focus my hearing on the receiver and can clearly make out Dolores screaming, "What the fuck do you mean, Jamie's brother is here? That can't be possible! He's...that can't be possible!"

I fix my eyes on the phone and see that Dolores is calling from Suite 511. I excuse myself while the receptionist is being grilled and head down the hallway.

Reaching for the door, Chester buzzes in my ears, "*If she's hot, can we fuck her?! Let's grab her by the pussy!*"

Shut the fuck up, Chester!

Keeping the father's form, I push the door open and as Dolores sees my face, she drops the phone. "It can't be. You're dead. Who are you?!" she cries out.

"Who are you?!" I scream back. "Sit down!" and she

quickly sits back into her large, black chair crossing her right leg over her left.

"How do you know that I'm dead?" I howl.

She adjusts her seat, her leg shaking vigorously. "I didn't kill anyone," she says calmly, despite her body and leg showing clear signs of anxiety and nervousness.

"Who said anyone died?" I remark.

Dolores responds quickly, "I received a call from my ex-husband, Jamie, a few minutes ago in a panic. He told me someone is impersonating his brother and that I need to be careful. And, while you do look like him, it's easy to tell that you're not. The only time you would ever *really* talk to me with that type of condescending tone is when you're fucking me from behind."

"*Polyamory is a beautiful expression where people can align themselves physically, spiritually and emotionally with a number of different partners simultaneously,*" Ophelia politely pontificates.

"*They didn't fucking know about each other!*" Chester roars. "*Clearly, Jamie found out and Dolores wanted to be with his big-dicked bro!*"

At that moment, Dolores uncrosses and re-crosses her legs, this time with her left leg over her right.

"*There it is!*" Brit yelps. "*Look at the bottom of her heels.*"

My eyes shift from Dolores' piercing blue eyes to the bottom of her raised high heel. While the majority of the heel is brown, there is a large speck of red on the bottom of the roughly fifty-cent-piece-sized heel. I look back into her eyes which are now startled with fright. "You killed them all, didn't you?"

"I don't know who the fuck you are, and I don't care. They'll never catch me. I have a perfect alibi and friends in government."

I smile and begin my transformation. First the high heels, then the body and brown hair in a tight bun, and finally I do my best to encapsulate her bitchy personality. As my lower mandible cracks into place, my piercing blue eyes find hers and I simply say, "You've already been caught, my dear."

I think long and hard about killing her or scorching her vagina, so that she can never use it again, but she hasn't seen my true face. I used the Scotch tape on her desk to seal her mouth shut and drag her out of the office into my car.

We drive back to the father's house where I leave her hog-tied in the backyard. Taped to her shoulder is an audio recording of her confession. She eventually tells me about how Jamie found out about the affair and his brother wrote him off as a result. She, in all of her pureness, had grown jealous of the family. She decided that if she couldn't have Jamie's brother then no one could.

Maybe I can do some good.

The Executioner

The mirror is a cracked version of who I used to be when things were easier, back when I could recognize myself. Every time I save a cat from a tree, blood rains down from the sky bursting out of euthanized kittens. Everything is gone, every semblance of my former humanity. I used to be able to see a small sliver of light in my own eyes. Surprisingly, during all my body transformations, changing my eyes hurts the most. Every time I even change their color, it feels like a malignant spirit is taking a hot poker and slowly sticking it into each one of my green eyes.

My eyes used to be a bright green. They used to be a window into a soul I could stomach. Now, they are often dark gray pools of sadness and despair. I thought death was the key to making the voices stop talking for good. I thought that through death, people would be able to find retribution -and vigor, but I severely underestimated the toll of being the executioner. With each drop of blood I drain out from my victim, I feel my body tighten even more. I feel the blood drain from my tarnished soul. And, of course, the thoughts only grow louder. I've acted so many times under the mask of righteousness.

Oh, my masks! My beautiful masks. Each one perfectly tailored and form-fitting. Each one covering a scar while cutting deep into my skin.

Despite all the noise, I'm so alone. I'm so very alone.

So Dramatic

Her convulsions started mid-story. I was telling her about how I beat the shit out of four grotesque gangbangers in a dimly lit alley near downtown Phoenix. Phoenix has the smallest downtown of any of the top-five metropolises in the United States. Having said that, there are plenty of dimly lit alleys and grotesque gangbangers.

I didn't know what to do when she started seizing. Foam was spewing from her mouth, and her eyes were as white as fresh cotton. Something must have triggered something because the nurses rushed in.

In a flash, I switched from me to a jumping spider, finding my place on a nearby light stand. For the record, I had been allowing Veronica to see my real face. She was dying after all, and I needed to feel like I could trust someone, like I had any sort of friend in this horrible incubus of life.

Doctor Dipshit came in a few minutes later, injecting her with a vial of some pharmaceutical company's best. Her seizure stopped and her eyes sealed shut. She was sleeping again.

After the team of medical professionals left, I spun a web and crawled down, resting on Veronica's chest. My eight were blurry, so I changed them all into small eagle eyes. Her stoic face was clear. It felt like being inches away from the Lincoln Memorial in Washington D.C. Overpowering and frozen, she looked like an angel; my sweet broken angel. God's perfect plan and a crime against humanity that her kind soul would be taken too soon. Her blonde hair was matted from sweat and her eyes had now glazed open, but the blue was gone. Her entire pupil was black, like oil. Her dime-sized dimples survived the ordeal, but they too were just barely hanging on.

I started to sob and, as if the tears were springing from the fountain of youth, she popped into life, throwing me off her onto the ground. I transformed back into me and sat by her side, holding her hands in mine. This powerful, brave little girl finally looked scared. She asked me if she was going to die. I told her, yes. She asked me how long she had to live.

Tetro buzzed, "*She will die within three days. It will be a very painful death...*"

I told her that she would die within three days and that her death would be very painful. That her heart would fail, and because she was too young to have a valid "*Do Not Resuscitate*" contained in a will, they would use a defibrillator to bring her back to life. Then the gagging would start.

I mimicked Tetro word for word. She would vomit for roughly six straight hours until her esophagus collapsed on itself. They would inject her with Zofran and Phenergan until she was a leaf hanging onto a branch during a windy morning. After the vomiting was contained, she would start bleeding internally. The bleeding would move from her kidneys, causing her bowels to evacuate; to her liver, up through her lungs and finally her brain. Eventually, they would use pentobarbital or thiopental to put her into a deep state of unconsciousness: a barbiturate-induced coma. Twelve hours later, she would be dead.

She winked at me and said, "Don't be so dramatic. It doesn't sound that bad." And we both smiled together.

I told her about how her family would be there the entire time, praying for her. She reminded me that her father or any of her three sisters hadn't visited her in over five months because they couldn't stand the sight of her plugged into so many tubes. She also hadn't seen her mother in years. I told her that at least they would be here then, and in that moment she started to spiral. She asked me if I would take her life. She was done. She didn't want to live anymore and she had made peace with moving forward to the uncertainty lay ahead. Then she asked me a question I'd never thought of before:

"Why do you care so much about justice?"

Brit and Chester tried to answer, but I wouldn't let them. I had to answer this question; I owed her that much. She'd listened to my stories for months about my version of justice.

"Veronica," I started quietly, "justice is the removal of pain and suffering from this world. Everything I've ever tried to do in my life has been to alleviate suffering. Sometimes, admittedly, I go too far. I allow myself to become the judge, jury and executioner."

I told her about the shaman in Peru who told me to use my gifts. I told her about falling off the wagon. I told her about how alleviating others' suffering caused the voices to quiet down. This was the first she'd heard of the voices. She knew about my powers, but she never knew the pain that permeated underneath. I could tell it brought her a bit of joy to hear about them and to hear about my struggle. I think it made my empathy for her feel more real.

She looked me in the eyes and rasped again: "Will you please alleviate my suffering? Please."

Ophelia whispered in my ear, "*Sir, the beauty of life is that each individual soul has a beginning and end. Each person comes into the world being birthed at the exact instant the universe has decided. Conversely, the universe must be the one to choose when we enter into permanent darkness. The allure and charm of life is in the eternal choices made within the confines of the universe. This* cannot be disturbed. Please, do not disturb the natural order. She has three days before she dies."

Chester never stopped spewing venomous words as he screamed, "*Do it you pussy! She fucking wants you to do it! Don't be such a goddamn pussy! You think you're so fucking justified in everything you do because you are ending suffering. End her fucking suffering!*"

Margaret took the moment to comment on my wardrobe collection and how she hated every T-shirt I owned.

Tetro buzzed, "*Woman murdering babies in Pyle Marsh, Bristol, England...*"

"Please end my suffering!" Veronica rasped again through her swollen eyes and tears. "Please, I'm begging you."

My purpose has always been to end the world's suffering. My version of justice is being doled out for the sole aspiration of stimulating vitality in this busted planet. I didn't need to ask her if she was sure.

Bending down and taking her in my arms, we embraced in a long, teary hug. She whispered in my ear how she wanted me to end her life. She was, as always, resilient and funny with her last request.

I spent the next hour transforming into different characters: Sheldon Cooper, Chandler Bing, Bugs Bunny, George Costanza, Liz Lemon and Leslie Knope. And so on. It was the most impromptu and star-studded Comic Relief event in history. Robin Williams would have been proud. Her tears had shifted into those of joy. And in that moment, when she was smiling the widest smile I'd ever seen on her face, I reached out and slit her throat.

The minute she stopped breathing, the five started screaming louder than I've ever heard them scream. They didn't stop for two straight days. Tetro buzzed like static on an old rotary television set with the volume on high.

I drank over fourteen liters of vodka in those two days. I can't even bring myself to tell you why I did it. I've only regretted two things in my entire life, and one was taking Veronica's life. I thought I was ending her suffering, I thought I was doing the right thing, but it didn't need to be done. Why the fuck would I trust her? She was only a little girl.

Now, I feel more lost than ever. Months have passed. I never visit the hospital anymore and I can't remember the last time I had a conversation with a human being. I'm slowly drifting into oblivion and all I can hear is Veronica asking me over and over again, "*Why do you care so much about justice?*"

I don't think I can hang on much longer...

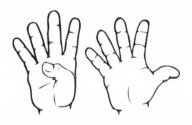

Unlucky stars

My biggest struggle, other than having to explain to Margaret why I will never order a fucking venti coffee (this is America and it's fucking large), is my overwhelming depression mixed with unbridled optimism. It's almost like being bipolar and mixing Red Bull and vodka, if you break it down to the nuts and bolts: a perpetually confusing depressant that has bursts of sanguine lucidity, coupled with a desire to fuck all the time and voices in your head that never shut up. I often wish I could just dive into one or the other instead of having to balance on a splintery and nail-infested beam. Despair and melancholy, while permanently gloomy, would at least be a resting point. I wouldn't need to struggle or worry. There would be no need to seek hope in people, places or things. I could live contentedly in hopelessness that this dark world will never be bright enough for me.

However, this is the contentious point of the struggle: where do the sharp nails start to be worth the tread? Where with each step can I delicately dance into cheer? Wouldn't it be nice? I have a boyish desire to see the world as we all once did, unoppressed from any preconceived notion that we were born into depraved immorality. Welcome to the world, here's your jacket of sin. Don't mind the thorns and be cognizant to ignore—and if at all possible, grow to loathe—the comfortable, suede lining stitched perfectly within.

The glossy, green-eyed me is a but a foggy memory of a past I'm not sure I ever fully had to begin with. Easier is the vantage that I can be cast into a living hell. When I close my eyes tightly, I can feel my skin burning. No matter how tightly I clench my peepers, I can never feel the joy of a rainbow. I drearily awake each morning without expectation of happiness and knowing that the world will ultimately be dark and cold.

Hell would be warm, cozy. After all, there would at least be a fire, right? I wouldn't need to bother with hope. Sitting back, roasting marshmallows next to Hitler and Mussolini and Pol Pot. (For the record, Pol Pot detested marshmallows.) There are times I think about going to see a shrink, but what would they say? They would tell me go have some fun, get laid and, "get out more."

Margaret always suggests those three little words: "*You should get out more. Just get out more. Why don't you get out more?*"

Where the fuck should I go, Margaret? I've nearly been to fucking Mars. Where should I, "*get out more*" to, you raspy cunt?!

People really mean that I need to meet a woman to "*get out more*" with. They don't understand I have fucking voices dictating my every destination. Everyone tries to set me up. It's either too much information about a woman's best friend or a guy's wife's friend whom he secretly wants to bang. The guys know every detail about my "dream girl." Somehow, they know everything about my future ex-wife, from where she does her nails to the size of her bra and waistline. Invariably, the husband's crush or the woman's adoration for her best friend blinds them to the fact that random woman X has already endured three abusive relationships, and she has that "little thing with her father." They all have little things with their father.

So, what in the fuck am I supposed to do? I find that men, especially me, battle society's social norms the same way women do. But, for some reason ours are accepted because they are seen as positive. We become the hero, staving off global disaster one twist of the pickle jar at a time. These are all great things until you're stuck working an 8 am to 6 pm job and your wife hasn't put her mouth on your Johnson in nine months. And then fucking what? We're supposed to just rise up again and live the same fucking life fifty years in a row finding pride in the fact that we can open a jar of goddamn dill pickles?

At least I'm not married.

Does anyone ever count their unlucky stars? This whole fucking planet is spinning on an idea of gratitude. The headlines are all the same: *"Be grateful to find happiness,"* or, *"Blending a healthy diet and mindfulness to find balance,"* or, *"Ten ways to give your partner the best orgasm of their life."* Maybe the key to this godforsaken beautiful twist of irony is to be ungrateful: counting all the unlucky stars that have been around for billions of years that are burning through all of their fuel.

Maybe the key to life isn't being grateful that Auntie Suzie celebrated another pointless birthday (for the record, Aunt Suzie died a horrific death at a very young age), but rather the key to life is seeing and embracing the undeniable fate that gravity will pull us into the ground the same way gravity pulls a star into a planetary nebula.

It's all a fucking disaster.

Heavy Parka, Thick Socks and an Ice Pick

I evolved in Peru, re-learning to intentionally set my mind to the present before my daily cup of coffee each morning, finding a mind-blowingly simple technique that keeps the squad at bay from babbling about peace, love and cock n' roll: I write on a sheet of paper every single day. Every single day I pick up my black ink pen—I hate using blue, red, green or otherwise—and I write my intention to be present each day. It gives me a small bit of hope.

I've also connected with nature in a big way. Ophelia too. She is distracted enough by the pine, jungle and hooker's green, that instead of gracing me with her gushing gab, she talks to the birds, plants and sunshine, singing and writing poetry to every Amazon lily, Peruvian sundew and yellow-tailed woolly monkey she sees.

The only time she really craved my attention is when she told me—as if I was taking notes or recording her to have the novella transcribed at a later date—about how nature is being destroyed, demolished and deprived by so many people. She used me as an example in her book citing that, "*Most people find that recycling is a waste of time.*" I love how I can turn into a cow, yet she still considers me, "*Most people...*"

However, she did manage to change my perspective

during the first few days in Cusco. Call it a Peruvian perspective permutation, if you will. Ophelia preached that nature is the source of life, giving me liquid to sustain my mostly aquatic physical form; how, like our physical forms, the wave of life is ever changing and uncertain, and without constant commitment to accepting that which cannot be accepted, the weight of the world will ultimately prove too heavy a burden to bear.

Candidly, it may not have been Ophelia at all; it may have been the black tar Ayahuasca my body is still using as gasoline.

My next mountain to climb was a literal four-day hike, up and down, and up and down, then down then up the Inca Trail. A hint of anxiety crept into my cerebellum as this would be the longest I'd been with other individuals—four days—in longer than I can remember, but I was grateful for the opportunity.

For the first time since the accident, I was excited to move my feet, excited for the opportunity to walk steps so few can muster, and I was grateful to be off the grid, alone from the world; disconnected from the cords that plug me into my cell phone, laptop and music. Like clockwork, each day I kept my focus on gratitude, and the team of misfits constantly ringing in my ears grew even more quiet.

My anxiety lowered as I consumed my second portion of hotel French fries, trying to keep my eyes open for as long as possible before leaving the next day. When I closed them, I dreamt of the peaks of the tall mountains, lost in the clouds, and the beauty in front of me: a sea of green trees looking like they were each individually placed by God's own hand. When I awoke, and after a breakfast of scrambled eggs, everything bagel and two cups of black coffee, I'd be floating in the clouds for real.

I woke up in a sweat. It was the closest I'd ever been in my life to having a panic attack. Well, in a situation that didn't include me laying in a grave preparing to die. I decided not to hire a porter to carry my bags because of my giant ego, perpetuated by

Chester constantly calling me a *"giant fucking pussy."* I can only presume it was an effort to maximize my anxiety.

The first thing I saw that morning was a text from our guide in reference to my decision. It said, *"You didn't hire a porter?!!!"* Three exclamation points are not very reassuring.

Part of me didn't want to go. I'd made so much good progress: I should have focused on staying well, right? I should have faked an injury and headed down to the market for some fresh fruit. That was the sensible thing to do, right?

I pressed on, deciding the absolutely fucking worst-case scenario would be four days of hell and struggle; and honestly, when you're me, what's another four days of hell? If at any point, I really wanted to leave, I could transform into a helicopter, or bat, or paper airplane, and fly away. However, my intention was to see the hike through.

Arriving at the trailhead, I was met with another wave of unfortunate feelings. Our guide, the bringer of good news, cautioned me that all of the clothes I'd brought would be too warm. Apparently, thirty degrees in Peru means Celsius, and the packed clothes would be more appropriately worn in Antarctica. This dumb American was ready to embark on miles and miles of hot trail with a heavy parka, thick socks and an ice pick. *Oy fucking vey.*

Thankfully, I was able to purchase a pair of shorts and a T-shirt at the general store and we made it through the first leg of the hike to our campsite.

We were greeted by thirteen Peruvians who had set up our tents and prepared dinner. The dinner was average: a stew full of curiously unnamed meats, potatoes, carrots and garlic, with a fig cake for dessert. The best part of the meal was a pre-dinner appetizer of popcorn, soaked with butter and salted to perfection. If the cook told me he developed a scientific formula for the perfect kernel of popped corn, and applied sixty-nine grains of salt to each kernel pursuant to his perfect formula, I wouldn't have been a bit surprised. The popcorn was that delicious.

I woke up the next morning cold, but for some reason it didn't matter; I was grateful to be waking up. To be honest, I don't like camping. People understand that there are hotels with big beds in existence, right? Auspiciously, I made a wise choice regarding my sleeping arrangement.

There were a total of eight newbies hiking the Inca Trail with me: Merlin, a 6-foot red-haired German with a quick wit and intelligence that far surpassed his time on Earth. He was an international businessman who had traveled to over a hundred and fifty countries and spoke four languages: English, German, Mandarin, and Sarcasm; fluently. Craig and Donna were the only people hiking that were coupled. Both hailed from England. Donna was blonde, about 5'7" tall and extremely sweet. Also, don't tell Craig this, but she had incredible legs; two of the best walking sticks I've ever seen in my life. Craig was a hockey player. He stood not tall enough to measure but could recite every Ricky Gervais stand-up ever, which made our four days' hiking together even more enjoyable. Rounding out the group of hikers were Talia and Dalia, twin sisters visiting from New Zealand; and Sarah, a New Yorker who had an attitude and an air of insecurity. The last two companions ended up sharing four long nights together as tent mates. John was a bisexual, forty-six-year-old man from Manhattan, New York. He had a sweet, labored laugh that reminded you of an older gentleman, but with a young boy's heart and determination. Robin was a twenty-four-year-old from Sweden who, even down to the dashing good looks, was a spitting image of Owen Wilson from the movie *Zoolander*. Owen Wilson was also in *Zoolander 2*, but I don't count that movie because it was so terrible.

Laying there the first night, we were all talking from our tents, which were in such close proximity they were practically hugging. Merlin was my tent mate. We discussed religion, politics, money, and women.

In the tent next to us laid Robin and John. We could hear their conversation loud and clear, and John, in all of his childlike honesty, said, "Robin, I just want you to know I find you extremely sexy. If you are into guys, I wouldn't mind being with you tonight." Robin, with all of his boyish charm said sweetly, "That's nice, but no."

The next morning, the hilarious conversation continued when John told Robin, in heavy detail, how he had the sexiest dream about Robin, and when he woke up he'd had his first wet dream in over thirty years.

Robin, after hearing the story, replied, "That's nice!"

Can't blame John for shooting his shot.

Day two of the hike was wildly intense. Our group, and my temporary best friends, hiked just over a mile at a steep incline for the first three hours. There were many times when I had to push my legs just to take another step. I could have easily transformed, but I needed to do this for myself. It would have been simple to transform my muscle fibers into a goat's without anyone noticing, but I was determined not to transform to make the hike easier. I wanted to experience this as me.

I often feel like I am faking each step in life, faking the endurance that pushes me forward. Now, feeling each step tug on my hamstrings, calves, and gluteus, it's impossible to ignore the effort; inconceivable to overlook the most meaningful muscle stretching during the fight to the top: my mind.

The most wonderful part of the hike was developing a new mental toughness. I knew before that my physical barriers were often a figment of my imagination. For example, even the worst pain known to man, stubbing one's toe on the side of the bed, can be curbed quite quickly if you focus your attention to the other ninety-nine percent of your body which remains unharmed. This hike was real pain, real struggle in ninety-nine percent of my body, and in order to reach the summit, I'd have to focus on the little things: the one percent.

At the summit, clarity hit me like a wave. Pride for persevering; salty tears of joy around everyone's eyes, witnessing our accomplishment. Some gathered together taking selfies, some sang songs and prayed. Our group came together, and all communicated one little thing that made us grateful. Mine was the popcorn from the night before. The perspective was earth-shattering; finding the same cheer in a handful of popcorn as we had marveling 5,905 feet above sea level into the brilliant sun burning above Machu Picchu.

The next few miles to the final campsite were almost completely downhill, a sweet reprieve from climbing to the peak. Despite my happiness and newfound resolve, I still had a small twinge of anxiety in my soul from being alone in Peru, and doing something completely outside my element. By happy chance, the third day of the hike was one of the best days of my life.

We woke up at 5:00 am almost at the summit of the Inca Trail. I awoke groggy and tired from the physical and mental wear and tear from just a few nights prior. However, all it took was a glass of coca tea and a stack of passion-fruit pancakes—by far the best meal on the hike—and I was off to the races. The third day was the longest individual day at sixteen kilometers. Being American, I have no idea what the distance was in miles and that was probably for the best.

The day took us up roughly one thousand ancient steps, about half the size of one of my size-thirteen shoes and down nearly nine thousand repurposed steps, large enough for my entire shoe. Each ancient step looked as if it were carved for a man standing seven-feet tall with size-three feet. The spacing was awkward and I'd be lying if I told you I didn't nearly fall two or three times.

By the third day, we had grouped off into smaller pods, as herds generally do, and my group of four hiked most of the forty-two-kilometer Inca Trail together. The foursome included me, Craig, Donna, and Merlin. Satisfyingly, the fivesome in my head were barely audible, and somehow almost pleasant, like light rainfall against a tin roof.

I was mesmerized at the beauty which came in the time shared with new friends, and the scenery all around. Most of the day was spent with my jaw open at the breathtaking views and smiling because of the calm stillness bringing me instant peace. It was one of the simplest days of my life, walking down the trail.

On the fourth day, we had the delightful irony of reaching the Sun Gate with the entire valley covered in clouds. The Sun Gate is the spot on the Inca Trail where the wonder is captivated. It's where people take pictures of themselves jumping, or naked, or in a fancy yoga pose. My plan was to take a picture of me jumping naked, doing a fancy yoga pose. However, like most best-laid plans, mine were foiled. Fog entrenched the wonder and I could only see my friends' faces who were standing about ten feet in front of me. I couldn't help but smile.

The moments shared with them along the hike were the real wonder. Staying present with each step and conquering the mountain filled my spirit. It didn't have to do with the placard associated with one of the Seven Wonders of the World. The richness of the overall experience I encountered kept my feet moving, and left a lasting impression far more important than a piece of stone in the middle of Peru.

The best part is that I thought I was cured.

Fifty Times

"Your blood is different."

"What do you mean, *different*?" I muttered in surprise.

I had donated blood once a week for seven straight months as part of my "giving back" to society. It really wasn't a big deal: my blood was O-negative, they give away cookies at the end and, after seven months, I was finally making progress with the cute, brunette nurse.

Nurse Anna looked at me in shock. "Your blood is..." she took a deep swallow... "almost cerulean. It's translucent, vibrant. When I first saw it, I couldn't take my eyes off the vial for over seven minutes. I was immobile, transfixed. It felt like I was being pulled into the universe with shooting stars, planets and meteors spiraling past me. The entire time I heard people, voices from my past and present, some even saying they were from my future. By the time I broke the trance, I was covered in sweat and it felt like I'd orgasmed fifty times."

"You orgasmed fifty times?" I spat. "And wait, my blood is what color?"

She put the vial into a box and handed it to me. "You have to take this away from me. I've been sucked in twice already. Both times, the sensation and hallucination lasted exactly seven minutes. The first time with the orgasmic feeling and the second was violent. I wasn't pulled into the universe. I was sucked into a constricting black hole. Nothingness and silence choked me until I couldn't breathe. Then, I could hear the whole world shouting at me, calling me names, telling me erotic stories, threatening my existence. By the time I broke the trance the second time, I was dehydrated from all the tears I'd cried."

I cautiously opened the box and saw the sky-blue vial of my blood. At first glance, aqua appeared to be deliberately moving within the bottle. Then, I noticed the strangest thing. As the liquid moved, one side stayed intact; bright, starry, airy. My body felt warm and I could feel love, bliss and joy emanating from the tiny jar. The other side was dark, slow-moving sludge. It begrudgingly moved at a different pace almost piercing through the lighter, airy blood. The vial was filled with equal parts of both and as they moved it reminded of a yin-yang symbol in motion, as if Salvador Dali controlled the laws of physics.

I closed the box and earnestly looked at Nurse Anna. She asked me candidly, "Did you see anything?!"

I flatly replied, "No. I didn't see anything."

As I closed the box and stood to leave, she screamed loud enough to give the other patients leave from their normal activities—usually crosswords or sudoku—to listen to her powerful voice. "What the fuck are you talking about!? The entire planet shifted. I could feel the concrete, earth and every layer of bedrock and humus vibrating underneath my feet, and you didn't see a thing?!"

She reached for the box of blood as I pulled the box more firmly into my arms. "I didn't see a goddamn thing, and I don't believe you did either. Goodbye, Anna." When all else fails, gaslight the shit out of them.

She cried and screamed after me as I walked out the door into the blistering heat. Phoenix was over a hundred and twenty degrees that day, but I needed to go for a walk.

"Guess you'll never get to fuck her now!" Chester roared,

while Tetro buzzed like an electric chainsaw through my internal
PA system:

"Suicidal man. Age forty-two..."

He was only .03 miles from my current location, so I
started walking in his direction.

*"...currently has .38 shotgun barrel in his mouth and is
screaming about how no one loves him."*

I walked toward his house and I was there in less than ten
minutes. The guy's house was gorgeous. You would probably
think that most of my time is spent in less than inspiring ghettos,
slums or rough areas of town, but surprisingly, people with
money have the same issues, and usually more, as broke-ass
motherfuckers from the hood. For the record, I do not condone
motherfucking unless it's consensual.

From outside I could hear the muffled screams of a
grown-ass man losing his fucking shit. I rang the doorbell and
yelled from the outside, "Housekeeping!" After a few attempts
and some fruitless knocks, I turned my right arm into a hydraulic
jack and broke down the door with a flick of my wrist.

I was pissed; his place was so much nicer than mine. This
motherfucker was bitching and moaning and suicidal, without
any idea how badly pain could really feel. He didn't have insects
and parasites burrowing into his soul, digging deeper into his
brain at every turn.

To the left there was a large living room with a baby grand
piano—a fucking baby grand—in the middle of the room. To the
right was an office with a large oak desk, sitting in front of
towering shelves lined with leather-bound books.

Down the hallway was a screaming little bitch whom I
was there to help. As I walked down the hallway, following the
maniacal and bipolar wailing, I saw multiple pictures of a
middle-aged man and a younger, blonde woman, around
twenty-nine years old. After passing a few more pictures of what

appeared to be his children, I reached the closed, bedroom door. I transformed into an old, white balding man and slowly turned the knob.

Doctor Depressed (hereinafter referred to as "DD") wrenched his head in my direction, and with the shotgun still in his mouth said, "Who the hell are you?!"

I smiled calmly and introduced myself as Joseph, his next-door neighbor. Sleepily, as if I'd just awoken because my neighbor couldn't handle his fucking shit, I said, "I heard screaming and knocked a few times before the door opened. Are you okay?"

DD removed the gun from his foaming mouth. "Do I fucking look okay?"

For the record, he did not look okay.

He put the gun to the side and sobbed uncontrollably while his body shook forcefully. He was sitting on the bed, and I cautiously asked if I could sit next to him. A light wave of his left wrist invited me over, and as soon I sat down next to him, he lunged toward me and fiercely hugged me.

He cried for exactly seven, uninterrupted minutes before blubbering, "Thank you for coming over."

Hours felt like minutes as we talked on the bed. He opened up about his fears, his shame and his guilt. Despite his outward success, I learned he was a doctor and that his car was also nicer than mine. He was filled with regret and anguish, and he described in painstaking detail his adorable aunt. She won the 1977 Little Miss Sunshine pageant in Norman, Oklahoma prior to marrying his uncle and moving to Phoenix, and raping him at the age of eight. I was the first person he'd ever told about the incident.

"I remember what happened pretty vividly. I was young, around eight years old. I was swimming with my brothers and sister at our aunt and uncle's house. They lived a few houses down from Mom and Dad and since they had a pool, we'd frequent their house during the summer months. This particular Saturday, I slipped running on the cool deck and split open my kneecap badly. There was blood everywhere and my sister threw up at the giant gash. Aunt Rebecca took me to the bathroom where she took off my blood-covered swim trunks. She used alcohol to treat the wound and used three stitches to sew the skin back together. She stood me up and I'll never forget the way she said, 'Good as new!' in her cheery Midwestern accent, right before she broke me forever. My pants were still crumpled to the floor.

"She said, 'Richard, would you be a good boy and pull Auntie's hair?' I was a confused little boy with my knee still hurting and my mind steeped in adolescence. After a few minutes, she showed me how to grab and pull a healthy portion of her blonde locks from the root. Every time I did, she let out a soft moan sending shivers slicing down my spine. Then, she pulled down her denim shorts and told me to put my tongue on her vagina. Apparently, I was bad at that too. She scolded me and had me stick out my tongue, 'Like a good boy.' With my tongue inside of her she stuck her right index finger in her mouth, wetting it before reaching around and shoving it inside of my asshole."

"My God. I'm so sorry, Richard."

"After the first time, I would make up every excuse in the book not to go to Aunt Rebecca's house. My stomach hurt, my throat hurt—one time I even faked appendicitis, but no matter what I did, at least once a year we'd end up in the same house and I'd end up leaving feeling ashamed and humiliated.

"The last time she molested me, I was twenty-three years old. I was visiting from college, in my senior year. I brought my beautiful, blonde girlfriend home to meet the family. She was a twenty-one-year-old junior, minoring in Spanish and majoring in Psychology. I was pre-med and finishing off a four-year career playing strong safety for the football team. We had been together for three years and we rarely had sex. It wasn't that I didn't find her beautiful—I did. She was gorgeous: long, flowing blonde hair, well-built. She ran track and the only thing stronger than her love of me was her love for running. The issue was that just about every time we would try and make love, the shame and scars of Aunt Rebecca would make it impossible for me to get hard, and of course, I couldn't tell her, so she thought it was her fault.

"Eventually my girlfriend, feeling so ashamed of her body, developed an eating disorder and I started drinking heavily. By the end of my senior year, I would regularly drink twenty-four beers per night. The only variation to my week would be when I substituted the last fourteen beers for a bottle of Jack Daniels whiskey. We were quite a pair. One the outside, we were the bells of the ball: smart, good-looking, poised for success. On the inside, she had a busted gut and eroded esophagus from vomiting for years and my liver was already failing due to my extreme alcohol consumption.

"When we were visiting for Christmas, the entire family showed up for dinner, including Aunt Rebecca. My parents had one of those long, wooden tables with twelve chairs on each side and one chair at each end of the table. I was about a bottle and a half of white wine in before my mother scolded me to, 'Slow down on the booze.' I called her a bitch and excused myself to the restroom.

After taking a piss, I opened the door to find Aunt Rebecca staring at me. She didn't even hesitate. I'll never forget the way she said, 'My pussy missed you, Richard.' I told her I didn't care and that I wasn't going to let her touch me again. She smiled and put on ruby-red lipstick saying, 'Now, Richard, I know you can't get it up with that little cunt girlfriend you have. She doesn't know how to *touch* the right buttons like I do.' As she finished her sentence, she reached for my penis and I don't know if it was the alcohol or the fifteen years of sexual assault, but I punched Aunt Rebecca in the face, breaking her jaw and nose. The police were called, and eventually I went to jail for twenty-eight days for assault and battery.

"After telling the prosecutors what Aunt Rebecca had done, my charges were mitigated. It turned out to be a 'he said / she said', and without proof, Aunt Rebecca ended up serving zero time in jail. Even worse, most of my friends relentlessly teased me because, 'She's not your biological aunt anyway, and she's super-hot!' Aunt Rebecca ended up dying a few years later in a car accident."

"I'm so sorry, Richard."

"Now, I have my perfect family. I'm on my second marriage, but my ex and I get along great and new wife is fantastic. My kids are great, and I have a good job, but I wake up crying every day and drink more than ever. Tonight, it was the anniversary of Aunt Rebecca's death, which my wife knows about. I took the day off work and was already two bottles of Chardonnay in. My wife came home and started nagging me about how she hates that I purchase Arrowhead water instead of the generic, store-brand water. Without thinking, I called her a cunt, and she came at me hard. She wasn't hitting me, just screaming in my face. Still without thinking, I took both hands and pushed her hard against the cabinet. The kids heard the screaming and were standing at the bedroom door and saw the whole thing. My wife left, taking the kids to their mom's house. She said she wanted a divorce."

"I'm so sorry, Richard."

"Thanks, Joe.

Richard broke down sobbing again, for another hour and twenty-eight minutes. During that time, we talked about his childhood and how to move forward. Eventually, he admitted he needed clinical help, and I drove him in his car to a rehab facility for alcohol treatment.

I left his red Mercedes there and as I was walking away, Tetro buzzed, "*Thirty-six-year-old man, hanging himself in Glendale. Even at top speed we would not reach him in time. He will die in twelve seconds.*"

I stopped cold in my tracks with the hot Phoenix sun against my face and burst into tears.

Small Mohawk

"*DHARMA!*" I scream at the top of my lungs as the tears pour out of my eyes. The words don't make it very far; they are trapped in the bubble surrounding me (six cups of water, one cup of dish soap, and one tablespoon of glycerin slowly stirred until the bubble forms). It jumped faster than I could move, engulfing me, my words and screams filling the space like pollution. I cough, trying to break the bubble. Nothing. Negativity surrounds me.

I long for the day when simple problems felt like anarchy, when my biggest worry was an inflated student-loan payment and whether I would make it to my yoga class on time; when the only voices I heard were my ghost and my time traveler. I wonder if they still speak. If they do, my ears fall deaf to their voices. The five clang around in my consciousness, constricting and constraining every concept without regret.

I openly weep as Tetro buzzes, "*Twenty-six point two tons of cocaine arriving at Port Everglades in South Florida in two days. Estimated worth: two billion one hundred million dollars. Forty-two smugglers on board. All heavily armed...*"

Chester chirps, "*That sounds like fun! Let's gooooooo!*"

On cue, because the time couldn't be less appropriate, and without anyone inquiring, Margaret reminds me about my father's murder. Like I need a fucking reminder.

Needing a distraction, I order a taxicab and Brit and I go

through the plan as we head to the airport. I think about transforming into a North American X-15 or gust of wind, but I have time and I'm dehydrated from crying so much. I need first class and a bottle or three of red wine.

Squeamishly, Brit tells me about how he wants this to be clean. His idea is that I creep in as a South American *Parotostigmus Scabricauda* centipede, and take our time biting each pirate and sending each patch-eyed or hook-handed drug dealer into immediate cardiac arrest.

He knows I want to make noise. He knows that. He always fucking knows that. I swear to Shiva he always starts with the worst fucking option, just so I don't go nuclear on these drug-smuggling assholes.

I make a slightly sexier suggestion that we steal the drug lord's Ferrari Enzo waiting for him at his Miami penthouse, and drive it directly on to the cargo ship, killing a few of the smugglers in the process, before transforming into the Stay-Puft Marshmallow Man, destroying the car and everyone on board. To my surprise, he's agreeable.

The plane is quiet. There is only one other passenger in first class: it is a man, middle-aged. He looks like he goes door-to-door selling insurance, or encyclopedias, or fertilizer. From across the aisle, he tries talking to me, but I short-answer him and shift my attention to the drinks and flight attendants. Both are less than inspiring.

Apparently, before the Phoenix-to-Miami flight, a bachelor party drank the entire first-class empty but for three bottles of house red wine. I order the three bottles and fuck the overweight flight attendant with the big nose in the bathroom.

We land early. The ship isn't arriving to port for another four hours. I transform into a charmer, standing 6'4" with carved abdominal muscles like Michelangelo working on a piece of marble. My smile is perfect, each tooth as if it were carefully positioned along the gum. I give myself a small mohawk and cover my arms with colorful tattoos. I take a limo to the W Hotel on South Beach, and when I walk in, I immediately go to the bar, purchase two bottles of champagne and sit on a comfortable leather couch in the corner.

The lounge is dark and empty, not one fucking woman in the entire place. Even the fucking bartender is a guy. The voices in my head are screaming and I need a release. I can barely see because Chester and Margaret are nonsensically arguing about the taste of blue cheese and olives. Margaret can't stand them and because of that, Chester feels the need to call her a cunt eighty-seven times over the course of seventeen minutes.

In my haste to find distaste for the situation, I overlook a man sitting alone in the darkest corner of the lounge. I can only make out his outline and the red glow coming from his Cuban cigar. I can smell the sweet tobacco even with a couple of hundred feet of distance separating us.

Tetro buzzes about a separate cargo ship arriving in ten hours, filled with a hundred and eight Taiwanese women; eight women per shipping container. The containers are each 8x8x8 cubic feet.

I finish my second bottle of champagne and stand up to introduce myself to my shadowy friend in the corner of the room. I approached the Shadow, and by the time I am roughly eight feet away from him, I hear two guns click. As I stop in my tracks, he stands up.

"Can I help you, young man?" His voice is coated with Colombian origin and cocaine.

"I was hoping I could trouble you for one of them sweet-smelling cigars," I spit in a Southern Texas drawl.

He lets out a hearty laugh. I'm unsure if it is due to the surprise of my accent or because of the audacity of my request. His chortle ceases, and I am close enough to see his sadistic smirk from the glow of his bouquet of tobacco. He maximizes every inhale, breathing in ten, fifteen, twenty seconds at a time before releasing a giant cloud of smoke with each exhale. The longer he sucks on his cigar the wider he smirks, the red glow eventually shifting from his cheroot and radiating from his fiery eyes.

"Come sit."

He offers me the finest cigar I've ever seen: a tightly rolled, million-dollar Gurkha Royal Courtesan. Each hand-rolled cigar is filled with rare Himalayan tobacco that has been watered only with Fiji water. Each piece is wrapped in a leaf of gold and the cigar's band is embroidered with diamonds, totaling up to five carats.

After a delicate cut, I gently bite the tip and light the golden claro. My senses are sizzling with sin. The Shadow and I sit together in silence for the first twenty-three minutes. He lights a new, million-dollar cigar as I memorize every inch of his face, how he sits and how he sips his Ultra-Premium Ley .925 Pasion Azteca.

The Shadow has the smoothest face I've ever seen; there isn't one crack, wrinkle or blackhead. Even though he is well over sixty-years-old and has probably inhaled pounds of tobacco during his life, he barely looks forty. The only thing giving his age away is his slightly receding hairline and his mostly salt, salt-and-pepper hair. The closest thing to an imperfection is a small mole on the left side of his chin. However, even on him it seems to have redeeming qualities.

"How do you live with yourself?" I opine.

His red smirk stares back at me. "There's an order to this world; a balance. Not many understand. I trust you understand it, though. Don't you?" he inquired softly and patiently.

As if entering into a marriage that I am questioning, I reluctantly say, "I do."

He continues, "Sheep without a shepherd flock aimlessly. Once in a great while the shepherd is not a lowly farmer holding a staff, but a god wielding a gold trident. I am that god, Mr. Karma. Can I call you Mr. Karma or do you prefer something else?" He speaks eloquently.

"People die because of your drugs…"

He snaps and interrupts me, "They die because of their choices! I don't make the orders. I don't tell people what to do. When I order someone dead their head ends up on a plate. These people you care so much about voluntarily put one of the most dangerous drugs on the planet up their nose for a short burst of euphoria. How the fuck is that my fault?"

As he speaks his truth, three gun clicks ring in my ear and I can feel one of the barrels on the back of my head. "Tell your men to back down immediately or this whole place…"

Before I can even finish my threat, he casually waves his non-smoking hand and the pressure from the gun barrel releases from the back of my head. "I can only assume you are here to sink my cargo ship arriving in two hours and fifty-seven minutes. Is that correct?"

He is one step ahead of me and I start to sweat. "That is correct, and what you need to understand is…"

He interrupts me again: "And what then?" he continues. "I lose my money and you are able to feel better about yourself? The stupid voices in your head will stop bitching and moaning? I will keep shipping. You are nothing to me but an insignificant speck."

How does he know about the voices? I know he is one step ahead of me, but perhaps it is so much more. How the fuck does he know about Chester, Margaret, Ophelia, Brit and Tetro?

"Tell me," his words spew as he spouts more smoke in my direction, "does the robot really tell you everything? Every single transgression born from man's mortality and you hear it all? Fascinating."

What the fuck is going on?

He takes another deep drag from his cigar. "I know you're a smart man. I know you will see my side of this particular gold coin. I don't ever directly harm anyone; they make the choice. I'm outside your scope of justice. You can't hurt me without hurting yourself even worse. After all, you wouldn't want Chester to learn a new cuss word. I can teach him how to say cunt in Colombian." Then he called me a cunt in his Columbian tongue.

I think back to the bottles of champagne. Did he slip something in my drink? I feel fuzzy and Chester is slurring. I look down at the glass table. It is covered in white powder. I cross my eyes towards my nose, which is also covered in white powder. Unbeknownst to my reality, I have been doing cocaine with Paulo Cohleco, the biggest drug lord in the world, for the last forty-five minutes, and in that time, the drug lord—worth an estimated fifteen-billion dollars—has convinced me that he is outside of my jurisdiction and we celebrate by doing what I only could presume is a fuckload of cocaine.

Brit must have shocked me because my body feels like I have been electrocuted with magnetic paddles and I instantly return back to the real world, aware of my precarious situation. He is right that I can't kill him, but if I'm not going to take his life, he will give me a favor. If I am going to spare his ship, his drugs and his reputation, he is going to owe me something in the future; something potentially worth more to me than all the pure, white cocaine on his transport.

Without delay, he agrees to my request and he offers me another smoke and another drink. I politely decline and stand to leave, shaking his hand. In my Southern drawl, I say, "Good running into you, friend."

He chortles and coughs as I walk towards the exit. Oxytocin fills my head as my eyes are drawn to a woman standing at the bar. She is wearing an off-the-shoulder beaded gown. Her blonde flowing hair dances past her shoulders; light blue tints her eyelashes as she winks seductively in my direction.

Chester chimes in, "*Watch where you point that thing! It's a loaded weapon! Zinger!*"

I fucking hate Chester.

She walks up to me and stops me before I can walk through the exit. "Hello, handsome," she whispers confidently. "Mr. Cohleco wanted me to give you something as a token of his gratitude." She points through the glass doors towards his brand-new Ferrari Enzo.

I smile and say, "And I can only assume you're coming with me.

Transvestite Turkeys

Veronica nearly spit out her orange juice. "So, what the fuck happened on the boat?"

The night ended up going down harder than the Titanic. Wreckage and dead bodies everywhere, without an iceberg to take the blame. I didn't help anyone; my morals were shaken, and my young, sick friend could tell. Veronica reminded me that there are echo effects to what we do and that I was merely being swayed by strong justifications of my own guilt and shame.

Thank fucking God for that little girl. I'd be a carcass floating in the ocean by now if it hadn't been for her.

She asked me for the gory details. I don't know how or why she became such a sick fuck, but in some way my stories, as gruesome as they were, must have provided her with a short reprieve from the monster living inside of her and her impending death. Fuck, I don't blame her. If my entire body burned like fire for four days a week because of radiation, I would want some sort of escape too.

She was so positive. The only thing she could never understand was how man struggled so, despite the simple gifts of life. For a dying girl, she could never understand why someone would ever hit their wife, rape a child, and so on. For her, she would give anything to simply walk, let alone have one person who cared about her. These people appeared to throw away everything simple because of a few bad minutes at work.

"So, here's what happened: first, I busted through the side of the ship. I planned on killing both of the guards, but as fucking luck would have it, I sharpened the metal too well and the fucking thing went straight through his eye socket. There was blood everywhere."

"Holy shit!"

"I know, right? Then, I had to figure out how to get to the top. Brit gave me detailed instructions on where the guards were on every floor. Usually, I'll transform into a bigger size in order to combat so many enemies. It's just easier."

"Remember that time you turned into a hundred-foot Samurai?!"

"Will you shut the fuck up and let me tell my story?"

We both laughed and smiled.

"Anyway, the ship's ceilings were only six-feet high, so I transformed into a five-foot furry blue beast with sharp teeth. The right side of my body was consumed with a blue flame: hot to touch, capable of disintegrating my enemies in seconds. The left half of my body was rigid ice. With the snap of the fingers on my left hand, I could take away someone's breath by surrounding them with an ice-cold death. As I approached the stairs, I could hear men running down. I imagine they knew who was attacking them because there were not just a few men sent to stop me, but every single man on board."

"Why do they all have to be men?"

"Holy fuck, Veronica. I don't know if they were all men. They could have been fucking transvestite turkeys for all I give a shit. They had guns and were aggressively attacking me. There wasn't time to introduce myself to the cunts. Anyway, all forty-three attacked me at once. I was at the bottom of the stairs and they were piling in from the top.

"Fortunately, only three men could fit through the doorway at a time, which allowed for some fun: I froze the first six with my left hand. One managed to pull the trigger on his gun, but not fast enough for the bullet to reach me before it froze. But my Elsa impersonation was too good and I accidentally froze the doorway. I used my right arm to launch a fireball through the doorway and at the six Anna replicas. As the ice melted away, one of the smugglers ran at me with a large machete, yelling something that sounded offensive. So, I extended my right arm towards his neck and grabbed him, lifting him up to the ceiling while my hand burned through him like a hot, seven-inch Santoku knife slowly cutting through a Taiwanese pineapple cake.

"After that, two more guards rushed at me; it was so funny. One of the idiots fell straight to the ground, vomiting because of all the blood and the smell of burning skin. But then, as I laughed and turned my attention to the non-vomiting guard, the vomiting piece of shit reached up and sliced my left arm with a machete. Margaret kept telling me how I shouldn't be so careless and I fucking lost it. I quickly transformed into a grizzly bear and sank all forty-two of my teeth into the guard's neck; he tasted like regurgitated chicken. Then, I got sort of stuck in the small hallway and another guard rushed towards me and a machete sank deep into my back."

"Why the fuck did they all have machetes?" Veronica inquired.

"I know, right? It was awful. It hurt, and Chester would not stop laughing at my pain. I tried standing but fell down because I forgot I was a giant, 600-pound grizzly bear and the ceiling stood only six-feet high. I fell to the ground and immediately transformed into an inland Taipan snake and lunged towards the stabber's neck, dispersing my poisonous venom into his jugular.

"I shifted my attention to the five men who were standing in front of me. For some reason, they were all shirtless and heavily tattooed. Chester and I thought the same thing and I asked the idiots why the fuck none of them were wearing shirts. For the record, they all ignored me and screamed something inaudible as they ran at me. Not one of them had a weapon, just decades of martial-arts training between them. I was no match for them in my scaly body, so I transformed from a snake into an Erymanthian Boar, running directly at the five with my sixteen long, pointed horns aimed at them. Each member of the band stuck onto my horns and I had thirty-four pirates to go."

"Are you almost done? My drugs are kicking in and I'm about to pass out."

"Calm your knees, I'm almost finished. Anyway, I made the boar too big and I was stuck, again, as eleven of my horns were buried into the side of the ship. My body was so massive that I was covering the entire doorway. No one could enter; however, they could shoot. Bullets tore into my skin and I screamed in pain."

"Did it really hurt?

"Of course it fucking hurt! I mutated again and was exhausted and losing a lot of blood. It was time to be efficient. I was having fun, but it was taking too fucking long. I reconstructed my body, standing 5'10" tall, just two short inches below the ceiling. My body was strong, muscular and covered with white fur. Lightning-black stripes covered my body, looking like they had exploded from within my burning soul. Instantly, I had a thirst for blood. My long fangs hung over my lower jaw and the men running towards me stopped in their tracks. They had all heard the rumors about me—everyone in the world has heard the rumors—but it's different when they are standing face-to-face with a man who can change form. They all knew they were about to die at the hands of Karma in the form of a weretiger."

"I'm tired and you're being dramatic."

"I know, right? But, I love dressing as the weretiger. The form adds an inherent thirst for blood which makes me between ten and twelve percent more aggressive; which for me, is equivalent to the rage aggressive alcoholics exhibit when their wife is telling them about her day at work. My claws are sharp as diamonds and my teeth as sharp as surgical scalpels. My bite is stronger than a Gila monster. When I'm in this form, I'm as strong as fifteen men, as agile as a world-class ballerina and as intelligent as a young Einstein.

"However, despite all the attributes, despite being a killing machine, an instrument of death, the thing I love most about this outfit is that I look like a fucking badass. The second-best thing about my striped coat is that I am unable to be killed. Rumors say a silver bullet may do the trick, but fortunately, I've never found out. Anyway, I ripped out more jugulars, I decapitated twelve of the men and used my strength to tear the rest into small pieces. At one point, I even tore off a guard's arms and used them to fight the remaining pirates. All the men on the ship were dead and my white coat was now red as I was covered in blood. At that point, I was feeling pretty good about myself because I knew the women were in the cargo containers waiting to be freed but, you know what happened next."

Veronica reminded me, "Isn't it funny that you can be absolutely, one hundred percent certain of a fact and within an instant it can turn to fiction? It's like how the whole planet believed the world was flat until one day it just...wasn't."

She babbled a bit more with her youthful ideas on philosophy before falling asleep. I tucked her in and slid out the window. I felt a little better and hoped that maybe talking to Veronica more consistently would do the trick.

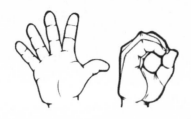

Can't

Irrational thoughts amongst rational chaos.

One second. Just a small sliver of the day allowing you to see a desperate example of an emotion.

When did I become so desperate to feel? When did I lose the ability to be present?

I can't do this anymore. I can't do this anymore. I can't do this anymore.

I can't do this anymore.

I run...so far. I push so hard into the walls. The walls are close to breaking. I can see the cracks forming along the mortar; they resemble the Tower of London in the cold. Built to withstand an army, built to protect a queen. And I push and push and throw stones and try to tear the wall down with my bare hands until my fingernails are cracked and bleeding.

I've huffed and I've puffed. I pushed and I pulled. The walls never come down.

I can't do this anymore.

I feel like I'm lying in the gutter. I can smell smoke. My mouth is dry and sticky. Rank. Like the smell of a bum trying to shit in an ashtray filled with smoked cigarettes. Hair covers my face. A desperate desire for a pair of shoes. I'd give anything just to have a job in the castle. The worst job. Any job. I'll clean the shit off their royal asses with my tongue.

I can't do this anymore.

I saw her laying there, motionless on the tile floor in their pristine kitchen. Her home, beautiful. It was near the base of Camelback Mountain. Twenty-foot ceilings. Glass chandeliers. Marble countertops. A six-foot island in the middle of the kitchen architected perfectly for her height. The whole house was built to accommodate her slender 5'8" tall frame.

She played volleyball. She started playing when she was nine. Life was always easy for her. She had good enough grades, glasses, had a real deer in the headlights look in high school.

She developed in college. Experimenting with some drugs, she joined a couple of clubs only to drop out weeks later, and she had an on-again, off-again boyfriend. She majored in business and minored in bullshit. She could talk herself out of anything and talk most people into something. She once stayed up all night memorizing the book for her World History exam because the final exam was the only class she'd attend that semester. She received a ninety-seven percent on the final exam.

She hit her stride at twenty-eight. Her hair was falling past her shoulders with cryptic curls. Her smile was a little broken but perfect in its own way. Her demeanor and strength carried her personality. You always knew where you stood with her. If she thought you were getting fat, she told you to your face that she thought you were getting fat. If you were marrying Mr. Wrong not only would she tell you, but she would stand up and filibuster during the wedding.

When she was thirty-five, she met the love of her life. He was a dancer and owned a pharmaceutical company. He was about to be recently divorced. They met online. She was a yoga instructor and auctioneer looking for a husband and he was looking for her. Within eight months he was divorced, and she had a ring on her finger. Their engagement lasted six months before they moved to the base of Camelback Mountain.

When I found her, she was lying in the middle of the

kitchen. Her head bashed against the six-foot island, floating in the middle of paradise. He had split her head open on the corner of the counter. Her face was so smashed in my hands all I could make out were her *almond eyes*. Two children, her twins, dead and in her arms. He laid next to his perfect family with a hole in his head and a 9-millimeter still hot in his right hand.

Grief is a greater burden without an available wall of vengeance to bang my head against.

I can't fucking do this anymore...

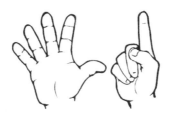

Chester

Dear Meatsack:

I really do fucking hate you! You're a coward and you still hide behind your own masks! You justify what you do as being for others! You're a fucking cocksucker motherfucker!! You'd also be fucking lost without me! We have some good moments! You know, it was my idea to use razor blades against that woman's labia, right?! I forget what the skank did, but you couldn't even go through with that, you pussy! Instead, you just bit her clit off! Also, fuck you for blaming us and resenting us all the time! We help you and you fuck it up by thinking if you change us, you'll change yourself! I hope one day you do put a gun in your mouth and pull the trigger!!!!!!

Love,

Chester

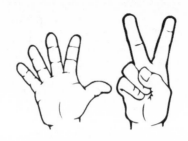

Ophelia

My love:

This struggle is serving a purpose. I've seen you lying in the bottom of dumpsters covered in urine. You've run through a small European town naked and drunk, yelling, "I'm going to be a mighty king, so enemies beware!"

You've helped a lot of people and changed the world, but this recklessness must stop. The judgement is never fully satisfied.

I love you. It brings me to tears that I can't remember the last time I saw you smile. You bear this weight like chains around your neck. Please, keep serving this purpose. Don't leave, not yet. We need you. The world needs you.

Love, -

O

Margaret

Sir:

I hate almost everything about you, except the way you dress. Whether you're a suave businessman man from South Africa, or a buxom Brazilian, poorly convincing people to do your bidding, you dress rather well. Although I have a strong suspicion that's mostly Brit's phenomenal taste in clothing shining through.

When you're you, your style is so childish. I know you don't have a lot of free time, but you could buy a new T-shirt every once in a while. And most men I know own more than two pairs of shorts (one of which I know for a fact you purchased over seven years ago).

I'm really not sure what you are doing anymore. Everything is dirty and you've let yourself go. When was the last time you even washed your car? Hell, when was the last time you drove it?

Your business is failing. I know you don't care because of this misconstrued crusade to find balance in the world, but a lot of people rely on you at work. You are a piss-poor excuse for anything but a selfish, self-centered narcissistic c-word. You want to know why I criticize you? It's because you're an awful human being.

Regards,
Margaret

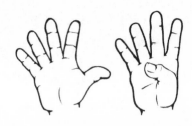

Brit

Sir:

I'm worried about you. You've become hard. You don't take care of yourself anymore. The last time you went to the gym was a hundred and eight days ago, and even then, you just walked around pretending to care and talking with old acquaintances.

When was the last time you even saw your daughter? You know you ignorantly forced her out of your life. Of all your forms, you pull off the ostrich most effortlessly, enjoying the worms as your head sinks deeper into the mud.

I'm so worried about you. We all are. I want you to know that I love you. I really do love you, but we can't keep going on like this. You deserve to be happy. You could try therapy again? That seemed to be working. Sure, it wasn't as gratifying as stopping a man from murdering seventeen people in a movie theater, but it seemed to work. I still remember you turning into Batman, taking three bullets in the chest and then tying him together using his arms and legs. That was so great, and you can be better.

You must be better. Not for us, or for the world, but for you.

Love,

Brit

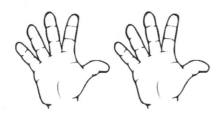

Time to Go

Dad has no remorse, no concept of the carnage he casts to the side. Obviously, I still love him, but he doesn't make it easy, knowing the things he has done; the things that he tries to justify as good and pure when without thinking, he mutilates and murders. Figuratively putting myself in his large shoes and understanding his perspectives is impossible. There is never a justification for killing an innocent woman. Never. He killed a woman when all she did was scream and suffer as she endured the punishment of her husband's fists. She didn't deserve to die and especially didn't deserve to have Dad kill her.

I'm not going to kill him obviously, but I have no choice but to turn him in. He cuts out women's tongues and breaks men's hands and painfully prods people with hot fingers as pokers until they wail in panic. He has never raped a woman, but he's intoxicated them to a point beyond willing consent.

He used to be such a wonderful father. He would wake up early and make eggs and flapjacks every morning. He supported me when I played piano and pretended to know when I messed up. Even though he had no clue about music and was likely tone deaf, I would let him think he knew what he was talking about just so he would stay in the room and keep listening.

"I love you. It's time to go, Dad," I utter as I transform into him, and he's staring into his own steel-blue eyes.

Caren: "*He's a good man, a hardworking man. He effortlessly loved you.*"

Anna: "*What are we going to do? Are we really arresting him? We're taking him to jail? Jesus, K. He's your Father.*"

Natalie: "*The whole world is going to go ape-shit, seriously, fucking ape-shit when we drag him into the precinct. Holy cow. What are they going to do to him?*"

Luca: "*I love him. I really love him, K. We have to visit him and take him cookies. He loves cookies. Chocolate chip.*"

Aviva: "*You have to admit it was pretty cool when he mutilated the nasty nurse.*"

This fucked-up world leads good people to fucked-up places. But it doesn't have to and Dad is flatly wrong. There's another side.

This world is compassionate and novel with each and every turn, and each and every moment is filled with love and adventure. My father has spent his existence fixating on the scars each person bears. But beauty runs deeper. He was a good man who was thrown out of the grave without any footing on which to stand, but I can't stand by and watch this mess of a human run wild on the Earth any longer. He's like the real-life incarnation of a burning Salvador Dali painting.

I repeat, "It's time to go, Dad."

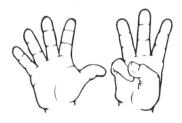

Third Musketeer

Dad always knew just what to say. I was young, just finishing my last season of youth basketball, but despite my youth, I vividly remember the memory. I had two best friends: Alanna and Adrianna. They were my very best friends in my very small world. The three of us were 4th-graders at the top private school in Phoenix. We didn't have a ton of money growing up, but Dad always made it a priority for me to attend private school. I never really knew why, but I was grateful he made that decision. He also cared deeply about me and my two best friends.

On this particular day, Alanna told Adrianna a secret and they left out their third musketeer: me. I couldn't figure out why they wouldn't tell me. I guessed that it could be embarrassment or fear, and no matter how many times I attempted to pry the information from my friend's grip they wouldn't move an inch. Eventually, I found out by a different friend that Alanna was being held back. The entire class was moving on to 5th grade but she was being held back and having to repeat the 4th grade because she couldn't pass math, science, history and English. The secret was immensely upsetting and my little mind couldn't understand why they wouldn't tell me. They were my best friends in the entire world.

Dad picked me up as he did every day, at 3:20 pm from school. And as he did every day, he asked me about my day. He knew my emotions better than I did and asked me why I was sad. At a snail's pace, I divulged the information about the secret. Then, Dad taught me about control. He told me there are things in this world that are within our control and there are things that are not. We don't get to choose. We have to accept the things which we cannot control and do great at what we can. He then told me about a gray area, which didn't resonate in my young mind. He said that sometimes some things look out of reach, out of my control, but with the right concentration and specific determination, I could control nearly anything, including my feelings and thoughts. He told me that anything that was inside me was within my control. He had no idea that one day I would be able to tap into other people's mind and control their thoughts.

My favorite days of my youth were our "daddy-daughter dates." We went everywhere and he always made a point to turn his cellphone off for the duration of the experience. We went to the opera and attended musicals regularly. He took me to sporting events and comedy shows. There was one time he dressed up like Harry Potter and took me to a magic show. Obviously, I was dressed as Hermione.

We ate at the same restaurant every week, Sammy's Steakhouse, where he would order a medium-rare ribeye with a baked potato, with extra butter. I would order a medium prime rib cut, twelve ounces of meat, with the house specialty: cheesy potatoes. He would always drink water around me; I think it was because my mom was an alcoholic or something.

He made sure I knew the difference between right and wrong, taking me on amazing vacations, teaching me about different cultures and about the world. By the time I was ten I had visited fifteen countries and thirty-five states. My favorite vacation was the time we went to Paris, Belgium and London over New Year's Eve. I was twelve years old.

Dad made me journal every day. I'd spend evenings writing about the Tower of London and drooling over the crown jewels. They looked like little -glowing orbs; every staff and crown covered in some of the most expensive minerals on the planet. My book was filled with stories of Belgium. Dad made sure we went to every chocolate shop in Brussels. My favorite was the hot chocolate from the Laurent Gerbaud Chocolatier. It is the only chocolate shop in the world where a patron can enjoy Forastero cocoa beans from West Africa. Dad and I sipped the hot chocolate as I wore my unicorn hat and he wore his mismatched socks.

We ended the excursion ice-skating on top of the Eiffel Tower on New Year's Eve. I stood on top of the iron lattice tower, crafted by Gustave Eiffel, screaming, "Happy New Year!"

I knew that I wanted to be like him, but I had no idea what he would become. I wanted to work hard like him, manage stress like him, take chances like him. But, despite it all, he went crazy.

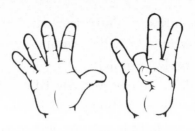

Cherry on Top

Watching Dad struggle has been the hardest experience of my life. Even as I learn to cope with these new voices, the most difficult part is hearing the screams from his bedroom. On his worst nights I can hear him crying into the pillow as he attempts to suffocate his tormentors. Dad interacts with them far differently than I do. I still don't know what or who they are. I imagine they'll go away someday, but what do I know? I haven't even had my first period yet.

Since it happened, I've done my best to keep the house tidy and clean, otherwise Dad would let stacks of clothes pile up so high they would press into the roof. I do everything myself: I feed myself, do mine and Dad's laundry, and the last time Dad helped me with arithmetic we were both using our fingers and toes. When I see him in the morning our interaction is brief and stale. I try to talk to him about an assortment of topics ranging from what's on his daily agenda to whether or not he wants a piece of toast. Before, he would politely decline conversation and pastries. Now, he grumbles and moans and spends his days buried in yellow pads covered in incoherent writing. Usually, I can only make it through a few lines of his writing before my stomach turns and I close the page.

Today, I am walking, alone to school, as I have for the last twenty-two days. Since the accident, Dad claims he's too busy to drive me.

"Too much to do! Need to figure this shit out! STOP

YELLING AT ME!" are his favorite new mantras.

Over the last three weeks, he's sent me two text messages, both lamenting my existence and telling me affirmatively that I should: "*Go to fucking hell*," which is especially odd and troubling because I don't think Dad believes in an afterlife.

My best friend brings me lunch every day; I see her in the distance. "Hey, Alanna," I softly mumble to myself as I realize even with a full shout, she would barely hear me.

As we get closer, she yells, "No lunch?!"

I holler back holding back tears, "No lunch!"

She gives me a side hug and rests her head on my shoulder and states, "I gotchu, weirdo," as we walk into our homeroom class.

DJ, the boy all the girls have a crush on, says hi to me, then Alanna. He's one of my best friends. Natalie always tries to tell me I should make a move, but I don't really know what that would look like or why the heck Natalie is talking in my head, so I try to ignore her.

We're learning about the 4th of July and my favorite non-president political figure: Alexander Hamilton. I know everything about him, but when Ms. Foss, my teacher, asked me a simple question about why Alexander Hamilton wanted a national government with complete authority, I stared blankly ahead as Natalie told me I should "*shag*" DJ, whatever that means.

Anna is worried that we're going to fail math, even though we have a ninety-seven percent with only one test to go, worth a measly three percent of our grade. Meanwhile, Caren won't stop talking about how we need to help Dad when we go home and check him into a clinic. Aviva keeps lamenting that school is "*boooooooring*."

The last voice, Luca, is telling me why I should be grateful for what is happening. How the heck am I supposed to be grateful while my Dad loses his marbles?

I didn't answer Ms. Foss's question and somehow, in what seemed like a shorter time than it takes to make macaroni and cheese, we made it to the last class of the day: science. The bell rings and for a moment I can't hear anything, especially the voices. It's peaceful and I can clearly see what I need to do.

I start my walk home, determined to help Dad. I have to help him, no one else will. His friends and girlfriend have left him, and he hasn't spoken to his law partner in sixteen days. I am going to walk home, look him in the eye and tell him that he needs to find help. There's no way he can turn away from me if I look him in the eye and tell him he needs support. He loves me so much.

He tells me I'm his everything.

As I arrive at our home I put my key in the lock and it doesn't fit. Our front door looks as if it's from an old, wooden cottage, with four small glass panes in the middle. The door handle has been changed. It used to be silver with chipped paint but now it's an ugly bronze that doesn't match the other fixtures.

I knock loudly as I yell, "DAD!" screaming wildly as if I've already seen the awful truth. Pounding on the door, my hand misses the wood, striking a glass pane. The pain doesn't faze me as I see an opportunity to reach inside and open the lock, as drops of blood coat the fallen glass. The door creaks open and the only noise is Dad's irrational shrill from the living room.

"Do it, you fucking bitch. Clean my fucking rug like the trash you are."

I walk into the living room and see a woman on her hands and knees cleaning the floors with a dirty rag and a bucket full of water. Dad is standing on the coffee table, which is covered in some sort of white powder, with a belt around his neck that is connected to the ceiling fan. As the blades spin round and round so does Dad's head while the belt winds tighter and tighter around his neck. The cherry on top is a naked woman with red hair kissing Dad's penis.

216

"Dad, what the heck are you doing?! Come down from there! You need help! I'm here to get you some help."

"What the fuck are you doing here, interrupting my activities?" he rages. "I fucking changed the locks for a fucking reason, you fucking stupid bitch! It's time that you fucking grow up and move the fuck on! Nobody likes a fucking crybaby!" Then he yells at the woman on her knees: "Did I say stop sucking my fucking cock?!"

"Dad..." is the only thing I can say through the waterfall of tears running down my face.

"You're right! I'm going to fucking do it, Chester! This is my house, and these are my fucking rules. Leave me the fuck alone!"

I try to speak but the words won't come out. All I can do is sheepishly point to myself as I am sure there is no way Dad is talking to me. Why would he reject my request for reassurance? He reaches up with both hands, unbuckling the belt before jumping down off the coffee table. Doing so, the entire house shakes forcefully.

"What language do I need to speak to make myself clearer, young lady?!" he yells as he grabs me by the wrist, opens the front door and shoves me outside. I'm not sure what was louder: the slamming of the door or Dad's last words to me.

Whenever I close my eyes, I can still hear him saying, "Leave...me...the...fuck...alone!!!"

I cried two days' worth of tears on the doorstep before I walked to Alanna's house, hurting and hearing Dad's words over and over again: "*Get out!*"

Alanna asked me what happened, but my voice has gone. Using a black felt pen and a clean white sheet of parchment paper, I tell her the truth, that nothing happened; that Dad had to go on a work trip and that he'd be gone for a long time. I can tell she doesn't believe me, but sometimes, I find that instead of being vulnerable, it's easier to lie.

Dad has done so much for me. I wouldn't be here if it wasn't for him. I need to figure out how to save him even if it means sacrificing myself. He would do the same for me, right?

"He would, K," Caren says. *"We all would do the same for you."*

What am I becoming?

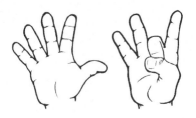

The Other Threesome

"K is doing well," I say stoically, as I talk to her mother over the wooden fence.

"Marvelous! That's so wonderful and fun!" she says with an airy tone, as if she is attempting to impersonate a pixie. "What grade is she in now?"

She talks to me as if we're best friends enjoying a sweet tea and lemonade on a porch in the American south. In reality, we're in the southernmost part of the state: Gadsen, Arizona, inches from the Mexican border.

"Umm..." I always stumble sheepishly over my words when I'm here. "She's in 8th grade." I try and smile, but emotion takes over and the best I can muster is a *Mona Lisa* grin.

"Wowzers! 8th grade!" Her voice is high-pitched and her piss-poor Miss Piggy impression stings my ears. "What a fun year! Does she enjoy school?"

"She does." I nod in the affirmative. "She excels. Her grades are perfect, she takes piano twice a week, Spanish once a week with a tutor, and she'll finish her basketball season in about two weeks."

"Basketball! How fun! Is she good at putting the ball into the basket?!"

"Yep," I reply coldly. "Listen, the reason why I'm here is because she graduates from middle school in three weeks and she'll be going into high school. The school is throwing a big graduation party and I know it would mean the world to K if you could make it. I'm not sure of the procedures necessary for you to leave here, but I'd be happy to talk to whoever will grant approval, sign whatever is needed and even drive you back afterward, so the cult, err, I mean congregation will let you leave for the day. It really would mean the world to her."

"Oh wow! A graduation party! That sounds so fun!"

My sigh is so loud, a few of the other members of the House of the Impact cult who are man and woman-ing the fields look over to see if K's mom needs any help from the tall grimacing man wearing black jeans, a black shirt and three wooden bracelets.

"Can you leave for a couple hours and attend? As I said, it would mean a lot to her and she's about to go into high school. She's becoming a young woman and honestly, I could use some help, a feminine touch to help her through her boy-crazed teenage years. I've talked to a hospital in Phoenix, and they agreed to help you out with whatever you're going through..."

"Why would I ever leave the compound?" she screams. "Are you here to hurt me?"

I hear husks of corn drop to the ground and other members of the Impact cult start running in our direction. "Why the fuck would I hurt you?"

My tone goes quickly from humdrum to agitated, exacerbating the situation. No matter how much inner work I've done, I can never seem to respond rather than react when I'm around K's matron. "You haven't seen our little girl in eleven years! Do you know how much it would mean to her if you came to her graduation? She would be over the moon! Over the fucking moon!!"

"I knew it! You're here to hurt me and take me away!" Her high-pitched shout alerts the others of her peril. "HELP!!!"

We lost her over a decade ago; right after K was born, her mom went missing in action. I'm not sure if she felt unworthy, too much pressure of being a parent at such a young age, or something else entirely. It took me over one thousand internet searches to find her and she's made the Impact compound her home ever since. The House of Impact is your run-of-the-mill work cult, mixed with some sex and the unequivocal hope that one day they may be so worthy as to sacrifice themselves to the White Elephant. For the record, I wish I were kidding about any of this shit.

Afelia, the White Elephant, is said to be over 300-feet tall, with dragon wings sprouting out of her back. Ironically, the only part of her body that resembles an elephant is her head. However, instead of one long, thick-skinned trunk, Afelia is gifted with seven trunks coming out of her colossal cranium. Her tusks extend beyond any of the trunks, with intricate carvings in the ivory. Rumor has it that once the entire Impact church is sacrificed, the prophecy within the carvings will come to life. Unsurprisingly, the only person who knows the prophecy is the leader, who promises daily that waiting for the White Elephant's destiny is, "worth it." The rest of Afelia's body is an amalgamation of animals and mythical creatures spanning the globe. Along with her broad dragon wings, she has a smooth lions' tail, the sturdy torso of a rhinoceros, and instead of legs she has seven tentacles that look like they should be connected to a giant squid or octopus.

The House of Impact members spend their days plowing corn fields and eating alfalfa, beans and corn. The House of Impact cult commander-in-chief, whose name I can never seem to remember, prophesizes that, "The way to a healthy life is eating and following the ABCs!" He means alfalfa, beans and corn. Unsurprisingly, in all of his years of leadership, he's neglected to tell his parish that the corn they mill produces food for prison inmates around the United States and, due to their free labor, the commander-in-chief is worth nearly ten million dollars. For the record, I really cannot accept that anyone would believe his bullshit.

Three extremely skinny men who look like they've been eating a strict diet of alfalfa, beans and corn are now within a sniper's shot of me.

K's mom abruptly blurts, "You should leave! Three against one isn't going to be a fair fight!"

I look at her and say, "You're right. They should have brought more people."

The first minion reaches me and tries to jab me with his right fist. I block the punch with my left arm and cold-cock the motherfucker right in the face. Blood shoots out of his nose and he squeals like a hyena. The other two reach me as the first minion runs to K's mom for consolation. Tweedledee manages to grab hold of my right arm as Tweedledum is trying to corral my left. Using my left hand, I maintain control over the fight, grabbing the back of his head and throwing him into Tweedledee, freeing my right arm.

One of them reaches for a husk of corn, firing it at my head. I snatch it out of the air and dismiss it to the ground before kicking both of them in the face with my right boot. In an instant, the pendulum swings far in the other direction. Another member, a much better-fed member, sneaks up behind me, taking the butt end of a shovel to the back of my head. I lurch forward, falling to the dusty ground. By then, the other threesome is bloody but back and kicking me in the face, shoulders, ribs, and legs.

After about ten minutes of having the shit kicked out of me, they retreat back to their job, knowing their punishment would be great if they didn't pick their days' worth of corn. I was beaten, bloody and covered in dirt.

K's mother walks over to me and places a hand on my back. "Well, that was fun! It's time for me to go back to work! Say hi to little K! She must be so big now. What grade is she in?"

I push myself up off the ground, wish K's mother well and

walk back to my car where I have a two-and-a-half-hour drive back to normalcy waiting for me.

K's mother is officially gone. This will be the last time I come back to the House of Impact.

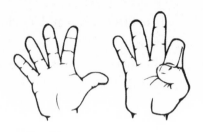

Good Dog

I'm two years away from my sweet sixteen birthday. It's been 438 days since I saw Dad, although it feels like three trips to Pluto and back. Alanna's Anatolian Shepherd, Amelia, goes for my left paw as I quickly move to the side and grab the scruff of Amelia's neck with my sharp teeth, causing her to let out a coy yelp. While we dressed in similar fur, if we were both heavyweight boxers, she would hail from Turkey and I'd announced my heritage as German.

He just left me.

Amelia and I have fought like this for the last year and a half. I know all of her moves and she knows two and a half of mine. She's a good dog. She bit me hard once and I've made her bleed three times. The last time Alanna's mom had to take her to the pet hospital because "some random dog"—shut up; I know it's dumb but it was the best I could come up with—"randomly ran up, like, randomly," and bit Amelia so hard that her jugular vein popped open like a water balloon.

I can't believe he just left me. What did I do wrong?

"*We should transform soon,*" the high-pitched voice says to me. "*Alanna and her dad will be home any minute from soccer practice.*"

What are these voices?

I nod affirmatively to no one in particular as I don my twisted, braided blonde hair and freckled face.

"Hey weirdo, how ya doing today?" Alanna's dad yells to me as the car door shuts. I smile and look down at the ground. It took a full rotation around the sun for me to smile one time. Two months after that, I smiled again.

The voice with the raspy tone, says, "*You're doing great, K. We all love you so much and can't wait to see what you become.*" The soft-voiced boy agrees with her.

Alanna runs up to me, gives me a big hug and uses her hands as two fists spinning slowly in opposite directions, before pointing her right index finger at me and then connecting her left fist to her right elbow, with her arm upright, and moving her right hand down to her left elbow. She smiles as she uses sign language to ask me, "How are you doing today?"

I haven't spoken in two years. I think I still can speak but my throat just won't work. The only place I can scream now is in my head.

Why did he cut me out like a cancer?

I take my thumb against my chest and waive my index, middle, ring and pinky fingers wildly in the air as I let Alanna know I am, "Fine."

She throws her arm around me and yells, "We got pizza!" My countenance lights up at the thought of melted cheese and salty black olives.

After we eat our pizza and say our prayers, Alanna and I hug in the hallway and go to our rooms.

Her mom and dad welcomed me into their home without hesitation. The night I fell at their doorstep, we went to a 24-hour department store and they bought me a bed, a wooden dresser and enough clothes to last me a week. The following week they bought me enough clothes to last me a month.

We spent the day trying to find dad, but he was gone. The house was in ruins, all his money and clothes were gone, and one time, after he'd had too many beers, I heard Alanna's dad say there was a streak of dried blood on the living-room wall.

As I lay in the bed, staring at the ceiling, I realize I've lost all hope; there's nothing left. I smile in front of my new family and can make do with conversation at school, but I've lost all my joy.

Did I ever have it to begin with?

I try to make shapes out of the white paint staring back at me, but the vaulted ceiling never moves. It simply stares back at me as if waiting to be surprised.

What do I have to offer? Why am I even here? Where did he go?

I wail between my own ears. My eyes close and eyelashes grip tightly to keep any tears from escaping.

A week's worth of questions keep me awake every time I try and sleep. Why did Dad tell me to leave him the fuck alone? Dad always said everything would be okay. That's what he said! His exact words were that everything would be fucking okay! Those were his exact words! The words almost creep out of my mouth as my lips crush one another.

Am I going to be okay?

My Friends

Dad probably loves that the newspapers call me K. I don't love K being my public name, but there's no reason to make a big fuss. As Dad always used to say, "*It's not the end of the world.*" However, I do wish the media would correct the story. They always paint him as some horrible human being who has never done anything good in his entire life. He raised me well and he should receive some credit for raising me. It's not his fault he doesn't know when to stop.

The most accurate description of the accident, shockingly, is told by a Fox News reporter. She actually figured out the exact date the accident happened. She knew the location, traced the wind burst and she knew two people were at the cemetery that night. Most reporters believed it was either one person or an entire cult and multiple people were affected.

She was obviously far from knowing the truth, but to her credit, she was closer than anyone else. She figured out Karma was my dad, and she even gave him a bit of understanding and empathy that the more left-leaning publications didn't. Somehow, she knew that his actions were a result of his brokenness and not simply because he enjoyed inflicting pain and cruel and unusual punishment. (Although, from what I can tell, he does enjoy imposing his will and if pain and cruel and unusual punishment result, he doesn't lose too much sleep.)

I also hate how some of the media outlets call Dad a killer. Anyone who does that much good doesn't deserve to be called a murderer. Having said that, murderers also don't deserve to live with basic freedoms. They should be able to breathe, but there is no constitutional right giving a person the ability to walk into a hamburger shop and purchase a goddamn hamburger.

My voices are different. I learned to take control of them pretty early on, by finding an understanding that I really don't have much control at all. Caren is compassionate; she sees the good everywhere and in everyone. She helps keep me sane. She is so powerful she can see slivers of light defying gravity and emanating from Pōwehi, a black hole nearly fifty-five million light years away from Earth.

Anna is so fucking anxious. She took me the longest to understand. I had to learn to accept her and her constant worrying. I never realized how unnecessary and burdensome anxiety could be until Anna would be up in arms about the simplest issues. She doesn't like riding in planes, trains or cars, she loathes ordering anything off the menu and she appears bound and determined to blare and bellow every time we transform. She always thinks we're going to transform into the wrong matter or material, or somehow be frozen in our new form.

Natalie looks at the world the way my father taught me to. She reminds me to stop and smell every rose as if it were the last piece of vegetation growing on the entire planet. While Anna anxiously questions our every move, Natalie marvels at our abilities and accomplishments. Everyday, Natalie glowingly recalls our hazardous adventures. She revels in our fight, side-by-side with the women of the Revolutionary Armed Forces of Colombia, when we were helping fight against inequality in South America. While my motivation was supporting South American women who were being raped and beaten for fun, Natalie was inspired by how we turned my tits into XM42 Flamethrowers and burned down the cabal's safe houses.

We brought much needed attention to the area too. The

media says with confidence that I am the reason the Colombian government signed a peace treaty demobilizing forces who were killing innocent children. They knew it was me. Along with the flamethrower stunt, at one point, I transformed into a four-hundred-foot gorilla and took out half their army, which was super fun.

Aviva is our fourth assembled member. She is fucking wild. She encourages me to run full-speed into the jungle without worrying about lions, tigers or bears...oh my. She is the one pulling the trigger whenever we are pushed up against the edge. She's not a woman, she's a goddamn warrior. She's also the only one who saved my life.

We were in Antarctica following a group of pirates who were hunting endangered species, specifically albatrosses, for fun. They had no agenda other than to laugh, giggle and shoot as many albatrosses as they could.

We had just finished tying up every pirate on the boat. At least, I thought we had just finished up tying up every pirate on the boat. My big speech about justice and the need to live hand-in-hand with the Earth, rather than with our neck on her throat was concluded and as I was calling the coastguard to come pick up the convicts, one fifthly fucking pirate who was hiding in the kitchen snuck up behind me and put a dirk, a pirate dagger, directly into my back, puncturing my right kidney.

As I spun around, punching him in the face and breaking his jaw, I slipped and fell over the railing. Fortunately, for me, there was a cannon sticking out of the boat below me which made the perfect resting spot for my head as I headed towards the water. When I hit the water, I was unconscious, half my face was falling off, and the salty water of the Southern Ocean was stinging inside from my kidney wound. Aviva, somehow, was the only one of us who wasn't seeing black and managed to flip me onto my back and move my feet until I was back on land. When I finally woke up, I was warm in the form of a polar bear—which Anna pointed out is silly because polar bears don't live in Antarctica; but I was happy to be alive and not overly concerned that we may be identified.

Luca, the last voice, is pure white light. His favorite word is love. Sometimes he sings lullabies when we're falling asleep, other times he'll recite ancient poetry as we embark on a long journey. He also claims he can see people's vibration moving through the atmosphere like waves floating in the air. He doesn't just see the bright side in people; he sees radiation as bright as the sun emitting from every being on the planet.

While Dad laments his team, candidly, I love my squad. We perfectly complement each other, and I couldn't be more grateful for them. This burden, this responsibility, this whatever it is, forced me to use my voice actively. Before the accident, I'd shy away from conflict. If there was an issue, Dad would take care of it or I could passively move through it without aggression. Now, I feel like I'm playing with house money.

I'm not burdened and not subletting my mind to five energy vampires. I'm empowered, I'm grateful and I'm the second most fucking powerful being on the planet.

Shart Your Pants

Dad would always say: laughter is the best medicine. At least once a week, we'd end up laughing to the point of tears, snickering and relentlessly playing pranks on each other. Once, he poured hot water on me while I was dead asleep and after that, each chance I had, I would hide behind every nook, cranny and partially opened door waiting to pounce and give him a heart attack. One time, I even hid Dad's office keys when he was going to the office. Forty-five minutes later, I received a text from Dad saying, "*I can't believe you hid my fucking keys... lol.*" For the record, his office was roughly forty-five minutes away from the house. We always tried to stay one step ahead of each other.

I cherished the times he took me traveling. We visited the Galapagos Islands, London, England and Glacier, Montana, in the span of one year. Better than any particular place was the enthusiasm for life we shared and a sense of adventure and curiosity. During the course of that year, Dad was attacked by a pelican—who he'd tried to attack first; he convinced a posh London hotel manager to give us an $8,000 upgrade; and he nearly fell into Avalanche Lake because he was trying to take "a cool yoga photo."

The "cool yoga photos," were neither cool, nor embarrassing. However, Dad was always trying to embarrass me anyway. He'd dance in public places and wear the most awful clothes. Somehow, seeing him lick trees and screaming, "Penis!" in a restaurant full of people gave me a sense of security and a sense

231

of knowing who I was. Even with teenage angst it was nearly impossible not to feel zesty when surrounded by such curiosity and joy. And even though Dad never talked about it, I know both were difficult for him.

There's sort of a blind ignorance that comes with any childhood trauma. The feeling is there: in the pit of your stomach, the furrow of a scared brow, being so shy you may shart your pants. But the logical reason behind the events—car crash, cancer; in Dad's case, murder—never really resonates, which caused my Dad to feel without knowing why, and never have a sense of who he was.

Lovingly, Dad would always correct me: "Our why is innate and ever changing, K. No matter where your heart sets, you'll always find a new sense of purpose, so long as you treat gratitude as a religion, be present, and when confronted with an issue, spend ninety percent of the time focusing on a solution, and ten percent of the time lamenting the situation. You're powerful, so powerful. And I am too. It comes from somewhere. We're all connected: you, me, our ancestors from a generation ago, and my great, great grandchildren who will laugh and explore life decades after I've departed into dust. There will always be darkness, and you are powerful enough to be the light."

Treacherous Marsh

"Where are we?" I mumble through my heavily chapped lips. The last time I blacked out I awoke in Spain. This time, I find myself in the green jungle, tall trees surrounding my being.

Anna is driving me insane. She keeps repeating: "*I want to go home. I want to go home. I want to go home. I want to go home. I want to go home. I want to go home. I want to go home. I want to go home. I want to go home. I want to go home. I want to go home. I want to go home. I want to go home. I want to go home. I want to go home. I WANT TO GO HOME!*"

The others and I, after hearing her new mantra at least a thousand times, collectively yell, "*Shut the fuck up!*"

That was one of only three times I heard Caren use the "F" word, and the other two times she was quoting lines from a movie. For some reason, she loved the movie, *Basketball* written by, and starring Matt Stone and Trey Parker. Aviva also loved the movie. Unfortunately, for me and the rest of us, it was where she learned the words, "*cum dumpster.*" Our lives have never been the same.

We wander through the jungle for hours. Sweat pours out of every pore on my body. I could transform into a dung beetle or a 747 airplane or a bald eagle, but something is keeping me in my natural form. A small tingling tugs on my thoughts, telling me to keep trotting through the treacherous marsh. My intuition is leading to whatever adventure or wasteland disease awaits me.

After walking exactly thirteen miles, my legs are burning

and Anna will not stop whining and informing us every few steps why she wants to go home, how her feet and head hurt; despite the fact that she doesn't have feet or a head.

Aviva, while simultaneously calling me a cum dumpster, keeps reminding me that we could simply fly out of the jungle and be home, whichever direction that may be, within a matter of hours.

I trudge along, intentionally moving us forward with each step. While Anna bitches and Aviva moans, Luca marvels at the world around us. He comments on the copious amount of colorful birds. He is the only of us that notices any of the brightly feathered creatures, our bounty of nature. He giggles with glee. The sound coats the air like an array of neon butterflies filling the surrounding space. He even finds the finches fascinating, with their flat beaks. Luca then leads a guided meditation for Anna, to calm her down. After fifteen minutes she is back to bearable and normal.

After hours of walking, the marsh finally breaks and we see the crystal-blue lagoon. To be honest with you, it is either a lagoon or a bay. I never did well in geography; however, I can avow the water is crystal blue.

At the edge of the water is a large tortoise with a long neck. He looks like one of those dinosaurs with a long neck. By the looks of him, he weighs exactly 1,257 pounds. He is massive. His tongue spins out of his mouth, elongating until he takes a cool drink from the bay. We are all transfixed. The six of us are drawn to the massive Tortuga. Aviva suggests we kill him and wear his shell. Unsurprisingly, none of the others agree. Anna is crying and wanted home. Luca thinks the slow leatherback is a simple message from God that we need to slow down, that the blackouts were connected.

I have no idea how we've ended up in the jungle. Hell, I don't even know what jungle we are inhabiting. I transform into an albatross and soar into the sky. To my surprise, the ocean is just a few hundred feet south of our position. We are in Ecuador.

Even more to my surprise, and everyone else's delight, I could see the small town of Tulcan about three miles to the north.

It is time to go home.

Ecuadorian Empanadas

Caren, Luca, Natalie, Anna and Aviva and I flew into the small island of Santa Cruz and I transformed back into myself as K. Walking through the town, we saw a number of locals who looked at me with reverence. They all recognized me in my black leotard and black mask. I was delirious from not eating for what may have been days. I was also breaking psychologically. I had no money on my person. I was dirty. I was lost. I wanted to cry.

In the distance, I saw Restaurante Mama Rosita. Walking in, a waitress quickly grabbed my wrist and escorted me to what she said was her, "*Mejor mesa*". It was the finest table in the restaurant. She brought me nearly their entire menu, despite me pleading that I had no money and could not pay. She didn't care. She said in her native tongue that I was, "*La reina que cayó del cielo*": the queen that fell from the sky.

After serving me four helpings of homemade Ecuadorian empanadas and ceviche, she went to the phone and spoke faster than a Texas auctioneer raffling off prized cattle. She hung up the phone and one small porcelain cup of espresso later a priest walked into the restaurant. The waitress pointed excitedly at me with blind fervor and the priest rushed to my table.

"May I join you?" he asked in perfect English, and one of the calmest tones I've ever heard.

He had a wonderful tranquility surrounding his being. His physical body stood six-feet tall and his skin was the color of rich caramel. His hair was a few years away from being completely bald, and if I had to guess, I'd put his age at sixty-three years young. He joined me and proceeded to thank me for my services. I informed him that I was unaware of the energy I expunged and the reason for his gratitude. He smirked and then told me he had heard stories of this God, but to witness me in action was truly a spectacle. I reminded him that I was no God. I simply did what I thought was right. And, in this instance, I had no idea what I'd done.

He took my sweaty hands into his frosty palms. Despite the balmy weather, his entire body was as cool as his perfect smile. His teeth looked like each one was carved from ivory. He smiled widely and in his perfect English, he told me how the ground started to shake, how the people were scared and that perfectly upright buildings were crumbling above the greatest earthquake their small town had ever faced. The small town of Santa Cruz was on the verge of being destroyed. The shaking stopped, but the true evil was coming.

The waves started to rise. The earthquake caused a ripple effect and a tsunami formed off the coast. He described the deluge as pure dread. It made the 1,720-foot wave in Lituya Bay, Alaska, look like the type of tide a small boy would ride while boogie-boarding on a summer afternoon in Mission Beach, California. Adam's ale surged towards the center of the city at 498 miles per hour. The priest told me he watched in despair, praying to a God that he doesn't know I don't believe in.

He called me a miracle; a thaumaturgy sent to Santa Cruz to stop the surge. He watched me drop out of the sky like a large drop of rain and that I hit the ground while breaking the sound barrier. He told me I ran to the front of the city staring at the 666-foot wave and started to grow. I widened and sprouted into a 7,000-foot-tall wall made of glistening gold. He said I made the Great Wall of China seem like a cheap piece of Ikea furniture. I wondered how he knew about Ikea. The waves bounced off me like ping pong balls against a stone wall.

I stood tall for nearly eight hours until the waters calmed, and the priest and his people were safe. After withstanding the strong current, I collapsed in my human form into the water. They thought I had died saving their town. He said they looked for me for four days. He couldn't believe I was alive. He couldn't believe I withstood that much force. Most of all, he couldn't believe he had met, and been saved by K.

Now, I need to figure out why I am having these odd blackouts.

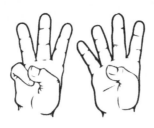

Scalding-hot Gravy

Grandpa's mother is odd. Technically, Webster's Dictionary and the law of physics would consider her my great-grandmother, but to me, she has always been simply, Aadya.

Throughout my youth, my father and I would eat three meals per year at Aadya's house. Each meal ranged from two to four hours in duration. Aadya had a strict regimen of pre-appetizer drinks, appetizers, pre-dinner drinks, dinner, pre-dessert drinks, dessert and then post-dessert coffee.

At the dawn of every festive dinner, Aadya—due to her immense hatred of her own name—would eagerly encourage me to come up with a creative nickname for her. Fun iterations were invented, including Oma, Nonnie, Gigi, Baba, Sweets, and so on. Ultimately, no matter how cute or imaginative the nickname was, Aadya would end up loathing the moniker and thoughtlessly yell at me to, "Just fucking call me Aadya!" before requesting that I pass either the carrots, green beans, mashed potatoes or scalding-hot gravy. Aadya's gravy was always scalding hot.

Some people made excuses that she was losing her marbles. I always told them I was unclear what alabaster and limestone had to do with anything, and frankly, even if she were suffering from dementia, she'd always been an asshole, regardless.

It's weird. My thoughts are generally tempered. I can effortlessly talk about my grandfather being brutally murdered, yet, during my yearly visit to wish Aadya a happy birthday and pay the invoice at Avenir Senior Living in Scottsdale, Arizona, I feel like an elephant trying to walk across a stage littered with marbles.

I hate being here.

Aadya has friends at the home where you discontinue normal life in an efforted attempt to be retired. Somehow people enjoy her company. Her friends don't mind when she is enraged that there are more Muslim doctors on her floor now than non-Muslim, and they turn a deaf ear when she rants and raves about her new neighbor being black, and how she lets the neighbor in her room but leaves the door open the entire time for safety, obviously.

"Hey Marmie, how's the gang?" I spit out apprehensively as I approach Aadya and her two best friends, Ethel and Agnes.

"Who the heck is Marmie?!" Agnes roars.

"It's Aadya. Sit down, dear. How are you? How's your father? What brings you to see your favorite great grandmother on this beautiful Friday afternoon?" Aadya says with more than an air of conceit. For the record, Dad's in prison, Aadya is my only great grandmother and it's raining on a Tuesday morning.

"I'm doing well, Oma. I'm here to pay your bill and see if you need anything for the next year. I spoke with all of your nurses and they said that 'God-willing,' your new pacemaker will last another ten years, and you should live just as long, if not longer. God-willing, it won't be longer. So, if that's all, I'll be going off now."

As I stand to leave venom spits out of her mouth. "You will sit down, young lady, and we will have a drink and appetizers!" She snapped her fingers at Lawrence, the resident "hottie" in the corner and he stands quickly to grab four glasses of Chardonnay with ice.

Lawrence is eighty-nine years old and from St. Louis, Missouri. He made his money in bitcoin before turning his attention to women and alcoholism. Lawrence has green eyes and no sense of smell. The women like Larry because he has the largest

240

and most satisfying cock in the entire building and, if I'm being -honest, he has a very cute mustache.

Larry approached as a perfect gentleman, kissing my left hand before gently placing a glass of Chardonnay with ice in my right. Ethel made a drifting toast which lasted three minutes and twelve seconds, that eventually was dedicated to, "better days and simpler times."

I drink my Chardonnay as fast as humanly possible and snap my fingers at Larry. In a flash, he hands me another drink and I ask Aadya what she wants to discuss before taking another large gulp of the fruity, smooth and slightly spicy crowd-pleaser.

"Well," she begins, "I'll be dying soon."

She appears to be displeased at the lack of emotion or surprise on my face as I snap my fingers requesting another drink from Larry.

She coughs. "I said, I will be dying soon!"

Ethel and Agnes do their best impression of someone pretending to be astonished. I crinkle my forehead and brow as if to say, "And, what's your fucking point?!"

"I'll continue," Aadya drabs on. "While I know I've been more of a burden than a blessing, I must inform you of one thing before I pass."

Before she says the words, she stands to look around the room as if she was the bride at a formal wedding about to give her speech. She raises her glass, looks me directly in my pupils and proudly proclaims, "You're just like your fucking father!"

Then she lurches forward, belching loudly as she grabs her heart and falls onto the glass countertop, splitting her face open just under her nose. Ethel and Agnes let out a collective gasp as Aadya breaks wind, immediately filling the room with a terrible stench. Even Larry covers his nose. The nurses rush over to stop the bleeding as hot red blood gushes out of her face.

I stand to leave and whisper, "Aadya, for the record, I'm

nothing like my father."

To my surprise, she vomits as blood drips down her face. "You're getting cold, K! You can't control it! No one can!"

Fuck you, Aadya. And happy birthday.

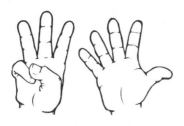

Happy Birthday to You

Each step pressed into the soft grass as I walked towards my grandfather's grave for dad's yearly birthday visit. I'd never met the man—never even really heard that many stories—but he always felt important to me, because he always felt important to Dad. So, once a year I aimlessly visited his grave at the base of the Mazatal Mountains, otherwise known as the Four Peaks.

Every year I sang a special birthday song to my dead grandfather. It was cheesy, but to me, simplicity is everything. And it's fucking beautiful when a group of loved ones take the breath out of their lungs in order to sing a song dedicated to you. I started singing softly:

Happy birthday to you,
Happy birthday to you,
Happy birthday, dear Grandpa,
Happy birthday to you...

It's funny how people take sincere acknowledgement of such a special day for granted. The words never seemed to be so meaningful as when I sat on the wet grass and sang Grandpa's special song.

On that particular day, the grave next to Grandpa's was empty. I flung my legs over the edge, laid back into the grass and rested my blonde ponytail on the upper left corner of Grandpa's mansion.

Happy birthday to you,
Happy birthday to you,
Happy birthday, dear...

...as a drop of rain fell into my mouth, causing me to pause. The stars shone in between the dark clouds looming behind them.
  ...Grandpa.

In an instant, a wind-burst sent me flying into the open hole, and a lightning bolt struck the tall oak tree. I screamed, "Help!"

I sat up and my spine lengthened almost through muscle memory, as my hands moved to rest on my knees. I could feel a connection everywhere. A pulsing, radiating energy bridging me to something, somewhere and someone else. Everyone else. I started to lose the feeling of the bridge, the radiating energy. My heart racing, my hands bound tighter and tighter and tighter, and I almost burst out of my own skin until I let out the biggest breath I've ever held in. For the first time in my young life, I felt clarity, the connection to the source Dad always ranted and raved about as a result of his meditations, and for a split second I could see through other's eyes, hear and feel everyone in the world as if my being was connected to the source and living inside of ten billion souls all at the same time.

I came back to consciousness nearly ten hours later, to the surprise of a maintenance man shaking the life back into me. By the time my eyes flickered open, he said he'd been trying to wake me for so long he was about to call the police. Dad and I did fall into the grave together but he was nowhere to be found by the time I was shaken back to life. With the solar wind and an enormous strike of lightning, we shifted into another plane where we shared space together with all the thoughts of humanity. It was an entire level of reality, filled with thoughts of bliss, love, hate, depression and every other thought and emotion filling the space where oxygen would ordinarily float.

The projected thoughts were almost glowing, giving off a powerful energy. However, instead of moving sporadically and chaotically, they danced in unison. The thoughts were moving into the graves, and the descendants of the dead were harboring the living's thoughts and pain. Almost as if a murmur came over a large crowd, the radiant formation of mental objects changed direction, and instead of diving into the depths of the Earth, they rushed towards Dad and me.

As the powerful force filled us with brilliant, intense spirit and power, I could hear Dad screaming in agony. I was, without a word, witnessing the changes moving through my body and casually observing the feeling of seeing through other's eyes. My cellular composition was changing; my mind becoming clear of every other distraction, as I allowed myself to drown in the feeling of not needing to think. I saw the potential of what I could become, and the people I could connect to, as every thought in the world filled my consciousness. In the matter of a few seconds, my possibilities were limitless.

Confused on what to do next, Caren, whom I would grow to love as well, spoke for the first time:

"*We should go, K.*"

And, without hesitation, we pulled ourselves up from the dirt and left the cemetery.

The Fucking Plebeian

Five days after Valentine's Day, Dad was disbarred. A few months prior, he'd lost his fucking mind in the courtroom. It started so fast, and there was no way to stop or slow his self-destruction. He was like a small pebble nestled in the snow, which in an instant, a squirrel confuses for a nut, causing it to roll slowly until the squirrel is caught in an avalanche and is rushing down the side of a mountain.

It wasn't shortly after that day in court that he went into hiding. The best description I saw on the news said that Dad "snapped like a ripe carrot."

The courtroom video showed Dad screaming, and I mean screaming, at the top of his lungs at Tetro for ruining his life and bankrupting his soul. By the time one of the members of the courtroom audience started filming on their smartphone, Dad was mimicking Tetro word for word, to the horror of the court.

At second fifty-two, Dad even said the words, "cum-guzzling" in a creepy, robotic monotone.

At minute four, Dad was playing intellectual tennis at breakneck speed, stuck in the middle of an argument between Chester and Brit. Of course, everyone just thought he was a nut with multiple personalities. I was the only one who knew Dad was simply trying to mediate a dispute between two of his best friends. The media portrayed a crying, shrieking middle-aged man yelling, "No, Chester! You're a fucking rotten cunt!!!!"

To be honest, it was not a good look for Dad.

At minute seven, the guards had finally held Dad down and they were waiting to sedate him. Dad was gagged, with venom spewing out of the sides of his mouth, and if I looked close enough, I actually think he was still trying to say, "cum-guzzling." Surprisingly, he never transformed. My best guess is that his mind was too powerful and wouldn't allow his body to transmute into something sentencing him to life in prison. For the record, Dad didn't break any laws. He just lost his shit, which thankfully is a forgivable sin in America.

His psychiatric evaluation was the next day. They asked me to attend. It was one of the last times I can remember seeing Dad somewhat normal. He tried to explain what happened to the doctors but the government healthcare system is a corona of disasters, and Dad's doctor didn't give Dad the time of day, diagnosing him with bipolar, schizophrenia, major depressive disorder, psychosis and Capgras Syndrome. My only guess was that the doctors needed Capgras Syndrome for doctor bingo that day. I later learned while waiting to talk to Dad that Capgras Syndrome is named for Joseph Capgras, a French psychiatrist who explored the illusion of doubles. Those with Capgras Syndrome hold the delusional belief that someone in their life, usually a spouse, close friend or family member, has been replaced by an impostor.

They brought me down a corridor longer than a football field to see Dad. He was sitting in a steel chair, shackled with a straitjacket and staggeringly sedated. His eyes looked like saucers and his pupils seemed to dance in imaginary moonlight.

I gently put my hand on his, which was dripping with sweat, and sweetly said, "Hi, Dad." I smiled and watched his breathing intensify and his despondent look suddenly shift to panic and horror.

He broke the trance instantaneously and started clamoring for a comforting cure. "K! You've got to help me! We

247

don't have much time!! The voices, oh my God, the voices! They hurt!"

I muttered, "I, I know, Dad. I hear them too. Here, try this. Find your breath and..."

He kept stammering, "My breath? My fucking breath? No, no, no, no, no, no, no, no! We need to escape. I need you to call Mr..."

"Father!!" I interjected, "Close your fucking eyes and find your breath!"

His eyelids closed and instantly, his sweat dried completely and his breathing leveled off. I walked him through exactly six minutes and sixty-six seconds of meditation before he opened his eyes. Regrettably, it was—this I'm certain of—the last time I saw his crystal-blue eyes. Furthermore, he looked at me with the last happy expression I ever saw on his face.

He spoke quietly and calmly: "I had my psychiatric evaluation an hour ago. It was a panel of five individuals, including, but not limited to, one attorney from the State Bar. I thought for a second I might make it through the inquisition but then Brit, the fucking Plebeian that he is, ruined the interview. He thought it would be a good idea to make a pass at the attorney from the State Bar and before I knew it, I somehow told her I liked her tits, and then called Chester a 'popped cherry' because of his maniacal laughter. After that, all hell broke loose, and they had to sedate me again."

"Oh, Dad, I'm so sorry," I said. "I think I can help get you out of here and then we can figure this out together. We can work on your breathing, go to a quiet cabin in the woods and figure out how we can both learn to love who we are rather than resent these new powers."

"Both?" he responded, shocked. "What do you mean, 'both'?!" His breathing and heartbeat had shaken back to life like a foreshock before the impending quake. "Do you hear voices?!

What do they say?! Do you hear Chester too?! Can you transform too?!"

Immediately, Dad started to transform into a 600-pound grizzly bear. The cuffs shattered off his wrists and he barreled towards the door, the weight of his new form crushing through the wood with ease as he bolted down the hallway. He looked like a drunk barbarian.

As he turned left towards the exits, I chased after him, but by the time I turned the corner he was gone. I sharpened my eagle eyes, scanning the room for any trace of my old man, but he was nowhere to be found. Knowing his capabilities, he easily could have miniaturized into a flying unicorn and gone in any direction. He was still smart enough to try and take control of his life and his new powers, but he was also stubborn enough to let it take him over.

I needed to find him. I needed him to listen.

OTF

One cup of black coffee, three hard-boiled eggs and my favorite Orangetheory class. I pretend to like that it pushes me to my limits, but I've been hit by a train and survived, and lifted one ton of Roca Sagrada over my head in Cusco, Peru.

If I'm being honest with you, there is a cute instructor. He stands behind me every time I squat, and every time I squat, I artificially enhance my gluteus maximus and puff my ass out a little bit. He's interested in me too. He has asked me to two concerts (Nelly and Justin Timberlake), three restaurants and an enchanting night of minigolf. To date, I have not listened to music with him at a concert hall, eaten a meal with him or hit the links, albeit on a smaller scale. Part of my mantra, part of why I think I can control it and Dad can't, is because I never give in to temptation. No matter how firm and tight and strong and beautiful his ab muscles are.

I leave, sweaty and exhausted, from holding in my lust for over an hour as I walk to work. I followed in Dad's footsteps years before I followed him into the grave. Despite his desperate attempts to send me into a different field, I became an attorney too. I'm in Mergers and Acquisitions. Don't tell anyone, but I was recently an integral part of the Amazon purchase of Whole Foods. Dad and I could take the form of sharks, but nothing felt more fulfilling than eviscerating an old white man in a board meeting. One time, I made the entire management staff at Oracle cry.

After work I go home, eat my usual blend of healthy food

and hot sauce and watch *The Office* on Netflix. I do this every night, except once a week when I go to my weekly girl's night with my two best friends. I also will, occasionally—and more often than Aviva would like— find myself out in the world transforming into bulldozers, bulldogs and bull-shitting my way around the world in an effort to help.

I keep my life very simple with few variables to keep myself from turning into Dad; to prevent me from falling into the pit of my own distorted ego. Every night I eat ground turkey, either in the form of a patty or mixed in with eggs. The shows I watch are all shows from my childhood. I watch *Friends* and *Seinfeld* and *The Office* on repeat, very rarely watching anything else.

Dad would always say, "Keep it simple, sassy," and I've taken that to heart with everything I do. It's easier to keep things simple. Because of Dad I know that something is inside me and rather than allowing it to come out, I live with dignity and try to do the right thing, no matter what, serving this world with gratitude and compassion.

I prepare for bed, brushing my teeth and meditating with my sound bowls for one hour. Hold on to your seats, but it is a nightly ritual for me. I've almost gotten back to the source, but I'm not strong enough yet. One afternoon, when visiting Kauai with Dad, we stumbled into a store selling sound bowls. Before the accident, he was a total hippie and he turned me on to all the same shit even though I didn't really appreciate it until I was older. I miss him.

When I heard the sound bowls ringing in my ears I was hooked. The vibrations always did the trick, clearing any bad vibrations and energy that had built from my long and stressful day. It was my outlet. I don't receive any satisfaction from instilling justice; it stresses me out, but I do it because it is necessary. Dad and I are very different in that regard. Dad fucking loves what he does and justifies every single one of his actions.

I check in with Aviva to see if there are any issues that requiring my attention. Aviva is like Tetro, except I am able to ask her questions and find out where there may be issues (rapes, murders, etc.) needing my assistance. She doesn't just spit shit all day hoping that something sticks against the wall.

I'm in fucking control.

It's been weeks since I've been out on a mission. There are the usual issues around the world, but nothing that necessarily needs me. I have been holding out lately for something: a nuclear strike, the next terrorist attack, something that would require me to flex my muscles and my intellect. I will leave the rapists and murderers, and people who callously throw gum on the street to Dad.

I fall asleep expecting to wake up as I do every morning with one cup of black coffee and three hard-boiled eggs. When I open my eyes, I am in a king-sized bed in Barcelona, Spain.

What the fuck happened?

Everyday Life

I woke up with my hair tangled, wearing my black leotard that I do not remember putting on. I take the hero thing a little more seriously than Dad. I have an all-black leotard with a black mask covering my eyes and forehead; it becomes skinnier as it loops around my ears. On the back, in white Bookman Old Style font is a single "K." Dad always transforms then leaves; he doesn't have a cape or cowl. He can be anyone at any time. But underneath the black piece of cloth on my face, like Dad, I do my best to change my face into that of the person who is receiving my justice. And, obviously, my ever-changing nail color is always perfect.

I do find it important that the K is a symbol. Firstly, because I am seen as an international inspiration to women around the globe. Young girls having someone to look up to? Count me in. Secondly, I do not want to be confused with Dad. I can't be. He's wanted for murder, even though I can't believe he actually murdered anyone who was innocent.

"What the fuck happened?" I asked the team groggily as I stood up. My room was huge. I discovered later that I had booked a suite at the W in Barcelona costing $3,432 per night.

Aviva yelled, "*We really did some damage last night, girl! I've never seen you that way before!*"

What the fuck was she talking about? I ate dinner, brushed my teeth, meditated, tried and failed yet again to connect to the source so I could tap into 10 ten billion souls for a second time—nothing out of the ordinary occurred last night. I felt perfectly fine and was in no doubt that there was a perfectly good and rational explanation for what happened.

Caren chimed in, *"It'll be okay. You're going to be okay. Stuff like that happens. Maybe you should try to have some fun once in a while so that you don't lash out that way in the future."*

Have some fun? Lash out? What the fuck happened? I wondered why they wouldn't give me a straight answer. I turned to Luca knowing that he wouldn't be able to feed me some bullshit or make more arbitrary statements. Luca dodged my questions before asking if I was sure that I wanted the information. After all, I'd fallen asleep in Scottsdale and woken up 5,781 miles away. He again gently inquired as to whether I wanted more information.

For a minute, I wondered if I should let the sleeping dog lie and simply fly or run home. But my anxiety was irritating me like a fly on my nose. I had to know. "Yes, Luca. Please fucking tell me what the fuck happened."

I'd fallen asleep in meditation after brushing my teeth. He said that the moment when I fell asleep there were three falling stars within twelve miles and the weather was 65 degrees Fahrenheit. I rolled my eyes and implored him to leave out the details and tell me what really happened.

With a laugh, I heard Aviva say, *"We took over. We needed to have some fun. You're so fucking boring."*

What the fuck? I was not boring. I had the top score in my Orangetheory class every day. This was how I kept control. I had meticulously created an environment where I could be in control of almost every outcome.

"That's the issue," stated Natalie softly, *"you don't ever live. You don't ever let us live. We need to see the world, have new experiences. While I do love the beauty and shape of the hardboiled egg..."*

We all stopped listening and I moved my thoughts elsewhere. Those fuckers had decided that I was too boring, so they'd taken over my body?!

I wanted to know everything and told Luca to tell me, in painstaking detail, what happened. Every fucking shooting star, how many cubes of ice were in my Diet Coke—I assumed I'd drank Diet Coke the majority of the evening—and the amount of times I'd politely rejected a gentleman at the bar.

As he started to conscientiously detail each moment, the haze over my memory cleared like a newly polished crystal. They didn't put me in the trunk and take the wheel. I was there the whole time, laughing, singing, dancing, fucking, and I could have stopped it.

Oh my God, I was fucking?

We'd started out by going to Orangetheory's house. I transformed into someone besides myself, because, awkward. Unsurprisingly, Aviva took the lead nearly the entire night. She talked me into transforming into a blonde bombshell. I looked about thirty-nine years old standing 5'8" inches tall with long, sturdy legs and giant breasts. I looked like I worked out eight days a week. My lips were big and pouty, and my face was wrinkle-free. My legs were ridiculously strong, and I hadn't flown in a while, so we jumped into the sky on the way to his house which was exactly four miles from my condo. Each jump took us about a quarter of a mile and we were there within thirty-four seconds. We knocked on his door (not before Aviva had removed all our clothes) and a startled Orangetheory opened the door, speechless.

Natalie took over and the sweet nothings trickled from my tongue. *"You're going to obey me completely. You will not talk this entire time. Once I am done with you, you will kiss me on the lips, walk me out and never mention this night to anyone. If you understand, nod now."* Orangetheory nodded. Natalie continued,

"Now, take me into your bedroom and remove all of your clothing."

About twenty-five minutes later I was out the door and feverish. He was not impressive. He came in about three minutes, leaving me to satisfy myself using the edge of his bed and my hand. Apparently, he traded in his intelligence and sexual abilities for muscles. I was hardly surprised, but it was disappointing, nonetheless. We needed to do something else. I felt like I was in heat and had an insatiable craving for something big and thick in between my thighs.

Surprisingly, Luca, that little fucking rascal, made the next suggestion and we were headed abroad. I transformed into a North American X-15 and we were on our way. The normal range of the aircraft is 280 miles, not far considering it travels at 4,520 miles per hour. However, with me at the helm, we had zero limitations. We went around the world four times just below the stratosphere for fun. I couldn't believe it. I felt like singing, "A Whole New World" from *Aladdin*, but it didn't feel right without my cats there with me.

After the fourth time around, Anna begged us to stop and we gracefully landed in Ibiza, Spain. We were like magnets drawn to the little island that appeared to be manmade and built out of a giant subwoofer, blasting techno music from every direction. Even the small coffee shops had people raising their hands to fist pump, jump, jump. Every club and bar felt like I was stepping into a Pandora's box with a plethora of sinfully delicious evil choices trapped inside. There were droopy eyes, smiles and sweat pouring out and emanating from every direction.

We made it to Club Heart shortly after Cinderella rushed out leaving her glass slipper behind on the staircase. To our surprise, the entire building was vacant, but for a handful of nicely dressed people. At Aviva's advice, we purchased the most expensive table in the club and ordered three bottles of something called Ace. It was an expensive champagne; so expensive that I went through my entire savings account that night. But if I'm being honest, we ran the club. Men and women surrounded me, begging for any attention from the foreigner holding three-of-a-kind Aces.

Among the people-pleasers and the beggars was the man I would make love to all night. He spoke no English, but it didn't matter. He was Brazilian and the only thing more attractive than his smile was his lust for me. Brazil and I danced and fucked everywhere in the club. Well, not everywhere. There was a janitor's closet on the fourth floor that honestly smelled like moldy cheese. Overall, he licked my pussy hanging from the swings on the third floor, he fingered me in the middle of the large dance floor as an EDM version of Belinda Carlisle's "Heaven is a Place on Earth" reverberated through the club on the second floor, and he kissed me goodnight like a gentleman on the first floor. Goddamn, his fingers felt good.

After two orgasms, we went back to my table and I blew him with the champagne pouring out all over his dick. Apparently, when you spend over a hundred thousand dollars, they let you do whatever the fuck you want. After he was finished, he kissed me goodnight and I sent him on his way.

Instead of satiating the desire, I felt thirsty; I wanted more. I ravishingly craved more. The bathrooms at Heart were big. Hired actors roamed the hallways wearing large, white wigs. They looked like they were transported via a time machine or wormhole from the Georgian Age. Near the corner, there was a men's area with a large, red bathroom door and a women's area with a large, blue bathroom door. There was also, to the left of both bathrooms, a private bathroom being guarded by two bouncers: one giant man and one small woman, barely five feet tall. She was the one collecting the money. Men and women who wanted to fuck or do blow—a term I'd heard from one of the criminal attorneys at work—would pay her a small fortune and have access to the large bathroom with the gross leather couch inside. I could only imagine how many living organisms were swimming underneath the cushions.

There was one man who kept going in and out of the private bathroom. He would walk around the club, furiously drink his cocktail like a trout, find an attractive woman and whisper in her ear. I transformed my ear structure to that of a moth and could hear every word he was muttering to the hopeless blondes, brunettes and redheads scattered among the aortic night club. He simply slurred in his Swedish accent, "Do you want to party with me?" Apparently, that was the access code into a twentysomething year old's nose and panties. Countless women followed him into the bathroom for enough time to fill two nostrils with the nose candy (a term I'd heard from the same coworker. Now that I think about it, I may need to have a talk with that guy).

I tracked my Swedish Fish, transformed into a gorgeous woman, and went into the bathroom. We stood eye to eye and he spoke English to me. I spoke Portuguese to him and seductively rubbed my nose with my thumb and index finger. He smiled and took a small Louis Vuitton bag out of his pocket and drew a thin line of white powder on the glass table sitting in front of the disgusting leather couch. I stared into his eyes without flinching an inch of attention towards the drug. I just stared and he knew I wanted more as he doubled the size of my slutty little portion.

It felt like someone took an ice pick through my nasal cavity to my brain. My senses were enraged like a group of foxes trapped in a small box. As I seductively snorted my second line, the Swedish Fish reached his hand towards my dress. I did not say he could touch me, and I grabbed his hand, breaking his middle and ring finger. He screamed into the bellowing base for all the deaf ears to hear. I could've killed this rapist by slicing off his head and using his remains like Jeff Dunham would use a puppet.

(And, I would have loved it, but I'm not a murderer. I'm not like Dad.)

We walked out and I gave him a deep, passionate kiss, he did give me a ton of cocaine, before finding a tall, nerdy guy to pounce on. We were in the private bathroom within minutes but this time white wasn't going up my nose, it was dripping down my chin. God, he was hot, and I wanted more coke. Tall and nerdy walked out first and went on his way.

Before I walked out, I transformed into a 5'7" Asian woman in a green dress and went back to my pseudo dealer with the anger issues and Louis Vuitton satchel of cocaine. He snatched me up and we were back in the bathroom. Six nostrils of nose candy later and me pretending to talk seductively in Mandarin I could see he was hard as a rock. Unfortunately for him, I had already begun walking out. He chased me outside and offered me fifty thousand dollars to stay. Fucking men.

My head was spinning now, plates were hanging everywhere and there were circus clowns asking me if I wanted a shot of *Jägermeister*. Outside of Heart I stared at the sky for what felt like an eternity. The moon was radiating energy and I could feel every pulse from inside the nightclub. Looking up, even the constellations were dancing with Orion bouncing around trying to find his pants and Vega was vacillating between scorching hot and seething. Clumsily, I started to change in the street, my legs first, cracking and expanding, my arms ripping through tendons and compressing, my lips splitting open.

My whole body transformed until I stood six-feet tall in the middle of the street. I was wearing black leather pants, a black lace top—with tits that I could have used to float from Ibiza to Barcelona—and matching black stilettos. I walked over to a 2002 VRSCA V-Rod Harley Davidson, formed my finger into a key and heard the lion's roar as I sharply twisted my finger. One minute on the beast, and I'd completely forgotten about all the men I'd fucked that night.

I revved the engine as the back tire spun, smoke filling the streets. People gathered around thinking it was some sort of gimmick. If I'd let go of the brakes, the beast would have been sent off at over a hundred miles per hour. My size-ten feet were firmly planted in the ground.

As the nightclubbers gathered, they started cheering incessantly. House music obviously blared at a perfectly upbeat tempo. I screamed for a straight minute, calling to the gods of life and death to meet me in the pit of hell, all of us, waiting, anticipating the unavoidable war. The engine roared. The people praised me and ultimately, I was really fucking high.

Luca started the story at breakfast and finished shortly after we ate dinner.

Holy fuck. I *was* too in control, I wasn't living. Every single step I took was calculated for a specific purpose. The team was starting to feel constrained, stuck in the box. They were forced to burst out like a fucking puppet.

I showered twice, cum still dripping out of me. I threw up a lot. I tried to eat some hard-boiled eggs in my hotel lobby while I retrieved a cab to head towards the airport, feeling awful about myself. If this was how I felt after one night, how must Dad feel after decades of this agony?

Dad tells me to leave him alone, but he needs to be stopped. Holy fuck, does Dad need to be stopped.

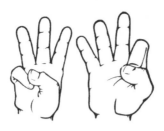

Single White Woman

Every time I see Dad in public I try and help him, but he yells at me to leave him the fuck alone. He keeps his real face from me and transforms into a vampire. I think he finds it hilarious because when I was a kid I was obsessed with *Twilight*. Today, here I am, running side by side with Dad; him dressed as Edward from *Twilight*—shut up, I know—and me doing my best Jacky Joyner Kersey impression. There's something about emulating a strong, black woman that really brings out the equally strong, single, white woman in me. We're chasing the same lead to Glacier Park, Montana. Dad always had a soft spot for the outdoors, and I am in the area visiting family.

The six of us run alongside Dad on the Going-to-the-Sun Road toward the Hanging Gardens Trailhead. Some anti-naturalist fuck who doesn't believe nature should be used by the public blew up half of Bearhat Mountain, killing himself, crushing thirteen and trapping sixty-seven hikers in a cave at the base of Hidden Lake.

"*This is so fun, going on a mission with Dad,*" Natalie chimed in.

"He's not Dad!" I bellow, but it is fun. Then, right as I am wondering if he's even noticed me yet, Dad notices me! I can tell. He's still in there! I turned my feet into skis and glide to the front of the ice face. We could go through it, or try and find a way down from the top of the mountain. Through seems easiest.

In my strong, black-woman form, I started to heat my hands to a million degrees Celsius and project heat through the ice. For the record, I don't think I'll ever hit nuclear fusion, but I think Dad can, and has.

The ice isn't melting. I transform my legs into two sturdy bighorn sheep hooves—which are more rubber than rock hard—and take a swift kick towards the ice to stabilize my bearings. Looking up I turn my arms into propellers and rifle my way up the side of the mountain. Not yet reaching the top, I hop around looking for a soft spot in the rock.

Aviva sighs. "*This is going to take foreeeeeeeever, K. Let's go to the top!*"

I transform into a northern goshawk and make it to Dad. He was using both arms as pickaxes and barreling down on the icy fragments.

"*Let's help him,*" Luca says softly.

"*Yeah! Let's clear the boulders!*" Aviva roared.

I enlarge my arms five times larger and ten times stronger than normal and start throwing the large boulders from the top of the mountain. Dad screams at me to stop throwing boulders but then asks if I can help him!

"I'd love to help you!" I yell back as I place the boulder down, and I nod, "a thousand times, yes."

Dad opens the cavern and I step in first turning my eyes into large spotlights, sending piercing light through the darkness. Dad comes up cautiously behind me. His eyes turn crimson and as if time has stood still, I can see the red atoms flying out of his eyes as I duck to save my life.

"*I hear someone! We're close!*" Caren shrieked.

I can hear them too; murmuring, crying, shivering. One of the perks about being able to be anything is my sense of hearing. Unless I'm at a concert or large gathering, my ears are tuned to moth-like hearing so I can hear a heartbeat from the next

262

room.

"*You never go to concerts,*" Natalie reminds me.

"Oh, shut up and let's finish this!" I wail.

Dad's laser eyes create a hole big enough for the trapped souls to run through. A young boy, roughly nine years old, escapes the cold and gives me a giant, polar bear-sized hug. We have saved the people trapped inside the ice. The little boy's firm grip loosens, and I see Dad turn around to leave, but I can't miss the opportunity.

"Dad! Can I see you? Please. I'm begging you. I want to help you. I miss you so much."

Without even looking back, he runs away.

Single White Man

"*Don't forget to transform into a vampire,*" Brit chimes in my ear.

"What?" I mutter through my alcohol-drenched flatus. I'd follow a lead after a few too many and am seeing double and hearing triple.

"*She's here, sir! Transform into a vampire! She loves that,*" Ophelia queefs from the rafters.

I think she is here.

"I bet he used dynamite, old-fashioned dynamite." Margaret pings. "Or maybe, it's a nuclear bomb."

"It's not a fucking nuclear bomb, Marge!" I bellow.

Why are my canines so sharp?

Two teams from the Mountain Rescue Association, established in 1959, have already attempted to free the hikers, but didn't haven't made a dent. The explosion started an avalanche, freezing a twelve-foot pane of ice in between the trapped souls and any member of the dedicated Mountain Rescue Association who prioritize saving lives through rescue and mountain safety education.

"Oh my God, Brit! Jacky Joyner Kersey is running next to us!" I spit as I slam face-first into a twelve-foot pane of ice. Every bone in my face shatters and bursts through the skin. Composing myself, I stand and rematerialize into a normal-sized man with brown hair, black glasses and a flannel button-up with my sleeves rolled halfway up. I look straight up at the remaining 6,127 feet of

Bearhat Mountain and think about the men and women and children trapped inside as I make it to the top while the woman tries to melt the ice. For the record, I know trying to melt the ice won't work.

While clearing debris at the top I notice the woman is next to me again.

Tetro buzzes, "*Woman about to be crushed under rock due to K removing stabilizing slab in seven seconds or less.*"

"STOP!" I yell in a fatherly tone. The freakish woman next to me drops the boulder in her arms and looks into my eyes.

That was weird. It must be the acid I took earlier.

"*Do you want to help or not?*" I yell over the icy howl of the wind.

The strange woman agrees to help.

"Then, listen to me closely! I looked through the mountain while running up and saw a series of tunnels. Once we pierce the second layer, which I'll finish in about twelve seconds, we can use the series tunnels to help everyone out of the cave! I need you to keep a light for me as I open the tunnel large enough for everyone to fit through!"

"*Go with the compact diode lasers and fiber diode lasers,*" Chester crows.

"Great idea," I compliment.

I transformed my eyes into CD and FD lasers and cut the rock to open up the crevasse large enough for the people—who hopefully aren't icicles by now—to escape. The woman with giant bug eyes is in the way! She is going to get herself killed!

This is why I work alone. Always alone!

I laser the last piece of rock and a half-frozen nine-year-old boy runs through the hole hugging the big-eyed creature. The hole is open, and everything is done.

I turn to run back through the crack.

"*Say hi,*" Brit implores.

"*Don't be a cheesy fuck,*" Chester chortles.

"*You would put the biggest smile on her face,*" Ophelia says.

Without looking back, still dressed in costume, I run away.

The Underground

I'm not my father. I swear to fucking God I'm not my dad, but I did kill one person. I will always regret it even though he deserved to die. I thought I was fully in control, yet everything slipped through my fingers, like I was trying to catch a gallon of water with just my hands. It took me months to find the house. Fucking months.

One of my passion projects, when I'm not advising the senior partner why he shouldn't buy bitcoin, is taking human-trafficking off the streets. A lot of human-trafficking is associated with prostitution, but what I found goes so much deeper. I found an elite section of society, composed of men and women, who trade women and girls like Bitcoin, using them in much more disgusting ways. There are no regulations in the Underground.

The women and girls of the Underground serve no purpose other than to satisfy the sick desire of the patron. They are crammed into safes for storage and hooked up to an intricate, yet terribly dirty, array of intravenous fluids to keep them alive and wet. They are monetized by an arbitrary figure simply known as "The Treasurer". He marks each victim using a hot iron with a lowercase "t". The placement on their bodies shows their worth. Plebeian women are marked below their waist. Equites are tagged above the waist to the neck. The elite, the Patricians—the true treasures—have the lower case "t" imprinted on their forehead just above and just between their eyebrows.

The women are beaten daily, regardless of rank and regardless of whether there was an infraction requiring punishment. They are raped in their mouth, their vagina and their anus. I assume if any other holes are made during the torture then those too are fucked. However, I can only assume, and I want to be clear that I have no first-hand knowledge of any other cavity or orifice used.

The large safes where the women sleep do not have any beds or bedding of any kind; no pillows, no fancy duvet covers, no windows. They sleep on concrete floors and the rooms don't have a bathroom.

I first read about The Treasurer in the *New York Times*. The publication published an article about eight women found dead in an apartment in Jamaica, New York. The women had two things in common: a small, "t" branded somewhere on their body and all of their skin had been shaved off. The most disturbing part of the article was the detail about when they found the skin in one of the spare bedrooms. Whoever was in the room had fashioned a makeshift grill and fried some of the skin like bacon. Half-eaten skin bacon covered the floor.

He moved around the city and was difficult to find. I had to go low and gross. I knew the bedrooms scattered around New York were simply lavish torture playgrounds. They weren't the Underground. Between the Fourth of July and Christmas day there had been ten other scenes found similar to the one in Jamaica, New York. All had various disgusting components and one connective tissue keeping all the tortures together: each woman was, yes, you guessed it, marked with a small "t" somewhere on her body.

It took forever to finally catch a break. The Treasurer was cruel but smart. He burned off all the women's fingerprints and removed all of their teeth. Evidence shows both acts were done while the women were still alive. There were no identifying marks and despite enough dead women sit on six juries being found; the police had zero warm leads. However, to be fair, I wasn't doing much better, but the big advantage I had was the "where."

I knew that he was burrowed under the city, so I began my search going through every subway, train tunnel and sewage drain. I had been inside every odious orifice of New York City and the only thing I had to show for it was a case of chlamydia that I must have contracted in one of the toilet drains. I also had used up all of my sick time and vacation time in the process. It was such a shit show, literally at times, but thankfully, The Treasurer finally fucked up.

We found her at a luxury apartment on 9th Avenue and Clifton. She was one of eight women. The other seven were found painted like animals with their throats slashed. There was a rhino, an elephant, a lion, a tiger, a bear (don't say it), a giraffe and a gorilla. Our woman, the survivor, was painted like a peacock.

The authorities wouldn't release any information, but undoubtedly, I was able to find everything I needed with some shoulder-tapping and miniaturizing. She was at the Mount Sinai Hospital in Manhattan with guards keeping a close eye on her. Two were guarding the door and one was inside the hospital room with her. I transformed into a miniature giraffe with wings, my favorite transformation, and flew through a small crack in the door.

The man inside was scrolling through Instagram on his phone. His feed showed a surprising number of male Asian ballet-dancers. I transformed into a Black Mamba, one of the deadliest snakes in the world, and slithered up the chair until I reached his neck. He noticed me, but I quickly bit down hard on his jugular, injecting him with a non-lethal dose of my neurotoxic venom. He wasn't going to die, but he would be incapacitated for a few hours. Moving across the room, I took my own form and was staring at Miss T, directly into her one eye. The left was still remaining, but there was a large white cloth over where her right eye used to rest. She was surprisingly alert. Her one eye was flickering and mouth was wet. I asked her what she knew, and she sat mute. She didn't have a language to speak. For one, her throat was slashed and any ability to talk was sliced away by the blade. Second, she was never taught English. She appeared to be of Russian descent, but she could have been Eastern European.

I grabbed the guard's locked iPhone and used his thumb to unlock the device, closed out of the surprisingly Asian-themed Instagram and used Google Translate to communicate with Miss T. She couldn't speak or write, but after thirty minutes, and her eagerly nodding her head when we were inching closer to the truth, I was able to find out The Treasurer's location.

She was one of his elite; one of the few that walked hand-in-hand with him on the streets. She was marked just above and in the middle of her eyebrows. She had been to his office; she had been to his home and she had met his children. In that thirty minutes, I had enough information to track the son-of-a-bitch and destroy the Underground.

The Underground was remarkable; a subterranean maze of torture; a Spanish speakeasy of discomfort and agony. Every single turn caused my stomach to twist. There were different torture rooms with movie-theater seating; stages of torture. One of the larger rooms had twenty-foot ceilings and eight rows of movie-theater seating. A 20x20 stage sat at the front of the room. On the left side of the stage stood a large, cast-iron toolbox. The front of the chest was impressed with a small, gold "t." Resting on top of the chest was a tongue-tearer. They looked like a large pair of scissors, but the tips of the tongue-tearer were dull rather than sharp. The torturer would prop open the tortured's mouth and rip out their tongue. The removal was not pleasant.

The back of the stage was lined with three wooden crosses, each cross coated with coagulated blood and a stench:

vinegar and vomit. There was a large trestle in front of the crosses with two brown ropes hanging down. The ropes were empty, but their use was clear. Saw torture. Women were hung upside down so the blood would rush towards their heads. Then, the two highest bidders would saw through a woman's body, starting at her sacrum. They would saw the woman to their abdomen and stop. Patrons of The Treasurer's elite would watch these women die and place million-dollar bets on how long it would take them to bleed all the way out. This room was currently empty, but that didn't stop the women's screams from being defeating.

I'd canvassed and mapped the entire facility. There was one elevator: the only point of entry. The elevator was attached to an old warehouse in Queens. The elevator went down for about thirty seconds before stopping at the facility. The facility contained seven torture rooms, including the large one, and four sex dungeons. The largest sex dungeon held four king-sized beds, two giant sex swings and a fifteen-foot wall lined with different sex toys. It looked like a garage that was made for fucking.

There was one other room in the facility. That room was only to be used by The Treasurer. I took the form of Miss T, slashed throat and all, and walked directly past the moaning, gushing filthy sounds that occupied the cavern. I walked straight to the door marked, *"Don't You Fucking Dare,"* raised my right hand and banged loudly at the steel door. From the inside I could hear muffled noises until the door popped open. An all-too-friendly 5'1" jester-like figure stood on the other side.

"Hellllooooooooo. Who is this?" His airy, high- pitched voice clowned its way to my ears. "Ooooooooh. Have you returned to me, my princess?"

This guy was out of his fucking mind. I walked towards him and as I got closer, he started hitting himself in the head, laughing the whole time and saying, "My little princess has returned! She has returned indeed! It's a rapture. What a glorious occasion! Charlotte, grab the webs and cookies! We must celebrate!" He took out a phone but before he could dial a number, I slapped it out of his hand.

"Do you even remember me?!" I yelled in English.

His maniacal laugh stopped, and his eyes narrowed. He had a way of staring into my soul yet looking deliriously past me at the same time. "Pleasure to make your acquaintance. I've heard a lot about you." His voice was now direct, albeit still squeaky like a tire. When he spoke, each sentence ended with him almost begging to take a breath. "You're going to kill me," he stated flatly, as if substituting broccoli for asparagus at a restaurant. "Instead of killing me with the buzz saw would you mind, only if it's convenient, using the tongue-tearer first? It's such a tongue-twisting treat." His voice now raspy and carefully annunciating each lowercase t.

I stared at him intently and told him that I was going to kill him. I'd never killed anyone before. It wasn't part of how I gave out justice. Killing was Dad's thing. But I had spent months chasing him; I'd looked a woman in the eye whom he had personally raped, then slashed her throat in hopes of killing her. He didn't even treat the woman as humanely as a cow on its way to slaughter.

He fell to his knees laughing. He wanted me to torture him, he wanted to sadistically feel the pain he'd become so accustomed to giving. I didn't give him the satisfaction. I walked up behind him, turned my hand into a bayonet and sliced his throat.

Caren screamed, "*What did you do?*" and I burst into tears immediately.

I couldn't believe what I had done. He was a monster, but what the fuck had I done? I was no better than my murdering father. I was no fucking better than the man I had grown to despise.

One Single Journey

I realized somewhere along the way what went wrong with Dad. When Dad and I connected to the source and the voices entered into us, encoding into our DNA, we had vehemently different reactions. I let myself become them, not worrying about them, and eventually I found peace with them. Dad violently rejected them and tried to do anything to keep them out. He did everything in his infinite power to stuff Alice's rabbit back into the hole before bursting into a flame of self-destruction and disappointment.

Dad's voices and powers came much quicker than mine. And fuck—Tetro, oh my God—if I had to hear someone tell me about bleeding assholes all day, every day, I'd probably need to drink too.

Mine were slower. They guided me along and I'd observe where their encouragement took me along my one single journey. At the beginning, I could kind of fade into them and lose my reality, allowing them to speak through me. Caren spoke to me first. Because of her we signed up and volunteered at the Emergency Suicide Prevention Hotline right after I received my driver's license. I'd fade back and she would ride the headset for the night, talking to broken men and hysterical women. Watching her showed me our potential.

Caren was on the phone with a male caller; twenty-three years old. He had a revolver cocked and in his mouth between his teeth. We could hear his teeth grind against the barrel as he yelled through his tears, "I'm going to do it!"

Caren spoke softly and within about twenty minutes, the caller had set the revolver down on the nightstand by his bed. She was listening to him talk about the pain his parents' fighting caused him. He cried about how he blamed himself. He wallowed in his suffering and shame.

Toward the end of the phone call, he was thanking me. He had texted a friend to come over and committed to checking into a rehab facility in the morning. He had used drugs for years to cope with the suffering. Weed, cocaine, pills, poppers, wiggle biggles, tiddly Tim's, crank, etc. It didn't matter to him. He hadn't smiled in such a long time that when he was laughing during the middle of the call he said, "I'm smiling. I can't remember the last time I smiled!"

Caren gently reminded him that he was probably still high, so it didn't really count and he laughed some more.

I saw the energy in motion that night. I felt it in the room, and I could see the molecules shifting. That night I realized how powerful I was. Dad revelled in taking lives, but my power lay in saving them.

Rose

I made it to Dad's condo before the police. Knowing Dad, he must have had some incriminating items—or at least a lot of drugs—that I wanted to remove before the detectives and the CIA agents arrived. I picked the lock with my finger and opened the door. Unsurprisingly, Dad was still a clean freak. When I was young, he would always say, "Cleanliness is second to Godliness." His simple plagiarized phrases all had new meaning now.

Dad's top-level penthouse was about 2,000 square feet with two balconies. Each balcony was covered in vines and red roses. He was obsessed with red roses. Growing up, I'd receive roses on my birthday, on my first day of school and every other Thursday afternoon. Dad even had a small tattoo of a rose on his left shoulder. Lazily but with intention, Dad never changed the rose tattoo despite his decided form. It didn't matter if he was posing as a panther, plane or prostitute, if you looked closely enough, you'd see a small, rose tattoo.

The condo was pitch black. I turned my palm into a Maglite, illuminating the entire room. In the middle of the room there was a large, black sectional couch split apart, with each section sitting inches away from its counterpart. There was no television, but speakers everywhere. I took a chance and yelled, "Alexa, play Spotify," and a blast of music filled the room. Tranquilly and fittingly, the song playing was a cover version of *Hallelujah* by Leonard Cohen. When I was a baby, Dad would sing the chorus every night as I fell asleep.

My initial investigation took me to the drawers and closets. Nothing, nada, zilch. To my astonishment, there wasn't a large pile of money or even a single rock of cocaine. The only piles I found were clothes stacked neatly in the laundry room.

I walked into Dad's office, which was littered with yellow legal pads. The only thing odd about the office was that Dad's most recent "to-do" list was over two years old. Dad was obsessed with his "to-do" lists. Every night he'd spend five to ten minutes meticulously making plans for the next day.

The kitchen brought more disappointment as even his fridge was harmless and mostly empty. Well, except for the twenty-four bottles of hard liquor from around the world. His best bottle was a 2011 Yamazaki costing nearly $120,000 in the stores. However, I'm not sure you can pick up a bottle of the sweet whiskey at Total Wine.

Caren, as if she were looking me directly in the eyes, gave me the first taste of advice before the others echoed behind her: *"Have a drink for him, K."*

Anna: *"We really should leave, K. We're going to be caught here and then it's all over."*

Natalie: *"Goddamn that's delicious whiskey. He has nearly 2.9 million dollars' worth of liquor in that fridge."*

Luca: *"We should focus on finding what we came here to find. You know it's somewhere in here."*

Aviva: *"Do you see that opening in the corner of the room?"*

I picked up the bottle of Japanese whiskey, popped the cork, and took a large swig from the bottle before walking over to the corner that caught Aviva's attention. The white wall looked as advertised. It was the only wall in the entire condo without one piece of art hanging on it. Dad's art collection was immaculate. My favorite piece he owned was *The Great Masturbator* by Salvador Dali. Dad would always try and pique my interest in the arts; however, I was more interested in math and science.

Personally, I'd rather see a line go from point A to point B than from crazy to crazier.

The opening in the wall was extremely small, peeking at me from near the top of the ceiling: it was barely the size of a dime. I pressed the wall hard, hoping it would pop open and I'd find a magic hallway or door, but nothing happened. The wall was completely solid. In fact, it was too solid; there wasn't one hollow point. This wasn't just a white wall floating in the abyss of Dad's penthouse; Dad had constructed a barrier between the living room and ... something. Well, he had someone construct the barricade. (Dad was a lot of things, but crafty was not one of his qualities. During my youth, most of his art sat in the garage because of his inability to properly use a hammer and nail.)

I transformed into an orb web spider from Samoa and crawled through the opening. The hole led me toward a long, small hallway. The opening was still only as big as a dime and the length was nearly ten feet to the other side. At my size, the trek to the other side took me nearly an hour. Below my feet was a thick layer of magnesium alloy: Dad was hiding something. The only way into this room was through the tiny hole Dad had prepared. I was inching closer and closer to the light on the other side, which was dim, but free-flowing through my small tube.

"*Holy fuck!*" Aviva blurted out when we finally made it to the other side. The room looked like an old dark room used for photography; however, there weren't any enlargers, easels, safelights, printing tongs, processing trays, thermometers, bottles, funnels or squeegees. The room was small, exactly eight feet by ten feet and had no furniture. The walls were made of the same magnesium alloy that separated the rest of the world from this chaos. There were scratch marks everywhere and maniacal scribblings where fingernails replaced pencils. Some of the explanation points were so poignant it looked like he skipped his nails and dug straight in using raw bone.

"*This room is impeccable!*" Natalie squealed.

Aviva nearly echoed her screaming, "*This is fucking looney bins!*"

Anna implored me to transfer back into a spider or into a fly or any other insect that could fit through the hole so that we could leave immediately. Meanwhile, Caren reminded me that this was the darkness living inside our father.

This was Dad in all of his dark beauty. I'd seen the Chauvet Cave, I've walked every inch of the ceiling at the Sistine Chapel. Nothing has made me marvel and stare as I did when I saw the room.

There was writing everywhere...

What a Crock of Fucking Shit

Some of the transcribed internal conversation was coherent and clever. However, most of it damaged me to my core. Just reading the words made me feel like I was the victim of an alcoholic father who took out his daily misery on my forehead and soul. It looked as if someone locked Kurt Vonnegut, Mary Shelley, Oscar Wilde, and Douglas Adams in a room, surrounded by ten feet of magnesium alloy with four typewriters, fifteen sheets of acid, and unfiltered Pall Mall cigarettes.

The rants reminded me of a burning rose: enchanted beauty with no choice but to fall victim to the flames.

"I hope I'm not too late. In my world, the clock possesses no hour, yet I constantly feel as if I'm biding my time, waiting patiently to be released from humanity's chaos. Once they stop, I'll find peace. Once I let them go, I'll find serenity. Once the world stops fucking destroying itself with guns and grenades and gossip and gerrymandering, I'll finally be unchained from this goddamn misery. I can't move fast enough. I can't fucking keep up with every rape, murder, molestation and gas-station complaint. I would bet most people are anti-suicide. In fact, I would bet the only people who are pro-suicide are probably unavailable for comment on the subject. I'd kill the five fucking fuckers if I could. I'd even kill, Brit. I'd gladly trade a thousand death penalties to rid myself of the insanity. Every day they tell me about babies being bludgeoned,

bodies being dumped into the lake and corporate fucks stealing trillions of dollars a year from hard-working Americans. It's like watching the fucking news twenty hours a day, and seven days a week. You think I'm fucking volatile? I can't be anything but volatile. WHO THE FUCK WOULDN'T BE A LITTLE VOLATILE? CUT ME SOME FUCKING SLACK, YOU FUCKING CUNT! The President did something dumb again. CNN's top new anchors are suggesting we deport him to the planet of Gazorpazorp despite the obvious risks of the President finding solace on the sun planet and eventually mating with one of the gorgeous Gazorpazorp Zorpies. I eschew government. If it were up to me, computers would run the entire country and food would be rationed based on a point system. If your name starts with any letter you receive full rations. If your name has the letters: k a r d a s h i a n, in that particular order, you receive zero rations and are publicly humiliated by having to live each day of your life on television. I've lost more sleep over the past four years than I've slept. My sleep and sanity are two things that my old self took for granted. He was such a lucky and righteous prick. He would set the fucking alarm at 5:00 am just to enjoy a cup of coffee. What a crock of fucking shit. I haven't enjoyed coffee in four fucking years! If you think I cuss too much, fuck you. If I could, I would run away to a distant planet where I could sleep. Obviously, it would be easier to run away to a city where I could sleep, but with the way my eyelids have been pried open like a fucking terrorist I would even settle for a town where I could sleep. I was once naturally wide-eyed. No pie in the sky was too wide for me to try and make it à la mode. Especially apple. People will argue the most important ingredient in apple pie is love. I would argue the most important ingredient in apple pie is apples. I walk around like a blind man. Never knowing when someone is going to push me, trip me or simply scream loudly in my face while they kick me in the nard dogs. In case the person reading this doesn't have access to UrbanDictionary.com, nards is another way for saying nuts, berries, genitalia, infinity stones, gonads, dangly bits, ankle clappers and lumpy plumpies. And so on. Before I die, I want to try and dissect parts of my body. I've never dissected anything before, but I would be a natural. I skipped sciences in high school and college and the only thing I dissected in law school were dissertations. Not quite the same as methodically cutting and tearing into raw flesh for the strangely understood purpose of preserving a decrepit meat sack. Who the fuck in their right mind would ever sign up to be an embalmer? I can't imagine there are many young boys growing up with dreams of being the next Frank Malabed. Although, as everyone knows, if you're going to embalm you may as well do it like Frank Malabed did. I would dissect my heart first. Bloody on the floor. Twisted. Unable to function. Octopus arms of black veins and arteries slowly trying to push thick sorghum into my nervous system, but pouring out all over the orange, shag-carpet floor. As my heart beats its final pumps, I can see my hopes and dreams floating in black sludge. If I try to pull them out, no matter how gently and precisely I use my fingers, the sticky syrup engulfs my hand burning off each and every one of my human identifiers. Who are any of us without our fingerprints? My hopes and dreams may as well be lodged into someone else's mind. I'll never reach them. They sit frozen in three-day-old quark-gluon soup."

There was writing everywhere...

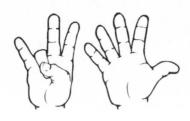

I Wept

The writing on the condo walls was captured through captivating calligraphy as the words jumped off the surface from every angle. Not only did Dad write an entire novel on these walls, but the calligraphy—oh my God, the calligraphy—was breathtaking. Each letter must have taken him hours. Along with the walls, Dad had composed his crazy on the ceiling. Every inch of the room was an altercation of alliteration except for the floor. The floor only had one word and each letter was as big as my hand.

"*'Control'?*" Natalie rang in my ear. "*Why did he write 'control' in the middle of the floor?*"

Then, as if ignoring the senile elder at the Thanksgiving table, nobody addressed Natalie and we all turned our attention to the surrounding walls and started to read:

"*The ultimate power is the ability to influence another person's behavior. The ability to change the course of events and swing the balance. Not just like a stupid fucking black and yellow buzzing bee providing oxygen for all to breathe, but providing a circumstantial change of circumstance. Giving the collective and the individual the ability to feel again.*

Our minds. So, delicate and devious. We build entire stories in seconds, putting up barriers between us and the never-ending pain and suffering we all lament on a daily basis. However, the walls are torn down even faster. People are robots, slaves to the process.

You're dying of cancer? Here's a pill.

You're hungry? Here's a processed piece of pepperoni.

There is an answer for everything and thought applied to almost nothing. We've lost our souls and the root of our foundation as a society. At least during the slave trade there was a sense of obviousness, a stronger, evil. The word "nigger," spitting freely from the mouths of righteous, god-fearing men as the waves crashed against boats coming from Senegal. People, fucking people, were being traded for rum and cloth and spices. SPICES!

Imagine living in a world where you purchase a pound of oregano for a human fucking being. Holy fucking God!!!!! Why did they do it? Labor costs? The economy has since settled since the abolishment of slavery on January 31, 1865. No, it wasn't because African Americans were cheap, it was about control. Sure, there was joy in cashing large cotton checks, but the real joy? The real sick, sadistic fucking pleasure was forcing a black man to chew the skin of his brother in a fight, or to bake in a hot box because he mouthed off. The real amusement and cheer included having your friends over for a sweet tea or lemonade and using John Coffey's wife as a Fleshlight.

But still, it wasn't the sex that made the trade so compelling. The sex wasn't the driving force behind slavery. It was the power to influence; the power to create chaos in the mind of an adversary; the power to exert will and control over another individual's free will; it was all for control.

We can control our minds, but only so far. The slaves couldn't see a sunshiny day. They were fucking baking—BAKING!!!!!!!!—in a hot box for mouthing off. The plantation owners, the fear-mongers, thought they were justified. There was no justice. They died rich and fat without recourse. They died of diabetes and heart disease from too little exercise and too much peach pie. They would never know the true terror of their actions. They would never be able to properly pay for the persecution and pillaging of life.

Too many people in today's world walk around with the same cotton-mouth grin as the slave owners. They beat and murder and rape without any recourse. Justice is no longer paid. The balance of the world is FUCKED!

Fucked, fucked, fucked, fucked, fucked, fucked and FUCKED SOME MORE.

I am the only one who can instill real justice.

I am the only one who can help people.

I am."

I had to sit down and stop reading. I knew the truth, but this was the first time I'd seen it firsthand. Dad had lost his fucking mind.

I wept. Silently and alone, I wept.

The Martyr

As Karma, my head has rested in alleys, trashcans, penthouses, and mansions: they are all the same to me at this point. There is no telling what the future may hold but if it resembles days of yore, I wish I wasn't coming back for more. Here, I lay in the grass outside Almond Eye's charming house. My head shakes back and forth, scratching the rough dirt against my forehead. Burying my toes deeper in the cool mud. Smelling cheese and flowers and citrus and wood and peppermint as they all drift into one ugly scent causing my stomach to turn even more. For the record, my stomach is *always* turning.

What the fuck happened to the days of sitting in the back of church with one eye on the large words projected onto a white blanket on stage and another eye on the cute brunette sitting in the third pew with the low-cut top?

"Jesus loves me this I know, for the Bible tells me so..."

The only thing I learned from the Bible was what not to do: don't steal; don't leave foreskin on your penis; don't you fucking dare touch somebody else's! People guarding other's opinions is stronger than the most powerful chains. Heavy are the chains that drag to the tune of "Amazing Grace." The sound from my pew tangled in a web of distracting thoughts. Why was my tongue glued to the roof of my mouth?

Jesus found good in his fellow man, or so it seemed. Whether it was an immoral woman enduring wrath of being a slut (I wonder if she was hot) or a man whose skin was flaking off like the most tender meat at Hawaiian pig roast, Jesus found the time to be kind. Then why does the weight of my shame feel so heavy on my shoulders? Why are they forcing me to bathe in my sin? For Jesus, or so it seems.

The pastor's lips moved slowly; repeating himself as his congregation waited with bated breath. "Let me remind you!" he said, as if speaking directly to me. "God so loved the world that he gave his one and only Son, that whoever believes in him shall not perish but have eternal life."

I took a sweet sip of the blood of Christ from a paper cup no bigger than a thimble which could fit on my enormous left thumb. How savory is the thought of finding yourself so lucky as to be the martyr? My lips finish off the dry cracker which I think symbolized the skin of Jesus or something. Not as sexy as the wine.

I made the rookie mistake of not eating the dry cracker first and then drinking the sour cranberry juice. Sometimes church felt like I was being held down and my hands were being ripped in half by 3x3-inch nails; being dragged onto a cross for the world to see my shame. "Show us your sin!" they screamed over pizza. "Feel ashamed and praise our god!" they sang in the green forest in Northern Arizona. Hanging there, lamenting existence while blood seeped from my hands.

I was born into sin; not just like, tripped-and-fell-and-murdered- someone sin, fucking *born* into it. One way in, one way out. My T'ed arms started to droop as teenage adolescence pierced my side with a long, jagged, sharp-tipped lance. I gasped for air. The only way to be clean was to drain my blood down my cross and be filled with the blood of Christ. I wondered if I raised my hand if someone would bring me more sour cranberry juice.

K helped me put down my cross. Born into sin; a bastard by any other name is still a rose. She helped me find purpose, passion, patience, perseverance and present; knowing there is truth to every story. God is love and love is everywhere. Crooked smiles. A long sip of coffee while your eyes drift over the cup to a sweet Rupi Kaur poem. A helping hand from your best friend. Performing a random act of kindness. Farting in the back of church.

I'd do anything now to find a home for my debaucheries and sins; a priest to listen to my bitching and moaning who will try and convince me that the Devil inside really isn't that bad. Fucking bullshit. Anyone who wears a robe in public shouldn't be trusted. What would it be like to have someone who *actually* *listens* to my pain; someone who hears the words italicized in my voice?

Neck sweat starts to conspire at the base of my scalp. Perspiring slowly and without warning, I find myself counting each bead of sweat as it falls down the side of my face. A thousand drops fill a gallon. A thousand gallons fill a pool. A thousand pools fill an ocean. A thousand oceans fill...wait...what do a thousand oceans fill?

Galaxies overhead blinded by the Sun's radiant power. Goddamn it is fucking hot, sweat now lining my crack like a lace G-string. Thank God for the weather. Otherwise, we'd be roasting like pigs or freezing like organs waiting to find a forever home. I hate when people say *who rescued whom*? Like you're a goddamn fucking saint for adopting an animal. Self-soothing comfort rarely is without selfish satisfaction.

Someone is going to find us here. Maybe that would be for the best. I'd be locked up with no one hurt and no hearts to slowly bleed of life. Unhappiness everywhere. Righteous optimism walking around with fake smiles like filling a beautiful cup of Colombian coffee with Splenda, Sweet & Low, or Spurina—it tastes fake. Smile for the camera you're holding. Fake optimism: the sweet relief from the bitterness, unhappiness, and pain we all hide behind our eyes.

If I look around my own shadows, and keep the windows to my soul shut, I can almost still hear my baby girl playing "Heart and Soul" on her metal xylophone.

Poetry and Children's Books

Dad could never discern quiet rage. He is brutal and callous; contrary to society's norms. When his eyes go green, his veins go red, bulging out of the sides of his neck and forehead. It is unbridled rage beating to the march of a Ludwig. I, on the other hand, like to think of myself as a sultry dance: percussion mixed with brass dancing through the dimly lit lounge, my hand running along the red Venetian velvet chairs stacked against the bar. It's after-hours.

If Dad loved his grandparents, I loved them more. One perk of being born young is being able to meet a lot of people who are very old. I can't see the faces of Fred and Yita, but I can remember how they each made me feel. Fred made me marvel at the expressive emotion and jubilation jumping off his face without sound. Yita was a wise fighter. Yita was a teacher and an advocate for deaf rights during the 1960s. She testified against large corporations, led deaf coalitions and wrote legislation passed by Congress. In her free time, she wrote poetry and children's books. They made an impact without ever making a sound.

Fred gave me my first hammer. He was a woodsmith. Craftsmith? What is the word? Carpenter. Carpenter! Fred was a carpenter. From the perch of Dad's arms, I would watch his wrinkled, smoke-scented hands make chairs and Arizona artwork: cacti, armadillos, cowboy hats. The best part of my Great Grandpa Fred was the smile on Dad's face when we were all together. We were always just so happy around each other, blissfully enjoying the sound of silence.

Being deaf gave Great Grandpa Fred and Great Grandma Yita a sense of freedom. I could feel it whenever I was around them. They just didn't care as much as most people. They didn't let being cut off in traffic or having over-cooked steak ruin their day or experience. Fred just smiled and laughed. Yita talked and kept them organized. Fred would tell the same story three times in four days and somehow it would get more interesting. Yita would sit with a young child and effortlessly give as much time required to complete a game of Memory.

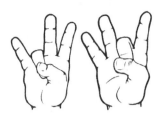

Golden Goose

I fucking hate yoga. Dad loved it, and I mean fucking loved it. Back when things were normal, one day wouldn't go by without him trying to convince me that chakras were certain, backbends were beneficial and that the reason he enjoyed practicing was the centering experience and oneness with life rather than the women covered in sweat and small clothing.

Dad's actions were becoming more and more unjustified. Some of the news stations wouldn't even report on him anymore because they found him too disgusting. He needed to be stopped. Either I'd talk to him and we could climb the mountain together or he'd resist, and I'd put him in prison.

Along with helping Dad, my blackouts were becoming more frequent, and I decided that it was vital that I take control of clearing out my past, specifically–*ding ding*–you guessed it, Dad. My grip was too strong around the barbed connective tissue between the torn-apart relationship Dad and I still reluctantly shared. If I didn't let go soon, my hands would be permanently thrashed from the wire.

I'd read about talk therapy and eye movement desensitization and reprocessing, which is just a fancy way of saying, "Look at these blinking lights while you ruminate about your past," but I knew if I could cut out the root of Dad in a positive way and change him or stop him the balance would be shifted, and I'd be able to let go of his ghost forever. One big shift and Dad would be fixed or the world and I would be free from the monster.

"Nat, cue me up. Where's the dirty in the yoga? Where's the suffering?"

Natalie took a deep, mindful breath, and I could feel her smiling within me, "*I think the rapes are rather appalling.*"

"*Rapes?*" Luca questioned. "*What's a 'rapes'?*"

"*Rape is unwanted sex!*" Aviva chimed.

"*Rape is dehumanizing. Rape is when one human uses hate to exert power and control over another person, villifying them in the most despicable way possible,*" Anna anointed.

"Yeah, it's all of that," I interrupted as I questioned Natalie about her suggestion.

"*Well,*" Natalie took another deep, mindful breath, "*Are you familiar with Guru Kumaré?*"

None of us were familiar with Guru Kumaré.

"*Kumaré was an Indian-born teacher from Calcutta. He emigrated to America with an idea for yoga: do it in the cold. His classes were structured with sixty-two asanas—physical poses—composed of the same sequence each class, and were held in rooms where the temperature was set at 10 degrees Celsius. He claimed the cooler environment allowed for blood to flow freely throughout the body without the unnecessary restriction of heat. In reality, he likes to watch young girls shiver in short shorts.*

"*For some reason, the fad caught on and he has opened studios all over the world and teacher-training centers in exotic locations. Well, it turns out Kumaré is a false god. Nobody knows this, but he lied about his prestigious teacher-training and plethora of awards. He's a master manipulator and a poor kid from Calcutta who's milking people's souls for profit and to get his dick wet.*"

Aviva was annoyed. "*Will you get to the goddamn point? Where the fuck does the rape come into play?*"

"*Well,*" Natalie said, before taking a deep, mindful breath, *"he's used his platform to make millions of dollars and ruin thousands of lives. The men at his retreats are treated like gods. They are encouraged to be violent and aggressive with the women; they are allowed to sleep past the rising of the sun; and every day they are fed breakfast, lunch and a three-course meal for dinner. The women are on a strict, structured regimen. They must practice ninety minutes of Kumaré yoga before the rooster crows, they are forced to be passive witnesses to sexual harassment, abuse and rape, and they are fed cheese sandwiches for lunch and dinner. If their hunger persists beyond the four pieces of bread and two slices of cheese, they are informed that, "Yoga isn't for fat women."*

"Oh, my goodness gracious!" Luca exclaimed.

"*And, this piss-poor motherfucker,*" Natalie said, before pausing to take a deep, mindful breath, "has gotten away with everything."

We made a plan to set up camp at Kumaré's biggest yoga retreat of the year. We'd lock up the dishonorable guru, take Kumaré's form, pretend to do some terrible things to the students, and eventually Dad would show up to save the day. Yoga, a trip abroad and rapes to stop – Tetro would buzz and Dad wouldn't be able to resist. I couldn't find a flight within the week, so we transformed into a AW101 Merlin helicopter donned with a red racing stripe down the middle. Kumaré was holding his largest yoga retreat in the Himalayas. There would be nearly eighty filthy men, three hundred and twenty sad, lonely out-of-their-element women who just wanted to feel love and practice yoga.

It took me half a day to fly to the mountain range west of the Pacific. I landed quietly outside the retreat center and could hear chanting from within the paper-thin walls:

"We all will love you. We adore you. You are exalted on the highest of highs. We are committed to our well-being which is first found in your eyes. Glorious Guru Kumaré...-"

"*I'm going to fucking vomit,*" Aviva crowed, and we all had a hearty, much-needed laugh.

"*Are you sure you want to do this, K?*" Caren asked. "*I don't have a good feeling about this.*"

Without hesitation, I took Kumaré's form, balled my fist and turned it into a diamond, breaking down the nearest wall. "You are all free to use your own will!" I stuttered loudly and without a shred of confidence.

"*What was that?*" Anna questioned. "*Why is your voice so shaky?*"

The room stayed quiet and I looked around for their holy instructor who was nowhere to be found. "*Where's Guru Kumaré?*" I erred, "*I mean, where am I right now?*"

Eventually, one member of the congregation pointed her shaky index finger towards the corner of the room where a plastic Buddha sat next to a door with a large neon, "Exit" sign flashing above and I quickly left and headed toward another area of the retreat compound. The place was fucking bigger than a mall in America. I was lost in an instant and asked Luca to point us in the right direction.

"*I can't place it, but go to the small storage shed at the furthest northwest corner of the compound. Something is off, but I feel his darkness there.*"

We trekked northwest and within the amount of time it would take to complete ten sun salutations were standing in front of a dilapidated shed with a crumbling roof. I listened closely and hurt a muffled yell. The minute my hand touched the sliding door it creaked loudly, and the entire structure fell apart. The only thing left was the golden goose sitting inside. Fastened to a chair, mouth tied with duct tape, wearing only a pair of soiled underwear, was the man I'd come to condemn.

What the fuck was going on?

He shrieked in excitement at the sight of me, thinking I'd be his savior. Little did he know, my attention on him was now diverted to whatever the fuck was actually going on. If he was tied up in the northwest corner of the compound, why was there a room of people chanting and worshipping as if they just received fresh instructions from their demi-god? I didn't touch the tape and was off on my search for the new Kumaré.

It can't be him.

Hearing spirited chanting coming from the south, I sprinted to the next structure, briskly opening the double doors. Guru Kumaré stood at his podium, raising his arms at the front of the room, and slimily slurped, "For whom do we have the pleasure of welcoming into our family?"

"Who are you?!" I cried.

Then, from his podium, Guru Kumaré slowly started to transform. First his feet, then his ankles, next his kneecaps, thighs, hips, stomach, chest, his neck, his cheeks, his lips and eyes and finally his forehead and hair. Kumaré had transformed into thirteen-year-old me. I was dressed as Kumaré with a diamond-covered right hand and my face—my fucking face—was staring back at me. Then his tone changed.

"Hey sweetie, it's good to see you again."

Electric Arm

"What are you doing here, Dad?" I spat back as I stared at my father who was adorned with my skin and my hair and my everything. I thought I'd surprise him and beat him to the punch yet here he stands before me holding the upper hand.

"Are you kidding me? Yoga, a trip abroad and rapes to stop? This is my 5th year in a row at Guru Shitbag's retreat!" He held his hands to the sky, palms up as if he were waiting to catch drops of rain. "The question is what are *you* doing here, K? I thought I told you to leave me the fuck alone!"

Dad's head twisted as if he were having a mild seizure and Chester spewed from the podium, "*You should have stayed away you fucking cunt!!!*" while hundreds of faces in the crowd grew more confused by the second.

Dad coldly interrupted, "Don't you fucking talk to her that way! I'll fucking kill you, you piece of shit!" Dad continued with his lecture focused on me now. "You have no goddamn idea what I go through every day. Even when I help people, truly fucking help people and not accidently kill a kid, nothing changes. Nearly ten billion people on this planet and a shadowed fallacy that my version of good or bad somehow makes a difference. Each time I move forward an inch, something, someone or somehow, I end up being pushed back a mile. My only goal was to help myself, feed my ego and quiet my friends so that I could live a fine life. No matter how many windy roads I traveled to feel fine, the conclusion of every journey was me running at full -speed into a brick wall covered in my own blood."

"You killed a child?" My heart descended deeper into a den of despair.

"Life!" Dad bellowed. "Your judgment is a fallacy. The idea that because something is bad there can be no good. This is your biggest flaw, K! You rejected my ideals and lost track of how there is no good or bad; there simply is. Existence is a dance of duality and your blind eyes don't make you more holy than us. Sure, I killed a boy and have indulged in the existence of being, but what other choice did I have? When the thread barely hangs there must be special attention given to the string."

In unison, Aviva and Caren screamed with me, "I rejected you?! You kicked me out of the fucking house before I even had my first period! Instead of helping me with the voices, you ran as quickly as he could in the opposite direction, intoxicating himself at every opportunity. I was just a little fucking girl!!!"

Instinctively and for the first time, my body started to grow to the size of my anger, and the temperature in my blood started to burn. It felt like every vein was connected to my stomach and a combination of exasperation, resentment and mania hit me causing me to curl over, writhing in agony. Painfully, I stood back up and roared, "I rejected you?!"

"Calm down, K. We can talk about this, but you have to accept some blame too! If you take a look at the simple facts of the matter..." Dad queefed before I quieted his bipolar, misplaced and incoherent guilting.

"I have to accept blame too?!!! You turned your back on me and didn't even bother glancing back in my direction. You would have given more attention to a nickel that fell from your pocket! After all we had, the closest relationship I've ever had, you didn't even bother to sit me down and have a talk! You didn't even bother to call me or text me! Instead, you let some women give you an asphyxiated blowjob and changed the fucking locks!"

In my fit of anger, I'd grown so big, my head was pressing hard against the ceiling which was starting to crack. Taking my two large, muscled arms, and still diamond-encrusted right hand, I punched two giant holes in the ceiling, freeing my head and causing debris to fall loudly against the ground. The congregation had shifted from silent with mouths agape, to panicked and running. At the front of the room, I could vaguely hear Dad yelling at me to stop breaking the building and that I was going to "hurt people."

What the fuck does it matter if I hurt people? None of this fucking matters.

Ignoring his plea and continuing to grow, I stood fifty feet tall with a crumbled building below me and my diminutive father still clothed in my skin. His countenance was disfigured, and his eyes were white with fire. He initiated his transformation, augmenting his body and his skin color to a light shade of blue with six additional arms, bulging with muscles, sprouting out of his back.

"You'll regret this, K!" Dad's scream echoed through the canyons of the Himalayas. "You have no idea how strong I am!"

Standing fifty feet tall, Dad's eyes locked with mine for the first time in years while nearly four hundred onlookers safely watched in the distance. Still looking like Kumaré I knew I needed more strength to have any chance in hand-to-hand combat with Dad. I began crystalizing my body until my skin was a three-foot barrier of solid gold. From my right shoulder and left shoulder, I multiplied my vantage points growing two full heads so that I could see in every direction. To match Dad, I followed up by growing three sets of new arms, bulging with muscles: one set out of my back, one set from my legs and the last set out of my ribcage.

As the sixth and final arm grew out of my left rib cage,

Dad punched me right in the face and I stumbled backwards nearly stepping on a few of the onlookers who apparently weren't as safely positioned as I first surmised. He didn't stop and he rushed toward me grabbing both my shoulders and slamming me to the ground nearly killing a short bus' worth of people. Little birds started chirping the moment my head hit the dirt and clarity hit me like the sun on a cloudless day. The only way to stop Dad was to put an end to his misery.

I reconstructed my back into a spring and launched forward with enough force to send Dad flying into some nearby trees. One large oak stuck into his shoulder blade and he was disoriented on his hands and knees. Running up behind him, I wrapped all eight of my strong arms around his torso squeezing him until I could hear his giant ribs start to crack. He immediately started to freeze his body from the inside until he was as cold as a glacier, and I had no choice but to let go, due to the stinging frostbite against my arms.

He turned around and transformed one of his right arms into the Sword of Excalibur and severed three of my arms. Screaming in pain, I swiftly cauterized the wounds and grew an electric arm out of my ribs. With my palm extended forward, my palm touched where his heart should have been, assuming any part of it was left, and sent ten thousand volts directly into his cardiac center. He let out a loud wail before falling into the grass, still fifty feet in size but now unconscious.

Standing above him, my five besties pontificated the perfect way to bring him into custody. His body was massive, but I couldn't miss the opportunity. I yelled at some of the students—surprisingly, despite the horror, none of them left—to grab as many drugs as possible scattered throughout the compound. We needed to keep him sedated and senseless. He needed another hit to the head, and I pulled two large oak trees—which were surprisingly rooted—and threw them at his head. To my dismay, that's when I learned Dad wasn't unconscious at all.

Two arms grew out of Dad's forehead, catching the large trees and throwing them to the side. He then transformed his hind legs into a horse and firmly kicked me in the front of both of my kneecaps, snapping them backwards. I howled in pain and collapsed to my fractured knees. Dad stood now roughly twenty feet above me, grabbed my last two remaining arms and cracked them in half at the elbows like he was breaking a crunchy Italian breadstick. I tried to fix the bones, but the break was straight through. These would have to heal on their own.

Tears filled my eyes and my form naturally became smaller and smaller until I was back to my size, dressed like K, with four broken appendages.

"Do you think any of this matters?!" Dad wailed from the skies. "Any of it?! You're such a fool, K! Maybe one day you'll see that we aren't that different after all, and that the only thing that matters in this cold, dark world is nothing at all. Your little half measures don't work. There either is or there isn't, and no matter how many bad guys you lock up there will always be more roaming the streets."

As I laid in the grass with broken arms and broken legs, Dad turned his arms into flamethrowers and incinerated Guru Kumaré. I'm not sure what was more horrifying: the screams of the false god turning into silence or the smell of his searing brown skin. My father, the person I loved more than anyone in the world, a man filled with love, compassion and tenderness, appeared to be lost forever. It started with him ghosting me as a kid and evolved into the monstrosity standing above me.

Then Dad spoke loud enough for astronauts on the moon to hear. "There is no God! There is only I! The judge, jury, executioner and afterlife. The only consequences rendered are after full control is received. I was once lost, but now am I found.

300

The six of us creating a perfect unity." His tone deepened. "And, young lady, if you ever try to attack me again, I will not only break every bone in your body, but I will take every breath from your lungs until the only words capable of escaping are my name! I told you to leave me alone!"

Then he was gone. There was no puff of smoke or powerful lift off into space using his legs for propulsion. In the simultaneous blink of my left eye and right, he was gone.

"It'll be alright, K," Caren consoled. "We'll find him. He's still in there. I know it."

"There's nothing left of him, Caren. My father is dead and the thing we just saw is a broken little boy pretending to play God."

I made a short-term home in the grass and broke down crying until my body was composed of only fifty percent water. It felt like he'd reached into my spirit and crushed everything inside.

I can't do this anymore. I can't do this anymore. I can't do this anymore!!!

He must be stopped.

Grandpa's Grave

Every year Dad would take me down to Grandpa's grave. I'd never met my paternal grandfather; rumor has it, he was murdered shortly before Dad was born. No one really ever told me how. In fact, I had only ever heard one story about the man, which was told to me by my great aunt. She was a lovely woman: short, Jewish, with curly brown hair and four Asian children. I may tell you more about them later, but candidly, I may not.

My great aunt worked in a hospital in one of the rough parts of town. She dealt with shootings, stabbings, broken limbs, eye-gouging, burnings, drug babies and the occasional cold. Her job was taxing and for years she efforted to obtain a nursing position which would alleviate her stress. Thankfully, she was eventually transferred to the children's cancer center where she worked with children who were dying. What a relief.

One day, after a particularly sweet boy named Charles passed of brain and spinal cord tumors, my great aunt called Grandpa, crying. She told him it was the hardest day of her life and that she was going to quit the next day.

After they hung up, she went back to work and then went to lunch at the cafeteria. Grandpa was waiting for her with her favorite dessert: a raspberry cheesecake. She told me about how they laughed so hard that she cried, and how Grandpa's sweet gesture reminded her of the life she lived in order to give back to those who couldn't. She was determined to grow stronger and give even more support to young boys and girls who were suffering. From that day forward, until he passed away, Grandpa brought my great aunt a raspberry cheesecake every Monday until he died.

My left leg hangs over an open grave on Dad's birthday at the cemetery where all of this bullshit started. My right knee still fused together and healing after a nasty infection led to four unexpected weeks in the hospital after my tussle with Dad in the Himalayas. My eyes close to meditate. Phoenix is currently sweltering hot and after escaping the hospital for a few minutes and hobbling across the street to an address marked: Rest in Peace. March 10, 1962 – March 24, 1984, I plopped down in the grass like an exhausted single parent after working a twenty-hour shift. At least that's how Dad would have said it. With the hospital bracelet still tightly cutting into my right wrist, my armpits are drenched in sweat as I hold my father's Smith and Wesson in my right hand.

Lying back, the ground is pulsating beneath me. I put down the gun next to me in the grass placing my now free right hand on my stomach. My left hand moves to my chest directly above my heart. Each beat slowly catching the rhythm of the grass dancing at my sides. Feeling myself breathe; I take a deep, less than mindful, yet long overdue breath. I can't remember the last time I took a breath.

Why is my tongue glued to the roof of my mouth?

After ten breaths I'm unsure if I even have a tongue. Looking down to see my tainted knee, I see nothing but colorful twilight. In the distance, traces of new color resembling the way a shooting star rips through the black night directly past my eyes and into my subconscious. Without the need for toes, tastebuds, or pupils how can I be sure that my eardrums carry any purpose.

On cue, a thought pops into nowhere, Aadya,

303

interrupting my heavy meditative trance, and I'm reading a book.

Wait, I'm reading a book?

My hands are old. Why are my hands old?

"My hands are not old!" Aadya screams. "And who the fuck are you?"

"Umm...it's me, K." I say without needing to move my lips which don't appear to exist anyway. Aadya reaches for a gun in the shelf, and I flicker back to my colorful oasis. Feeling my belly rise under the fingertips of my right hand and my heart racing under the fingertips of my left hand. Suddenly, Alanna dances across my sanctum and I'm staring down at a sweaty black yoga mat and two hands that don't need to worry about a sun burn. "Hello?" I ask curiously. Alanna stands up and I can see a room full of people staring at my friend. "K! Is that you?!"

"It's me, Alana!" I scream without vocal cords. "Can you hear me?" My friend confirms my suspicion as she falls onto the floor confused, but not before she interrupted her yoga class by yelling, "Yes I can hear you! Where the hell are you!?" Bored while people rush over to Alanna with cold towels, I fade back into my new, colorfully vivid sanctuary. I knew it was possible! I knew I could use the connection to the source to connect me to others. And holy shit they can hear me?!

I wonder.

"*Try it.*" Caren spoke slowly.

An unusual feeling washed over me and with urgency I was staring out of a peeling-open left eye. Without much in view, I fell in deeper into the tantric state and tapped into the other available senses. I could smell wood floor cleaner, feel bloodied and scared knuckles, each finger painfully uncomfortable against the hard wood floor and my lips coated in drool. Somehow, I ignored my ears and as if plugging a loose electric guitar plug strumming a loud E into a speaker a fire alarm started going off. The sound was so heavy I couldn't feel any of the other senses anymore. Floating in Dad's subconscious I could hear his voices. A maniacal robot spouting off Satan's best stories, a man's voice which kept using the word cunt, two woman who were in the middle of weighing the pros and cons of owning a cat and a British man begging me for help.

"Dad!" I yelled. "Wake up!"

His left eye shut again, and I could feel his head bang against the hard wood floor. "Dad!" I yelled hoping for a response from someone I lost long ago. "Are you anywhere in here?"

"Is that you, K?" Dad spoke with sincerity as I rummaged through his subconscious. "Where are you? I can feel you. I took a lot of mescaline today. Do you know what mescaline is?"

"Umm...no, Dad." I stuttered, "I don't know what mescaline is."

"*Do you want me to take over, K?*" Caren interpreted, "*I bet. I can help.*"

No. I have to do this myself.

"Dad, I love you so much. I miss you so much. What happened to you? Why did you leave me?"

Dad bellowed and I could feel him twisting on the ground. I almost lost the connection as his stomach seized in pain.

"I couldn't help you. I couldn't help anyone. I'm so ashamed of what I've done. You have no idea what it's been like for me. It's all I can do every day to numb the voices and suppress the pain for as long as possible."

"Dad, *everything is okay*. Everything you did is forgivable. I forgive you. Let me help you by teaching you to use the tools you already have in your toolbelt. I met your friends, Chester, Brit, all of them. They're nice. I can help you, but not here, meet me at the cemetery."

"I can't, K." Dad spoke as my heart raced in my physical body and I knew we didn't have much time as I couldn't hold the connection much longer. "I've killed people. Innocent people. I've walked in empathy in thousands of shoes that squish with blood during each step. I've even hurt you. I'm so sorry I can't believe I hurt you. Oh my God! I have to go. I'm so sorry, K. I'm so sorry I failed you."

As I fell out of meditation, I could feel Dad's brain circuits seek an indulgent tool to forget our psychic exchange. My right hand reached away from my stomach and I grabbed my Father's Smith and Wesson.

I had no other choice but to do what came next.

Fuck It

Hope has been a fleeting disaster in the wind. Brief belief for short spurts but ultimately and unanimously I'm always declared the loser. Born to be gallant and wild wearing a bulletproof vest only to feel the Kevlar tighten around my chest every second of the day. My breathing sounds like a cracking exhaust pipe hoping to hold on for as many miles as possible.

"*Woman, escaped from hospital, sitting at Paradise Memorial Gardens near the base of Four Peaks mountain in Arizona...*" Tetro buzzed. "*Putting her father's Smith and Wesson 500 Magnum in her mouth. She will pull the trigger in five minutes and fifty-five seconds.*"

I haven't been out of the condo since killing Guru Kumaré. Pain and tragedy are never intended but when two cars are driving towards each other at 300 mph there is bound to be a messy collision. My days consist of masturbating until my favorite towel is soaked with at least four loads of semen and drinking drain cleaner (at this point, it's one of the only things that can really fuck me up). Words burped out of my mouth with the stench of vodka and weed: "Should we go?"

I peel open my left eye and realize I'm lying face down on my kitchen floor with my lips and cheeks coated in drool. The clock on the wall is blurry, but even with 20/20 vision the hour of the day would be irrelevant.

Oddly, Brit says, "*You have four minutes left before she kills herself, sir,*" as matter of factly as if he were ordering dry toast at a cockroach-infested diner. He always leaves directing the disaster to Tetro.

Standing up, suspicion creeps out of my subconscious. I need to go to the cemetery as fast as possible.

"*Try*," Chester takes a hard swallow, "*try turning into electricity. I think that will work.*"

Before O could suggest an option, I am standing in the cemetery surrounded by nothingness. My ears ring at the cock of a barrel, and I don't need eyes in the back of my head to know who is standing behind me. "Put it down, K," are the only words my worthless mouth could muster.

"*Woman will kill herself in three minutes and twenty-three seconds at Paradise Memorial Gardens...*" Tetro tormented.

"PUT IT DOWN!!" I scream, still staring in the other direction.

Through the howling wind I can hear her faint whisper, "Turn around and look at me, you monster."

Sparkling at Chester's suggestion, my form augments backwards until two bright electric eyes are staring my little girl right in the face. Floating ten feet away from her, her expression is motionless, and I can't find a single dimple on her face. Gobs of water begin falling from the sky, making the distance between us seem heavier with each and every large drop. She doesn't have to say a word.

From the static shock my form takes, I begin to shift. First, my clunky, large feet that cause me to trip over myself at the worst possible moment. Next, my long bulky legs and torso with arms dangling to the ground. Growing a spine, broad shoulders and skin to house my dimples, I stare into her blue eyes with mine. "Please take the gun out of your mouth. I'm begging you, K."

"Don't call me..." I could hear her teeth cracking around the barrel... "K. Tell me about them. I want to know about them! Why are yours so bad?"

"I'll tell you about them! Will you please take the gun out of your mouth?"

Tetro buzzes, "*Woman's brains will be shot all over the cemetery in one minute and eleven seconds...*"

"Tetro!" I wail to my daughter. "Tetro, is the worst. They're all the fucking worst! But...ummm...he just told me you were going to blow your brains out." I howl louder than the cyclone surrounding us.

"What else?" she snaps back coldly.

My whole body is shivering. Sobbing uncontrollably, I continue, "Chester yells at me all the time! He makes me want to take a gun and blow my brains out. Every night, reminding me of every morning's sins. From spilling milk to going too far. He calls me a cunt every day. I'm so sorry, K. I'm so damaged and broken. I'm such a goddamn fucking monster."

"Don't fucking call me, K!"

Tetro buzzes and my hands shoot up pleading for more time on the clock. "Brit helps me with my daily life. Honestly, I would have killed myself long ago if it weren't for him. I think when I'm sleeping, he whispers words of advice. O, her name is Ophelia, but I call her O. We all call her O. She is good. She held onto me for so long trying to help me see the good that was left." I'm now talking faster than my lips can move. "Margaret bitches at me all day. She numbers the strands of my hair and gives me a daily update about which locks are going gray. There are five in total. How many do you have? Oh my God. I'm so sorry, K."

What have I done? Tetro begins his countdown at ten; by seven, K and I are inches apart, and I'm on my knees begging and pleading for her to put down my gun. Wild promises that I will turn myself in, stay away from the drugs and stop using my powers for anything at all. Her cool blue eyes narrow and she knows that I'm lying through my tears. "*Six...*" rolls off Tetro's titanium tongue as I reach for the gun and her steel boot connects with my jaw spilling blood immediately. As I start to transform my right arm to grab the gun, Tetro jumps from six to three and I recoil back to my knees, begging where I belong. "This is me!" I scream over Tetro teasing the number two with blood and tears running down my face. "You're my baby girl!"

"*One!*" Tetro, Brit, O, Chester and Margaret say in harmony.

My eyes close and I pray to no one in particular screaming over the sound of a gunshot and triumphant thunder. The deepest pain I've ever felt buries into my chest. Two large titanium fingers lodge their way inside of me: one clogging my aorta, which, if she moves a crumb in either direction, will cause my entire body to fill until I drown in my own blood and the other is puncturing my lung wide enough to allow the drops of heavy rain to interrupt my belabored breathing. As I close my eyes to drift into space, she transforms into me, and I hear her say to no one in particular,

"I love you. It's time to go, Dad."

He Wept

I visit him from time to time. They keep him in a hidden asylum in the Arizona desert forty-two miles south of Yuma. He's kept amongst criminals and terrorists captured around the world. On any given day, there are at least a hundred of the most gruesome individuals on the entire planet locked inside. Currently, there are a hundred and five total patients at what is known as the Arizona Bloomingdale. Eighty-seven men and eighteen women are in the asylum because of me. Fourteen of them were smuggling various drugs; six of them were torturing tigers; forty-two of them drugged a woman at a bar and gangbanged her in an alley; three were six hours away from killing the Italian President; nine were found releasing a toxic chemical into the water system in Vietnam, and the other thirty-one had done something measuring between things you don't repeat at a dinner party and fucking god-awful.

The building resembles the Bloomingdale Insane Asylum built in the 1820s, almost to the shingle. There are three storeys made of brick containing few amenities or furnishings on the outside and large chimneys sitting on the top. It's in the middle of the Arizona desert, connected to zero accessible roads.

The outside of the asylum looks out of the early 1820s, but the inside is state-of-the-art. Dad has his own cube: it's almost cute. His floating cube is very surgical. He is connected to feeding tubes and a continued IV drip of a special, non-FDA-approved drug called Happy Days which suppresses his ability to transform.

311

The drug was created especially for him. I allowed the doctors and scientists to use my blood and plasma to create the drug.

He's strapped down to a table, despite the combination of drugs leaving his body nearly catatonic. His eyes are open twenty-four hours a day and seven days per week. The doctors tell me he should be nearly comatose and unable to stay awake. I crack a wry smile.

"He wept," said Helga.

"What do you mean he fucking wept?" I screamed, smiling into the phone.

Nurse Helga, the medic in charge of administering my father's daily drug cocktail told me my father cried from 1,100 miles away. I made friends with her about five years ago. She updates me once a month about any ongoings or goings on with Dad's incarceration. Mostly— frankly, every—conversation Helga and I had for five years consisted of no new updates other than people who attempted to kill my father, increases or decreases in his medication dosage and whether she'd met that special guy.

Nurse Helga is a fifty-seven-year-old woman who lives alone and eats submarine sandwiches six days per week. Her favorite sandwich is a twelve-inch meatball sub covered in mayonnaise. On Friday, she treats herself to the tuna because it is, "Fresh on Fridays," according to the store manager, Thomas Emele (pronounced Emily).

"He just cried motionless for almost twelve hours. Tears were streaming down his face so fast, it looked as if someone had turned on the faucets to his eyes." She spoke in her sweet southern drawl.

"Did you increase his medication? Did you decrease his medication? I anxiously spit out as many questions as I could before Helga interrupted me. "What do the brain scans show?"

"I know, I know you're going to be very curious about the goings-ons and the ongoings. I had prepared for that and sweetie I just don't have that information for you. If you want it, I am sure you can get it, but I can tell you with my own eyes, your father laid there looking like a corpse, peaceful as a dove on an olive branch, crying out his entire soul. He wept, K!"

He wept.

Made in United States
North Haven, CT
15 April 2022